First to Fall

C. L. Pattison worked as an entertainment journalist for twenty years, before re-training as a PCSO with Hampshire Constabulary. Today, she writes psychological thrillers from her home on the south coast of England. Her previous novels, *The Housemate*, *The Guest Book* and *The Florist* were all eBook bestsellers.

Also by C. L. Pattison

The Housemate

The Guest Book

The Florist

C. L. PATTISON

FIRST TO FALL

HEADLINE

First published in 2025 by
Headline Publishing Group Limited

1

Cataloguing in Publication Data is available from the British Library.

Paperback ISBN 978 1 0354 1551 9

Typeset in Sabon LT Pro by EM&EN
Printed and bound in Great Britain by Clays Ltd, Elcograf S.p.A.

Headline's policy is to use papers that are natural, renewable and recyclable
products and made from wood grown in well-managed forests and other
controlled sources. The logging and manufacturing processes are expected
to conform to the environmental regulations of the country of origin.

Headline Publishing Group Limited
An Hachette UK Company
Carmelite House
50 Victoria Embankment
London EC4Y 0DZ

The authorized representative in the EEA is Hachette Ireland,
8 Castlecourt Centre, Dublin 15, D15 XTP3, Ireland (email: info@hbgi.ie)

www.headline.co.uk
www.hachette.co.uk

FIRST TO FALL

Mystery surrounds deaths at sporting hero's home

January 31, 8.32 a.m. GMT

An unconfirmed number of people have been found dead at the home of legendary German figure skater, Lukas Wolff.

Several bodies have been recovered from the property, which lies in a remote part of Bavaria, close to the Austrian border. The victims' names and nationalities have not been revealed.

Local police chief, Udo Gutenberg, confirmed that an investigation was underway but declined to say if the deaths were being treated as suspicious.

The tragedies are thought to have occurred during a prolonged blizzard – one of the worst in Germany's history. The extreme weather left large parts of southern Bavaria effectively cut off from the rest of the country and without electricity for several days. The local government has been criticised for its apparent lack of preparedness and for delays in restoring power and mobile communications to the affected areas.

Unconfirmed reports suggest that Wolff, 44, was hosting a training camp for promising young figure skaters when the deaths occurred. The authorities were only made aware of the grim situation after one of the survivors made a gruelling journey on foot to raise the alarm.

A spokeswoman for the sport's governing body, the International Skating Federation, told Reuters: 'The Federation did not endorse – nor does it have any knowledge of – a training programme hosted by Lukas Wolff at his home in Germany. If such a programme were in operation when these shocking events occurred, Mr Wolff appears to have been acting in a purely personal capacity.'

Wolff, a five-time German national champion, was a gold medallist at the 2008 Olympics in Beijing and is best known for a spectacular sequence of skating moves called 'the Grim Reaper'. The name, which was first used by US skating commentator Kurt Macatee, is a reference not only to the distinctive hooded jersey Wolff wore when he debuted the sequence in Beijing, but also to the high level of risk involved.

After retiring from competitive skating in 2015, Wolff carved out a successful career as a coach and went on to train several national champions. In 2022, he announced he would be taking a break from the sport, citing mental exhaustion and a wish to pursue other interests. Since then, he has rarely been seen in public.

More details soon . . .

Four Weeks Earlier

1

My first visit to an ice rink was a disaster. It was the beginning of the summer holidays; a classmate's eleventh birthday party. As one of the least popular girls in my year group, I'd been surprised to receive an invitation. I found out later I was a last-minute substitute, a way of making up the numbers because half the first-choice guests were abroad with their parents. *My* family never went on holiday. For one thing, we couldn't afford it; for another, Mum was barely capable of organising a packed lunch, never mind a week on the Costa Brava.

The memory of that day is burned indelibly on my brain. After being kitted out with my boots, I took to the rink feeling reasonably confident. It was only frozen water, for heaven's sake. How hard could putting one foot in front of the other be?

I'd barely managed two wobbly circuits when a teen-aged boy, skating too fast, caught me with his elbow, sending me flying. My classmate's mother helped me up, compounding my humiliation as she roughly dusted the ice from my bottom. Worse was to come when I complained that my wrist was hurting. Sighing in a way that left me in no doubt what a massive inconvenience I was being, she helped me off the ice. Nothing broken, just a slight sprain, the rink's designated first-aider declared as he handed me an ice pack. Probably best if I sit out the remainder of the session.

Not wanting my friends (and I use the term loosely) to witness my disappointment, I made my way to the far end of the rink, where a group of kids was having a private lesson in a cordoned-off area. I leaned on the guardrail to watch them, marvelling at their balance and poise. One girl in particular caught my eye. She was three or four years older than me, long-limbed and graceful, with silky blonde hair tied in a high pony.

After a little while, she broke off from the rest of the group and began practising on her own, directly in front of where I was standing. I watched, mesmerised, as she launched effortlessly into an upright spin, arms pressed close to her body. It was one of the most beautiful things I'd ever seen. I'd watched figure skating on the TV, but this was different. This felt as if it was just for me.

All too soon, the girl was flinging out her arms, an action I noted with keen interest had the effect of slowing her rotations. As she came to a dead stop, I couldn't contain my emotions any longer and burst into applause.

'That was amazing!' I gushed as the girl looked over at me and smiled. 'Is it as difficult as it looks?'

'Not really, it just takes a bit of practice,' she said, coming over to me. 'How come you're not skating?'

I held out my arm, the ice pack still pressed to it. 'I fell over and sprained my wrist.'

'Ouch,' she said with a grimace.

'It's my first time at the rink as well,' I added, in a bid to garner more sympathy.

'That's bad luck,' she said. 'But don't let it put you off. As soon as your wrist's better, you should get back on the ice; that way, you won't have a chance to develop a phobia.'

'Yeah, I'll do that,' I told her, even though I seriously doubted anyone would ever invite me to the rink again.

'You should think about taking some lessons; it'll help build your confidence.' She jerked her thumb towards an older woman in a fur gilet, who was clearly the group's teacher. 'My coach runs a beginners' session on Saturday mornings. She'll have you whizzing round the rink like a pro in no time.'

'Really?' I said disbelievingly.

'For sure – and all the other kids in the class are really nice. Even if you decide skating's not for you, at least you'll have made some new friends.'

'OK,' I said, nodding eagerly. 'I'll ask my mum when I get home.'

I sometimes think of that moment, combing it for insight, for thought, for some sort of intuition. But I never find it. All I see is an unhappy girl, unwilling to admit how

lonely she was, grabbing at something bright and colourful as it floated by.

At first, Mum was reluctant. Being a single parent, who
flitted from one poorly paid job to another, she didn't
have much spare cash. But when Gran offered to chip in,
she agreed to sign me up for lessons. Gran had been a
surrogate parent to me my whole life. Her son, my dad,
had died in a motorbike crash two months before I was
born. She'd stepped in to save the day more times than I
could remember and it terrified me to think what my life
would've been like without her in it.

Despite my inauspicious start, I took to skating
immediately, quickly mastering the basics: how to skate
forwards and backwards, how to do a snowplough stop,
a bunny hop, a ballet jump, a two-footed spin. My first
coach, the woman in the gilet, was wonderful. A percep-
tive and nurturing woman, she saw in me a child with
promise, a rare determination and a desperate need for
stability.

At eleven and a half, I was a relative latecomer to the
sport. Most of the other kids who trained at the rink had
been skating since the age of four or five. But, according
to my coach, I had an advantage.

'You're a natural,' she used to tell me. 'Your build,
your arm span, your leg strength, your single-mindedness
– everything about you is perfect for skating.'

I was fearless too. If my coach asked me to try something new, I wouldn't think about it long enough to get

scared, I'd give it a go straight away. I'd usually fall the first time, but, unlike a lot of the other kids, I wouldn't whinge about it; I'd get straight back up and try again. And I'd keep trying until I had it down.

I discovered that I wasn't afraid of pain. Quite the opposite – I felt a perverse satisfaction in my ability to make myself suffer. On any given day, my knees, hips and shoulders would be various shades of blue and green, but I was proud of my bruises. They were a badge of honour; evidence of my bravery; proof that I was somebody worthwhile.

For me, the rink was a place of freedom, an escape from the chaos of my home life. Gliding across the frictionless ice with the wind in my face felt almost like flying. And I adored the classical music my coach liked to play in our training sessions. The sensation of it was physical, like warm water being washed over a gaping, bloody wound, agonising and cleansing and curative all at the same time.

Keen to progress, I worked harder than any of the others in my class. After training, I always stayed behind to practise. Sometimes, I'd sit in on the advanced classes, watching from the sidelines and sucking up every bit of knowledge I could. Back at home, I watched endless YouTube videos of all the greats: Boitano, Hanyu, Kwan, Witt, picking apart their routines and trying to work out what it was that made them special.

On the advice of my coach, I took up running to build my cardiovascular fitness and bought some second-hand weights to improve my muscle strength. Within six months, I had been promoted to the intermediate class; another nine months and I had joined the advanced skaters.

Eventually, my coach felt I'd outgrown the group classes and told me I needed more specialist tuition. She recommended me to another coach she knew called Eva, who, once she'd seen me skate, agreed to give me weekly training sessions for half her usual fee. Eva was a lot tougher than my previous coach and sometimes we clashed, but her methods paid off and soon I was knocking out double toe-loops with ease.

Before long, Eva began encouraging me to enter competitions. I refused at first; I was too self-conscious. To me, skating was a private act and not something to be shared with others. Eventually I gave in, lured by the promise of a bejewelled costume and the possibility of prize money.

To my surprise, I found that I enjoyed performing in public. I loved everything about it: the applause at the end of my routine; the judges' praise; the smile on Eva's face when I placed in the top ten; the warmth of her hug when I was top five.

At first, the competitions were regional ones, but soon I was making a name for myself at national events, winning a junior bronze medal at the British Championships and placing fifth in the seniors' competition a couple of years later. I had never competed internationally, however, even though Eva said I was good enough. It wasn't the lack of desire, but the expense. Ice skates weren't free. Neither were costumes. Coaches, choreographers, physical therapy – they all cost money; money that Mum and Gran could ill afford.

With more financial investment, I knew I could've gone further. I wasn't bitter though, far from it. I had already achieved more than I ever thought was possible for someone like me. But now that I had finished full-time education I'd decided, albeit reluctantly, it was time for skating to take a back seat. Mum had been supporting me for long enough; I needed to start giving back.

When I told Gran I was hanging up my boots, she tried to talk me out of it, insisting it would be 'a waste of a God-given talent'. She even offered to cash in her Premium Bonds, saying it would be enough to fund another half year of coaching. I refused her kind offer; she had made so many sacrifices for me already.

Career-wise, my options were limited. I would have loved a backstage job in the performing arts – stage design, or theatre management – but with two very average A levels and a diploma in business administration, I knew I didn't stand a chance. Instead, I applied for dozens of entry-level office jobs. After a handful of interviews, one employer made me an offer. I would be starting in two days' time: customer services trainee at the city council. The thought of wearing a headset all day and listening to people complain about their bins not being emptied didn't exactly fill me with joy, but what choice did I have?

In readiness for my new job, I'd spent the afternoon shopping for suitable business attire. My budget was modest and I was feeling pleased that I'd managed to find everything I needed in a single, purposeful pillage of our local charity store.

Mum was on a late shift at the warehouse where she worked in order fulfilment, so the house was empty when I got home. There was a pile of mail on the doormat, mostly junk by the look of it. Stepping over it, I went to the kitchen, dropping my shoulder bag and my two reusable totes on the floor. As I filled the kettle at the sink, I heard the sound of a key in the front door. I smiled when a voice that was as familiar as my own called out, 'It's only me!'

Gran's flat was three streets away and our place was like a second home to her. She used to have a lovely house, not far from the sea, but soon after I started primary school, she moved to be nearer to Mum and me. That way, she'd be able to keep an eye on things; make sure Mum was holding the fragile edifice of our home life together.

'Hi, gorgeous,' she said as she appeared in the doorway. She put a stack of post on the table. 'These were lying on the mat.'

'Thanks, Gran, I would've picked them up myself, but my hands were full.' I opened the fridge and took out the milk. 'Tea?'

'Ooh, yes, please.' She pulled out a chair and sat down at the table. 'Did you find what you wanted at the shops?'

'I think so.' I bent down to open one of the totes and pulled out a pair of navy trousers to show her.

'Very smart,' said Gran, reaching out to stroke the material. 'So, how are you feeling about your new job?'

'A bit nervous, to be honest. There are a bunch of us trainees starting on the same day, so at least I won't be the only one who doesn't have a clue what they're doing.'

The lines on Gran's forehead pinched together. 'You know, I never imagined you working in an office, Libby.'

I tossed the trousers over the back of a chair. 'You're not the only one.'

'Are you sure this is what you want, love?'

I felt a dull ache in the pit of my stomach. 'I just think it's the right thing to do.'

Gran's face remained immobile. I could sense her disappointment. Ever since I started skating, she had been my number one fan. She'd travelled to every competition, stayed up half the night sewing Swarovski crystals onto my costumes, kept a scrapbook of clippings that contained every local newspaper article that had ever mentioned my name. 'I just think it's such a shame to give up skating when you've put so much hard work into it.'

'I'll still skate,' I said, opening a cupboard and taking out two mugs. 'I just won't be having lessons, or competing.' Even as I said it, I knew it wasn't true. I wouldn't be going back to the rink. Ever. It held too many memories; too many painful reminders of what might have been. At the same time, I knew a fragment of it would always be embedded in my heart, like an icicle, prodding me painfully at certain moments when I least expected it.

As I dropped teabags into the mugs, Gran started telling me about a recent trip to the vet's with Betty, her Siamese cat, who had just been diagnosed with cataracts. I sensed that she wanted to say more about my big life decision, but, recognising my discomfort, she had tactfully decided to change the subject.

As I set a mug of tea and a half-open packet of biscuits in front of her, she got up from the table. 'Just nipping to the loo,' she said. 'Back in a mo.'

I sat down with my own drink and began to riffle half-heartedly through the pile of mail that Gran had picked up. Amidst the pizza flyers and the final reminders, one item stood out: a thick cream envelope that felt expensive to the touch. Even more curiously, it was addressed to me.

It was probably from the council, I thought to myself as I eased my finger under the flap; another HR form that needed filling out. Nothing to get excited about.

2

By the time I heard Gran's footsteps coming back down the stairs, I was in a state of shock. I could feel the blood dancing in my veins, the hundred-beats-per-minute drumbeat in my chest. My face must've been white as a sheet because the first thing Gran said to me was: 'Is everything all right? You look as if you've seen a ghost.'

My mouth suddenly felt very dry. I took a gulp of tea. 'Have you heard of Lukas Wolff, Gran?'

She sat down and helped herself to a chocolate digestive.

'The Olympic figure skater? Of course. He used to have that signature trick, didn't he? What was it called again?'

'The Grim Reaper.'

'That's it,' she said as she dunked the biscuit in her tea. 'I remember watching it on the telly. I'd never seen anything like it before.'

I pushed my mug aside. All my nerve endings were tingling. I felt like a catapult pulled right back. 'No one had,' I told her. 'And you'll probably never see anything like it again.'

Over the years, plenty of skaters had tried to replicate the Grim Reaper, but, to date, no one had managed to pull off the sequence in its entirety – at least not in competition. A Serbian skater had come closest at one of the Winter Olympics, I forgot which year – but he messed up the penultimate jump and landed awkwardly, breaking his tibia and a handful of ribs.

I cast my mind back to when I was twelve or thirteen, remembering all the skaters I used to idolise, Lukas Wolff among them. 'I used to have a poster of Lukas on my bedroom wall, right above my bed. Do you remember?'

Gran smiled. 'Your bedroom was covered in posters; I never knew who was who.' She took a sip of tea. 'Why are we talking about Lukas Wolff now anyway?'

I straightened my shoulders; took a deep breath. 'Because he's invited me to train with him in Germany.'

She gave a little chuckle. 'Course he has.'

'I'm serious, Gran. He's written to me; the letter was in that pile of post you brought in. I opened it while you were upstairs.' My voice quivered; I could scarcely believe it myself.

I pushed the sheet of watermarked paper across the table. At the top was an eye-catching graphic of a castle; it looked like something out of *Grimm's Fairy Tales*. Underneath it, the words *Schloss Eis* were printed in a stylised font, although I had no idea what they meant.

Gran's lips trembled. 'I haven't got my glasses; you'll have to read it out to me.'

I cleared my throat. '*Dear Libby, I trust my name is familiar to you. Although we've never met, I know that you are a uniquely talented skater who, to date, has failed to fulfil her true potential. In an attempt to rectify that,*

I should like to extend a one-time offer: eight weeks of personal tuition at my home in Bavaria. All coaching sessions, accommodation and food will be provided at my expense for the duration of your stay. The dates provided below are non-negotiable. I appreciate this leaves you with little time to clear your schedule, but that is intentional on my part. If you know anything about me, you will know that I demand nothing less than full commitment, and the kind of student I am looking for is one who is willing to make themselves available at short notice.'

I looked up. Gran was staring at me, her mouth wide open. Then she broke into a smile.

'So, when does he want you to go?'

I scanned the page. I hadn't bothered to read down that far; I was still struggling to process the fact that an Olympic champion had reached out to me. 'Wow. When he said short notice, he wasn't kidding. I have to be there a week on Friday.' I read the final sentence aloud. *'Kindly confirm your acceptance or rejection of this invitation via the email address provided.'*

I laid the letter back down on the table and ran my fingers over the handwritten signature: *Lukas Wolff.* As far as I knew, he hadn't been involved in the sport for several years; I actually thought he'd retired. It begged the question *why?* Why would Lukas Wolff make such a generous overture to a virtual unknown? How did he even know I existed?

'I guess you'd better start packing then,' said Gran.

I blinked hard several times. I had my future all mapped

out; there was no room on the blueprint for a self-indulgent trip overseas. 'But I'm not going. I'm about to start a new job, remember? If I don't show up on Monday, the council won't hold the position open for me.'

A furrow appeared between Gran's brows. 'Don't tell me you're going to prioritise a minimum-wage job over the chance of one-on-one coaching with a sporting legend. Think what this could do for your skating career.'

'I don't have a skating career, Gran. It's over. *Finito*. I've moved on.' As I said the words I felt a slight clutching of my solar plexus.

She rested a hand on my forearm. 'There's nothing stopping you changing your mind, sweetheart.'

'I'm not denying it's a very flattering offer, but it's come too late – and anyway, the letter might not even be genuine.'

'It seems kosher to me, and who would want to play a trick like this on you?'

I gave a heavy sigh. 'Even if it is legit, what about the cost of this little jaunt to Germany?'

'Lukas has offered you free bed and board, hasn't he?'

'Yes, but there's still my travel expenses.'

'A flight to Germany can't be that much and I'd be more than happy to make a contribution, you know I would.'

I looked down at the tablecloth; picked up a few spilled grains of sugar on the end of my finger.

Her voice softened. 'Come on, Libby, I can read you like a book. What is it you're not telling me?' When I didn't reply straight away, she added, 'It's your Mum, isn't it?'

Gran was right; she usually was.

'If I leave her on her own, I'm worried she'll relapse.'

Mum hadn't had a drink for almost four years – her longest stretch of sobriety to date. She was what you might call a high-functioning alcoholic. Even when she was at her worst, she was always able to care for me (just) and hold down a job (albeit a pretty undemanding one). That wasn't to say that living with her was easy and when I was growing up, life at home could be chaotic; unpredictable. The smell of booze was part of the fabric of my childhood. Mum used to hide bottles of vodka around the house – inside cereal boxes, between towels in the airing cupboard, behind the toilet cistern. Whenever I found one, I'd pour the vodka away, fill the bottle with water and then return the bottle to its hiding place. She must've noticed, but she never said anything.

At school, I always felt different to the other kids. I still feel that way, if I'm honest. Keeping Mum's addiction a secret was all-consuming. Gran was the only person who knew. I didn't breathe a word to anyone else – not the few friends I had, or the teachers, or my skating coach. I was terrified that if social services found out, they'd take me away. I wasn't scared for myself, I was scared for Mum and what would happen if I wasn't there to protect her.

When Mum was sober, she was amazing. Kind and loving and fun. When she was drunk, it was like living with a different person. She'd get very emotional, tell me that she just wanted to be loved and list all the bad things that had ever happened in her life. It was true that she'd been through a lot – her own parents had died, of breast cancer and a heart attack, three years apart when she was only in her twenties. Then there was the tragic death of my father, a man she always described as the love of her life, when she was pregnant with me. Bringing up a newborn baby on her own was tough and she did her best, but it wasn't long before alcohol became a crutch.

Mum's binges always ended with her either falling asleep or passing out. Even if it was really late and I had school the next day, I'd force myself to stay awake so I could keep watch over her. Every hour or so, I'd hold a small mirror up to her face, just to check she was still breathing.

She tried to kick the booze numerous times. Sometimes she went months without a drink. But no matter how many stints in rehab she had (most of them funded by Gran, using the rapidly dwindling proceeds from the sale of her house), she couldn't seem to chase away the demons that led her to self-medicate. And each time she relapsed, it was as if she took with her a layer of my skin, leaving me frightened; anxious; vulnerable.

The turning point came when I was fifteen. Mum got arrested for drink-driving on the way to work. She usually caught the bus, but that day she was running late and she stupidly decided to take a chance. She knocked someone down on a pedestrian crossing, although thankfully they only sustained minor injuries. The magistrate had some harsh words for Mum as he issued a twelve-month driving ban and a community order, telling her that if she hadn't been my primary carer, she would've got a custodial sentence. Fortunately for all of us, it was the wake-up call she needed.

'You don't need to worry about your mum; I'll watch out for her,' Gran said, her grip on my arm tightening. 'You've been looking after her your entire life, Libby; it's time to put yourself first now. Fate has thrown you this wonderful curveball and if you don't grab it with both hands, you're going to spend the rest of your life regretting it.'

When she said that, I felt a faint, high buzzing in my ears, like a pressure-change on an aeroplane. I knew in that moment I was going to Bavaria.

3

'How much further is it?'

The driver made brief eye contact in the rear-view mirror. 'Fifteen minutes.'

His words came as a relief; it felt like I'd been travelling forever. First there was the coach journey to Birmingham Airport for my flight to Munich. Then two connecting trains to a station with an unpronounceable name, where I waited for a pre-booked taxi that arrived forty-five minutes late. I was pleasantly surprised to learn my driver spoke English, but he wasn't very communicative; I don't think he'd said more than ten words since he picked me up.

At least there was plenty to look at through the window. Mountains, forests, lakes, picture-book villages filled with charming, timber-framed buildings. Bavaria was undeniably beautiful, but I didn't think it would be this cold, even in January. While I was waiting for the taxi, I'd had to dig in my suitcase for an extra layer and a pair of gloves. It was just as well I'd taken Annett's advice and packed plenty of warm clothing.

Annett was Lukas's personal assistant. She'd responded to my email acceptance within minutes, although her reply had been scant on detail. In addition to a clothing advisory, she sent me directions to Lukas's home, her mobile phone number and a request that I notify her of any dietary requirements. There was no information about the tuition itself: no schedule, no description of the training facilities, no list of expectations or performance goals.

The vagueness of it all had made Mum a little concerned. Like Gran, she was thrilled I'd been presented with such a wonderful opportunity, but she was understandably nervous about packing her only child off to Germany to live in a strange man's house for two months. Being a five-time national champion didn't preclude him from having dishonourable intentions, she was quick to point out.

To help put her mind at ease, my coach made some enquiries. Eva had been hugely disappointed by my decision to quit skating and she was delighted that Lukas's offer had prompted a change of heart. She spoke with Annett at length on the phone and was reassured by what she heard. She also exchanged a couple of emails with Lukas's sports agent, and apparently everything checked out.

The only remaining mystery was why, of all the thousands of skaters he could have chosen, Lukas had extended his offer to *me*. Sure, I'd won a few competitions, but I wasn't that well known in skating circles, especially not international ones. Eva did come up with one plausible theory: that Lukas, who was famed for his unusual training methods, had devised a brand new regimen and wanted to trial it on a relative unknown, someone from outside his home country. Should the whole thing turn out to be an abject failure, a skater like that would likely feel less aggrieved than a more high-profile candidate; less motivated to whinge about their disappointing experience on social media and bring Lukas's name into disrepute.

There wasn't much time to prepare before I left for Germany, but I'd crammed in as much online research as I could. I came across an old TV interview with one of Lukas's former protégées – a Czech skater, who'd been forced to retire at the age of nineteen after a nasty accident during training. It left me in no doubt that Lukas was a hard taskmaster, who pushed his pupils to their limits. The Czech woman didn't explicitly criticise Lukas, but it was all there if you read between the lines. It might have put some people off, but not me. In my short life I'd already learned that nothing worth having came easy and I was up for any challenge, the harder, the better. I had no idea what path my life would take when I returned to England – as I suspected, the council had refused to push back my start date – but I would worry about that when the time came.

'We're here.'

At the sound of the driver's voice, I leaned forward, craning my neck through the gap in the seats to see through the windscreen. Up ahead lay a pair of tall metal gates and beside them a sign that read *Schloss Eis*.

'What does the name mean in English?' I asked my driver as he lowered the window and pressed the button on the intercom.

He paused in his gum-chewing just long enough to spit out two words: 'Ice Castle.'

The translation made me smile. What better name for the home of a skating champion?

As the gates swung open, the car moved forward and we began to make our way along a meandering gravel drive, lined on both sides with a well-coiffed yew hedge. At first, there was no sign of any building, but then, as we rounded the next bend, a vast mansion reared up in front of us. I'd never seen anything quite like it before.

Just like a real castle, it had turrets. One sat at the centre of the building, directly above the entrance portico. It was circular, with a conical slate roof, topped by an ornate weather vane. Two further turrets – these ones square and squat, with pagoda roofs – guarded each end. Each of the third-storey dormers had a miniature version of the same pagoda roof. The glass in their arched windows looked almost black in the gathering dusk and the shades were pulled low, giving the mansion a sleepy, half-eyed gaze. I recognised it immediately. It was the castle I'd seen depicted on Lukas's letterhead. Not a fairy tale after all; it was real.

As the taxi drew to a halt, I held my phone up to the window and took a quick picture. After adding a caption: *Disney World, eat your heart out!* I posted it on the family group chat.

The driver and I both got out and I watched as he heaved my suitcase out of the boot. After pulling up the handle for me, he cast a suspicious, sideways look at the castle.

'Will you be OK here?' he asked.

Resisting the urge to ask him why I *wouldn't* be OK, I nodded and tipped him a few euro.

As he drove away, I started dragging my suitcase towards the portico. It was a cheap one of Mum's that she'd had since she was a teenager. One of the wheels caught on a flagstone and I swore under my breath as I wrestled it free.

When I got to the front door, there was no sign of a bell or a knocker, but almost straight away it opened to reveal a woman who looked to be in her late thirties. She was small and curvy and sensibly dressed in thick corduroy trousers and a chunky sweater that looked as if it had spent as little time as possible in the transition from sheep to clothing.

'Libby,' she said. Her cheeks tightened as she smiled. 'I'm Annett. Welcome to Schloss Eis.' Her German accent was soft and made me wonder if she'd spent time in England.

I smiled back. 'It's great to be here.'

Taking the suitcase from me, she wheeled it inside. I wasn't invited to follow her over the threshold, but I did so anyway.

'Did you have a pleasant journey?' she asked.

'Not bad, thanks.'

As she parked my suitcase against the wall, I stared around the imposing entrance hall in awe. It felt like I'd just stepped into a film set. Although the fabric of the building was clearly old, everything in the room looked straight off the delivery truck. A colourful rug, a console table with elaborately curved legs, matching gold lamps that were perfectly positioned to highlight the room's stunning architectural features. I had the strange feeling that if I touched anything it would fall down, like painted wooden scenery, revealing the true world concealed behind.

'This is an amazing home,' I remarked as Annett joined me in the centre of the room.

'It is, isn't it?' she agreed. 'It was built at the turn of the twentieth century for a member of the Prussian nobility. After the Second World War, it functioned as a sanatorium, and then as a nursing home for scarlet fever patients. It lay derelict for several years, before being bought by an international hotel group. I believe it operated very successfully for several decades and then, in the early 2000s, it was purchased by a wealthy financier, who converted it back into a private residence.' She had her spiel down pat; I wondered how many times she had delivered it.

'How fascinating,' I said, drinking in every detail. 'Has Mr Wolff lived here long?'

She gave a long, heavy blink, as if it was an effort to keep her eyes open. 'Perhaps you could keep your questions for another time, only I'm about to serve dinner. If I'd known you'd be arriving at this hour, I would've told the catering company to deliver a little later.'

'Sorry about that,' I said, caught off guard by her critical tone. 'The taxi was late picking me up.'

'It's no problem. The other skaters are in the library. I'll take you through to meet them – unless you'd prefer to go to your room first.'

I frowned. 'I'm sorry?'

'I thought you might like to freshen up after your journey.'

'No . . . I didn't mean that,' I said, feeling flustered. 'You mentioned there were other skaters.'

'That's right. You're the last to arrive.'

On hearing that, I experienced a sinking sensation. At no point in any of my – or Eva's – dealings with Annett had there been any mention of other participants. Nor had they been referenced in Lukas's original invitation. In the absence of any evidence to the contrary, I'd just assumed I'd be the only one.

'So Lukas is coaching a few skaters, is he?' I said, working hard to conceal my disappointment.

'Yes, one of the invitees was unavailable due to injury, but everyone else managed to clear their schedule.'

'How many of us are there?' With any luck, there'd only be two or three.

'Nine, including you.'

Shit.

'Are they from England too?'

'No, we have a variety of nationalities.'

My heart plunged again. I could probably hold my own against skaters from my home country, but internationally? Not a chance.

'So would you like to go to your room?' Annett

prompted me. 'You won't have time for a shower, but you might like to change your outfit.'

I shook my head, aware that I was on the back foot. The others had been here for several hours. They would've had time to acclimatise to their surroundings, to size each other up. I'd already arrived later than planned; I didn't want to waste another second of this experience, especially now I knew it wasn't just me and Lukas. 'No, it's all right, I'm happy to go straight to the library.'

Annett led the way down a brightly lit corridor. In the distance, I could hear excited chatter, peppered with the occasional explosion of laughter. It made me feel a little wary; my friendship group back home was small and I'd never particularly enjoyed socialising en masse.

Finally, we arrived at a door that was wrapped in brown leather and secured with brass rivets, like an antique trunk. The minute Annett opened it, everyone in the room fell silent.

The library had the same stage-set feel as the entrance hall, with floor-to-ceiling shelves lined with old books – far too many for one person to have read. At the centre of the room was a pair of matching sofas and several armchairs, ranged around an imposing fireplace. Occupying the seating were eight people, all roughly my own age – four female and four male, the vast majority of whom I had never seen before.

'The last member of our group has arrived at last,' Annett told them. 'This is Libby Allen, she's from Birmingham in England.'

'Actually, I'm from a small town in Shropshire, about sixty miles west of Birmingham,' I corrected her. I could feel myself talking too quickly, the way I always did when I was nervous.

'Oh,' Annett said stiffly. 'My apologies.'

There was a brief, slightly awkward silence before she spoke again.

'You'll have to excuse me; I need to get back to the kitchen,' she said, her hand already on the door handle. 'I'll leave you all to introduce yourselves to Libby.'

Instantly, one of the guys sprang to his feet. He had deeply tanned skin, offset by light brown eyes. 'Hi, Libby,' he said, extending a hand towards me. 'Nathan Carter.'

His soft southern drawl sent a pleasant rush of blood to my nether regions.

'You're American,' I said, stating the obvious, as we shook hands.

'Sure am. Ever been to the US?'

'No, but I've always wanted to.'

He flashed a smile. 'Well, if you ever find yourself in Tennessee, I'd be glad to give you a guided tour.'

The girl who had been sitting next to him on the sofa got up. 'Gabrielle Dupont,' she said, taking my shoulders and placing a quick kiss on each of my cheeks.

'I know you,' I said. 'Or at least I've heard of you. You were the youngest ever competitor to land a triple Lutz at the French Championships.'

She smiled, revealing her dimples. 'Yes, it was a long time ago; I'm working on my quads now.'

I had serious jump envy. The Lutz was one of the hardest jumps to master in skating. The only triple I'd ever landed cleanly in competition was the much easier toe-loop. It made me question, yet again, why on earth I'd been chosen.

'I expect you've heard of me too.'

I half turned over my shoulder. The speaker was a slender man with angular features; his accent sounded Eastern European.

'Alexander Nowak, *enchanté*,' he said with a theatrical bow.

I briefly considered lying, before deciding to come clean. 'Sorry, no, I don't think I have.'

His nostrils flared momentarily. 'No matter.'

'Alexander's the former Polish junior champion,' said Nathan. He gave the other man an amused, sideways look. 'It's just a shame he crashed and burned at the Warsaw Cup.'

'I was recovering from an Achilles injury,' Alexander retorted.

'Yeah, man, whatever.'

Before Alexander could think of a comeback, another woman stood up. She was Asian. Petite. Bursting with energy.

'Melissa Chen, from Shanghai.'

I was familiar with that name too. Famed for her amazing flexibility, Melissa had a sublime, hyperextended Biellmann spin that only someone who was half-human, half-elastic band could pull off. Judging by the diamond studs sparkling in her ears and the expensive watch on her wrist, she was also pretty wealthy.

'I won't bore you with a list of my achievements, because, frankly, it would take too long,' she said in perfect, accentless English. She winked at me. 'Only kidding. It's a pleasure to meet you, Libby.'

Her handshake was cool and very firm. I got the impression that behind the delicate appearance and kittenish manner lay a core of solid tungsten.

As she retreated, another skater waved his hand, but didn't bother to get up from the sofa.

'Gerhard Völler,' he said. 'I'm German, in case you hadn't guessed by the accent. Welcome to the team.'

To his right, a familiar face smiled broadly: Flora Kavanagh. She was Irish; we'd competed against each other six or seven times. On nearly every occasion, she'd placed higher than me, but I'd beaten her to the podium the last time we met. We weren't friends exactly, but we'd chatted a few times in the locker room.

She stood up and came towards me with her arms outstretched. 'Hey, Libby, it's good to see you again.'

'Likewise,' I said as we hugged.

'If I'd known you were coming, I'd have suggested we meet at Munich airport and travel the rest of the way together.'

It seemed I wasn't the only one who'd been kept in the dark about this being a group training camp.

'Yeah, that would've been fun,' I said as we drew apart. 'Cheaper too. I can't believe how much the taxi from the station cost.'

She gave my arm an empathetic squeeze, before turning to the only female skater who had yet to introduce herself. She was sitting slightly apart from the others in a wingback armchair, her legs elegantly crossed at the ankles. She had the cool beauty of a glassy lake on a freezing day. You wanted to stare at it, to admire the view, but you were afraid to touch it in case you got frostbite.

'I think you know Saskia, don't you?' Flora said.

Who didn't know Saskia Blair? She was a thoroughbred in the world of skating. Her mother, Joanne, was a former Scottish national champion and the country's most successful female skater ever. After competing at two Winter Olympics, she retired from the sport – prematurely, many believed – to start a family with her hedge-fund manager husband.

Saskia had been skating since the age of three. Her first pair of boots had to be custom made because they were so small. She kept them in a display case in the family home in Edinburgh, where she still lived. I knew all this because Saskia slavishly documented her life on social media and, even if she didn't know it, I was one of her twenty-odd thousand Instagram followers. Flora and Saskia were related. Second cousins, to be precise – another fact I had gleaned from Saskia's Insta.

'Of course,' I said, smiling through my envy. 'I loved your short programme at the Oxford Open. The choreography was brilliant; I'm not surprised you won.'

'That's *sooo* sweet of you to say,' Saskia gushed. 'Remind me – where did you place?'

My neck started to burn. 'Eleventh.'

'Really . . . that high? I thought you were in the teens somewhere.' She looked at me like I had some kind of a problem, which I supposed in her eyes I did. A deficiency. A lack of status.

Just then, Annett appeared to tell us that dinner was ready. The announcement was welcome since I hadn't eaten a thing since the over-priced ham and cheese toastie I'd purchased on the plane.

We followed her as she led us down a series of disorienting corridors.

'Have you worked for Mr Wolff long?' Gabrielle asked as we rounded a corner.

'Nearly six months,' Annett replied.

'Do you live at the castle?' another voice chimed in.

'Not usually, but I'll be staying here for the duration of your stay.'

'What happened to Mr Wolff's previous assistant?' Nathan enquired cheekily.

Annett drew in a breath, as if she was about to say something, but then expelled it. 'I have no idea, and I don't think it's any of my business.'

By this time, we had arrived at our destination: a large

dining room, decorated in shades of oatmeal and taupe. At Annett's urging, we all took a seat at the egg-shaped table.

'You do know I'm allergic to soy,' Gabrielle said as Annett went over to an industrial-looking trolley in the corner of the room and began removing plates from its shelves.

'Yes, I received your list of dietary requirements,' Annett said, as she carried two plates to the table. 'No soy, no dairy.'

She set one of the plates down in front of Melissa, who immediately wrinkled her nose in distaste.

'Would you mind asking the chef to cook my salmon a little more, only I prefer it well done?'

'Mr Wolff doesn't have a chef,' Annett replied. 'Your evening meals will be prepared by an outside catering company and delivered daily.' She put down the other plate in front of Flora. 'He doesn't employ a housekeeper either, so you'll have to take care of your own bedrooms. Cleaning products are available on request and you can help yourself to towels and bedding from the first-floor linen cupboard.' She gave Melissa a pointed look. 'Do you think you can manage that?'

'I guess I'll have to.' Melissa was clearly unimpressed. 'Will Mr Wolff be joining us for dinner?'

Annett continued ferrying plates to the table. 'I'm afraid not. He's away on business; he won't be back till tomorrow.'

'When's our first coaching session?' asked Gerhard.

'I'll be distributing a schedule first thing in the morning,' Annett said as she served up the last two meals. 'Until then, I suggest you relax. Once training starts, you'll have precious little time to yourselves.'

She went over to the minimalist sideboard. On top of it was a mini fridge filled with bottles and beside it, a tray of glasses.

'Libby; what can I get you to drink?'

I beamed gratefully. I drank alcohol rarely – and never at home, for obvious reasons – but right now a drink was exactly what I needed to loosen the tight knot in my stomach. The other skaters seemed nice enough, but there were still too many unknowns for my liking, too many sinkholes waiting to open up and swallow me whole.

'A beer would be lovely, thanks.'

A muscle twitched in Annett's cheek. 'Alcohol is banned during your time here, at Mr Wolff's request.'

'Oh,' I said, feeling as if I'd failed some sort of test. 'A fizzy water then, if you have it.'

As she continued taking drink orders, I glanced at the man sitting to my left. He was the only skater I hadn't spoken to yet. There was something prickly and defensive about his body language. His shoulders were high and his lips were compressed into a thin line.

'I'm sorry, I didn't catch your name earlier,' I said, even though he had yet to offer it.

'Frederik Bakker.'

He shook my hand – a single, dry pump.

'How was your journey here?' I asked him. It was wildly unimaginative, but small talk had never been my strong point.

'Good, thank you.'

'Did you have to travel far?'

'Maastricht.'

'That's in the Netherlands, right?'

'Yes, it's in the south-east.'

After that, the conversation stalled and Frederik started to eat, forking green beans into his mouth in a rapid, anxious motion as if he was expecting his plate to be snatched away at any moment.

Laying a crisp linen napkin across my lap, I started on my own meal. Despite Melissa's criticism, it was actually pretty good – the salmon moist and flavoursome, the vegetables roasted to perfection.

'Enjoy your food,' Annett said when she'd finished serving the drinks. 'Dessert's on the trolley, help yourselves; I'll be back later on.'

As the door closed behind her, Nathan, sitting opposite me, put down his fork and leaned back, resting one arm on the table and placing the other on the back of Gabrielle's chair. As he lifted a hand to smooth back his dark hair, a ripple of muscle announced itself under his slim-fitting shirt.

'Bit of a buzz kill, isn't she?' he said, flicking his eyes towards the door.

Gerhard threw him an arch look. 'This isn't a holiday camp. We're here to work; to *learn*.'

Nathan held the German man's gaze. 'Last time I checked, learning and having fun weren't mutually exclusive.'

'I dunno, from what I hear Lukas Wolff is a bit of a slave-driver,' said Flora.

Gabrielle nodded her agreement. 'A friend of a friend shares a physio with someone Lukas used to coach. According to her, he likes to push his pupils to breaking point – and not just physically, but mentally too.' She pushed her salmon skin to the edge of her plate. 'Not that I'm complaining; this is a once-in-a-lifetime opportunity. I wouldn't have come if I wasn't prepared to work hard.'

Nathan picked up his glass and took a mouthful of grape juice. 'Did any of you know there'd be other skaters here?'

'I did,' said Saskia. 'But only because Flora told me she'd been invited too. We guessed there might be others, but we didn't know for sure.'

'I had no idea,' Melissa admitted. 'And, personally, I don't appreciate the deception. It should've been made clear from the beginning that we'd be part of a group.'

'Would it have made any difference?' asked Alexander.

'I'd still have come, if that's what you're asking. I just think I would've been better prepared.'

'I feel the same way,' I said in a small voice.

'So why do you think Lukas is doing this?' Nathan said, not addressing anyone in particular. 'And what's so special about *us*?'

Gabrielle flipped her sheet of silky blonde hair over

her shoulders. 'This is going to sound crazy, but it did occur to me that this could be the lead-up to some sort of reality show.'

Frederik stared around the room, wide-eyed. 'You don't think we're on camera now, do you?'

'No way,' Nathan scoffed. 'No production company would film us without our consent. If they did, we could sue their asses off.'

'It could be a dry run though,' said Gabrielle. 'So Lukas can see whether or not the idea's viable before he floats the idea to the TV companies. If the show goes global, he stands to make a small fortune.'

Melissa made a face. 'I don't think so. Based on what I've seen so far, Lukas doesn't exactly need the money – and anyway, he's famously private; almost reclusive. There's no way he'd want his home all over the TV.'

'Maybe he just wants to give something back to the sport,' said Saskia. 'To give us the kind of opportunity he wishes *he'd* had when he was coming up through the ranks.'

I swallowed the slice of courgette I was chewing. 'Frankly, I don't care what his motivations are; I'm just looking forward to working with him.'

I meant it too; it was just a pity I had to share the experience with eight of my contemporaries.

As the evening wore on, I found myself becoming increasingly withdrawn. I wasn't shy as such, just deeply introverted – the sort of person whose inner resources were depleted by social interaction. I was doing my best to stay positive, but my earlier optimism was coming apart like a fraying hem. With every passing minute, another thread came loose.

As Nathan started to tell us about his recent audition for Disney On Ice, I had to pinch the skin on my inner arm, twisting it a little, just to keep myself present. When he revealed he'd be joining the US cast of *Encanto* as soon as he returned from Bavaria, the others cheered and clapped. It was certainly an impressive achievement; Disney skaters were some of the best in the business. I cheered too, a split second behind everyone else, like an alien desperate to appear human.

It came as a relief when, just before nine, Annett returned and offered to show me to my room. As I followed her up two flights of stairs, an unsettling realisation was solidifying in my brain. I was seriously out of my depth here. I had never won a national competition, only once placing in the top three – and, unlike the rest of the skaters, I had never competed overseas.

I had no idea what Lukas Wolff had in store for us, but in that moment it felt as if I was crouching down in front of a huge wave, just waiting to drown.

4

I woke just after seven, having slept surprisingly well. My room was small, but spotlessly clean and very comfortable – the mattress just the right firmness, the sheets crisp and fragrant.

When I checked my phone, there was a message from Eva. She wanted to know if I'd arrived safely. I meant to text her yesterday, but with all the excitement, it had slipped my mind. My reply assured her all was well and downplayed my disappointment at discovering I wasn't Lukas's only house guest.

Afterwards, I went over to the window and hoisted the Roman blind, squinting as the light flooded in. My room was on the second floor, up in the eaves, and afforded excellent views across the grounds. On impulse, I unfastened the catch on the window and pushed it open. The morning blew in on a chill breeze, thick with the scent of pine trees, shocking me wide awake.

When I'd arrived, I'd been so dazzled by the castle itself that I'd failed to register its surroundings. But now I saw how lovely they were. Directly beneath my window was a formal garden – an expanse of gravel laid out with low, clipped box hedges and flower beds arranged with fierce symmetry. Beyond it, the dewy lawn was dotted with well-maintained shrubs and the occasional piece of classical statuary. To the right was a tennis court and beside it an octagonal summer house with a wraparound veranda. If the grounds looked this good in the wintertime, I could only imagine what they would be like in spring and summer, with everything in full bloom.

Before I came here, I don't think I had really appreciated just how wealthy Lukas was. His home was absolutely stunning and so secluded; the perfect hideaway for a man who valued his privacy.

Dying for a pee, I pulled the window shut and headed for the bathroom. Having my own en suite was an unexpected luxury; it was like being in a hotel. But before I got there, I noticed a piece of paper lying on the thick pile carpet. Annett must have pushed it under the door as I slept; the promised training schedule, no doubt. I picked it up and took it with me to the bathroom.

As I'd expected, the schedule was pretty full-on. The group was to have five coaching sessions per week with Lukas, all of them lasting most of the day, with time set aside for conditioning and strength training.

Given the castle's remote location, I assumed the nearest rink would be some distance away and that arrangements had been made to bus us there and back every day. The thought made me slightly on edge, as I had a tendency to get car sick in larger vehicles.

It wasn't clear from the schedule if we would be on the ice that day, since the only activity listed was 'team building'. The words alone were enough to make me shudder. Suffice to say, I was not a natural team player. It was one of the reasons I had always resisted any suggestion that I might like to try pairs skating. It was true that partnering with a boy whose skill set was superior to my own might have taken my skating to the next level. But if and when a performance went awry, I would much rather I only had myself to blame.

Setting the schedule down on top of the cistern, I peeled off my pyjamas and stepped into the shower. Annett had advised that breakfast would be served at eight sharp, so I had a bit of time to get my game face on. As the powerful water jets pummelled my body, I practised some deep breathing techniques, the same ones I used to settle my nerves before a competition.

When I went to sleep last night, I'd been feeling quite dispirited. I'd always had an unfortunate tendency to dwell on past failures, to focus on my weaknesses, rather than my strengths. It was like picking a scab – painful and irresistible at the same time. If I wanted to do well here, I had to change my mindset. Stop my thoughts sliding down the grooves my subconscious had carved on purpose to lead me into this trap.

'I *am* good enough,' I said, listening to the sound of my voice bouncing off the tiled walls. And then, just in case my subconscious hadn't been paying attention, I said it again – only this time a little louder.

By seven-forty-five, I was ready to head down to breakfast. As I pulled my bedroom door to, I caught sight of Gabrielle, emerging from a room further down the corridor. Clad only in a skimpy nightdress, she was barefoot and her hair was all messed up. We made eye contact and she gave me an embarrassed smile. I opened my mouth, intending to ask if she'd slept well, but before I could speak she'd stepped back into the room and closed the door behind her.

It was only when I was halfway down the stairs that I realised why she'd looked so sheepish. When Annett had shown me to my room the previous night, she'd mentioned that Alexander and I were the only skaters on the second floor. It could only mean one thing: that he and Gabrielle had spent the night together. Whilst I was no prude, I couldn't help feeling shocked at the lightning speed of their union. It really was none of my business though. I was here to skate; what others did in their downtime was up to them.

The dining room was empty when I got there, but a buffet breakfast was laid out on the sideboard. It all looked very wholesome: muesli, fresh fruit, oat milk, plain yoghurt and thick slices of dark rye bread.

I was heaping cereal into a china bowl when Nathan appeared. His hair was slicked back and he was dressed in technical gear – hiking trousers and a pale yellow top that contrasted pleasingly against his olive skin.

'Morning,' I said brightly. 'Did you sleep well?'

He joined me at the buffet. 'Not really. It's way too quiet here.'

'I know what you mean; I'm used to waking up to the sound of traffic back home.' I gestured to the breakfast things. 'I'm guessing we just help ourselves here.'

'Yeah, no point waiting for the others; half of them are probably still asleep.'

'Gabrielle's awake, I saw her a few minutes ago, up on the second floor.' I hesitated, not wanting to sound like a gossip. 'She was coming out of Alexander's room. I think they might have been discussing the schedule.'

Nathan gave a snorting laugh. 'I doubt it. Those guys have been sleeping together for years.'

My eyebrows shot up. 'Gabrielle and Alexander are a couple?'

'It's more of a friends-with-benefits kinda thing. They live in different countries, so they only get to hook up when they're competing at the same event. They think they're being discreet, but it's one of the worst-kept secrets in skating.'

I drenched my muesli in oat milk. 'Do all the skaters generally stay in the same hotel when you're competing overseas?'

He gave me a quizzical look. 'Surely you've stayed in enough of them to know.'

I took a spoon from the cutlery tray. 'I've never competed outside the UK.'

'Why the hell not?' he said in surprise. 'It can't be because you're not good enough – because if that was true, you wouldn't be here. There's no way Lukas Wolff would waste his time on a skater with no talent.'

I bit my lip, wishing I hadn't said anything. 'I guess it all boils down to money. I've never had any kind of sponsorship and my family isn't that well off.'

He reached across me for the neatly labelled thermos of coffee. 'Yeah, competing overseas is pretty expensive. My family aren't loaded either, but I was lucky enough to get an athletic scholarship.' He poured coffee into a mug. 'Want one of these?'

'Please.'

'Sit down and I'll bring it over.'

I carried my cereal bowl over to the table and slid into one of the upholstered chairs.

'How about you, Libby? Are you dating anyone right now?'

I gave a little cough, wrong-footed by the change of subject. 'No,' I replied. 'I've been single for a while.'

The truth was, I'd never had a proper relationship. Just a series of entanglements, all of them complicated and unfulfilling. Not wanting to sound like a loser, I reached for some sort of justification. 'I haven't had the time, to be honest; most of my weekends are spent at the rink.' Or at least they used to be. Now that I'd quit skating I really had no excuse.

Nathan brought the coffee over to the table, going back for some fruit and yoghurt. 'Same here,' he said as he sat down beside me. 'I was with my last girlfriend for two years, but we broke up over Christmas. I think she got tired of playing second fiddle to my skating.'

Just then, the door opened and Saskia walked in. She was wearing a full face of make-up and skintight active-wear that showed off her toned body.

'Hey,' she said as she sashayed into the room, some-how managing to suck all the oxygen out of it at the same time.

Nathan raised a hand in greeting, while I managed a half-hearted 'Hi'.

Saskia went over to the sideboard. 'Is this it?' she said disdainfully.

'What were you expecting?' Nathan asked her.

'Something hot – porridge or a poached egg.' Sighing, she helped herself to a wedge of melon from the fruit platter.

'Morning!'

We all looked up as Flora walked into the room. In stark contrast to Saskia, her face was bare and her hair was pulled back in a messy bun.

'Mmmm,' she said as she caught sight of the breakfast buffet. 'That looks amazing. Get me a coffee, will you, Sas?' She came over to the table and flopped down in a chair. 'God knows I need something to wake me up.'

'Didn't you sleep very well?' I asked her.

'No. My bed was super comfy, but I was just too excited.' She grinned at us both. 'I still can't believe it . . . I'm actually in Lukas Wolff's home.'

'I wonder when he's going to grace us with his pres-ence,' said Nathan.

Flora thanked Saskia as she put down a mug in front of her. 'At today's team-building event I expect. What do you think we're going to be doing?'

I took a swig of my own coffee. It was stronger than I usually took it and the hot, bitter liquid scoured my throat. 'I don't know, but the schedule said to bring a coat, so it must be an outdoor activity.'

'Personally, I can't see the point of it,' said Saskia as she joined us at the table. 'I thought we were here to skate, not play silly games.'

There was a burst of noise outside the door and then suddenly the other five skaters were spilling into the room. As the air filled with competing voices, I found myself retreating back into my shell.

5

By nine-twenty-five, we were all assembled in the entrance hall, five minutes ahead of schedule. I was still struggling to orient myself in the vast property and was surprised I'd managed to find my way there without taking a wrong turning.

On the dot of nine-thirty, Annett appeared. After the briefest of greetings, she led us outside to where our transport was waiting. Not the minibus I had been expecting, but a pair of battle-scarred 4×4s.

On seeing them, Melissa visibly recoiled. I guessed she was probably used to travelling business class. 'Are we really going in those?' she said.

Annett's face betrayed no emotion. 'If you don't approve of the arrangements, you're welcome to stay at the castle.'

Melissa's face lit up. 'You mean we have a choice?'

'Of course. However, I must advise you that non-participation in any of the scheduled activities will result in you being terminated from the programme with immediate effect.'

Her words were bruising, but at least we all knew where we stood now. There were only two options: do as we were told, or go home.

'Fine,' Melissa sighed. 'I just hope these things have seat belts.'

'Will Mr Wolff be travelling with us?' asked Alexander, as he shouldered his backpack and walked towards the nearest 4×4.

'No, he's coming directly from his business meeting in Stuttgart; he'll meet you there.'

'And are we allowed to know where "there" is?' asked Gabrielle as she followed Alexander. I noticed how he offered her his hand as she mounted the vehicle's side step.

'It's not far,' was all Annett was willing to divulge.

After ushering Nathan, Gerhard and Melissa in behind Gabrielle, she directed the rest of us to the other 4×4. It was only when she slammed the door shut behind us that I realised she wasn't coming too. I was actually quite glad. Whilst Annett was undoubtedly efficient, I didn't find her particularly friendly or empathetic. It was as if some tech company had made a simulation of the perfect PA, but her settings were ever so slightly off.

On leaving the castle, our 4×4s headed in a northerly direction, away from the local train station and the pretty villages I'd passed on my inbound journey. Nobody said very much. I didn't know if the others were just tired or if, like me, they were inhibited by the presence of our chauffeur – a man with a thuggish buzz cut and e-fit eyes.

Our vehicle was in front, the driver expertly negotiating the twists and turns in the narrow road. Mile after mile unspooled before us, with no manmade structures in sight. No houses, no shops, no farm buildings. Just endless fields and trees, with the ever-present Alps in the distance. It only served to reinforce just how isolated Lukas's home was.

We'd been travelling for less than half an hour when our driver took an abrupt left-hand turn, leaving the metalled road behind us. My stomach turned somersaults as we bounced along a deeply rutted track, flanked by impenetrable woodland. Very quickly, the track disappeared and suddenly we were cutting a swathe through tall grass and bracken. The view was the same wherever I looked, and it occurred to me that it would be very easy to get lost out here.

As branches scraped across the windscreen, Flora and I exchanged an uneasy look. I wondered if she was thinking the same as me: *what has any of this got to do with skating?*

Finally, we emerged into a small glade. The driver nosed the 4×4 into a patch of nettles and killed the engine.

'Where the hell are we?' said Saskia, as she peered through the mud-splattered window.

Frederik pursed his lips prissily. 'No idea, but this is definitely not what I signed up for.'

'What do we do now?' Flora asked the driver.

He stared straight ahead. 'We wait for further instructions.'

Saskia opened the door, saying she needed to pee. As she scuttled off into the undergrowth, the rest of us got out to stretch our legs.

Moments later, the second 4×4 pulled up. Gerhard, sitting in the front passenger seat, was opening the door even before the vehicle had come to a standstill. His eyes were shining; he was clearly loving every minute of this. Melissa and Gabrielle less so, judging by the looks on their faces.

'Isn't this amazing?' said Gerhard. 'I love the outdoors; I can't wait to see what Lukas has planned for us.'

'It had better not involve hiking,' said Saskia, looking down at her pale pink trainers. 'I didn't pay two hundred pounds for these, just for them to get covered in mud.'

Nathan pulled his neck warmer up over his chin. 'Whatever we're doing, we need to get moving before we freeze our butts off.'

He had a point. The temperature was barely above freezing. The sky was a veil of grey and clouds were closing in on all sides, dark and ragged.

I heard the sound of twigs breaking underfoot and turned around, thinking it must be Saskia, but instead I saw a youngish man emerging from the trees. He was wearing black, base-layer leggings and a waterproof jacket in a retina-scarring shade of yellow.

'Hallo, skaters,' he said cheerily. 'I'm Bruno and I'm going to be your guide today.' He made a lavish sweeping gesture with his arm. 'Please, follow me. Mr Wolff is waiting for you.'

At the mention of our host's name, I felt a rush of excitement, tinged with trepidation. I was keen to make a good first impression and I knew I was only going to get one shot at it.

Most of the other skaters followed Bruno into the woods, but Flora and I hung back to wait for Saskia. The three of us then had to play catch-up, dodging tree roots and fighting off brambles that tore at our clothes. There was no path to speak of, but Bruno strode confidently forward, clearly familiar with the terrain. After only a short distance, the trees began to thin and the ground beneath our feet grew rocky.

As we started to climb a steep slope, I slipped on some loose shale. Muttering an expletive, I lurched forward, grabbing Flora's arm to stop myself from falling. It was then that I saw a set of tracks in the dirt – not human; animal. A bit like the paw prints of a dog, only longer, with clearly defined claw marks. Flora saw them too because she pointed at the ground, looked at me and Saskia, eyebrows arched in a question mark as she mouthed the word '*Wolf?*' In unspoken agreement, the three of us picked up our pace, trying to close the gap between us and the others.

Ever since we'd begun our ascent, I had been aware of a noise – a sort of gentle whooshing sound. At first, I thought it was the wind in the trees, but then I realised it couldn't be, because it kept getting louder and louder, until eventually it became a roar. It was only when we reached the top of the slope that I discovered what it was.

Twenty feet below us lay a river, swollen and roiling. Even from this elevation, I could see the foaming white-caps, feel the spray on my cheeks as the water smashed its way between enormous boulders that were jewelled with emerald-green lichen.

Melissa gave a delighted squeal. 'Wow, would you look at that!'

'Awesome, isn't it?' said Bruno. He frowned slightly and scratched his eyelid. 'It isn't usually this fast-flowing, but we've had a lot of rain in recent weeks.'

He let us admire the view for a few more moments before turning away from the river.

'Come with me, there's something else I want to show you.'

I felt a twinge of irritation. Stunning as it was, I didn't come to Bavaria for the scenery; I came for Lukas Wolff.

We retraced our steps for a short distance, before Bruno veered left, picking up a narrow trail. We followed it in single file, the noise of the rushing water making conversation all but impossible. For ten minutes or so, we continued parallel to the river, but then Bruno turned back towards it, leading us up a steep embankment. What I saw when I reached the top was like something out of a horror movie.

I found myself staring into a large granite basin where the river water had collected. But this was no serene pool where one might, in warmer weather, enjoy a spot of skinny-dipping. It was a boiling vortex of water flowing in a downward corkscrew as detritus from the riverbank tumbled through it in a death spiral. Reeds and saplings that once stood tall near the banks had been smashed completely flat by the force of the clashing currents.

We all gazed at the whirlpool in silence, mesmerised by its power. The dense wall of fir trees on the far bank had cut off the light and the water looked almost black as it charged around and around before finally finding an escape route over a series of rocky steps and continuing on its way.

Nathan was the first one to find his voice. 'That's wild, man,' he said, shouting to be heard above the whirlpool's deep-throated rumbling. 'It's almost like that water's alive.'

Bruno's lips turned up in a half-smile. 'The locals round here have a special name for it. Roughly translated it means *the witch's cauldron*.'

Melissa gripped the sides of her designer coat tightly around her neck. 'What makes the water behave like that?'

'It's all to do with the irregular topography of the river bed,' Bruno explained. 'It causes water moving in two different directions to come into contact with each other. They can't continue to travel at the same speed and direction, so they're forced to rotate instead. This is actually a tributary of the larger river you've just seen.' He pointed to the opposite bank. 'That piece of land is an island. Another tributary runs on the other side of it; the water there is much calmer. The two tributaries come together half a kilometre downstream and the river continues on to the Danube and from there to the Black Sea.'

'How interesting,' said Gabrielle, her teeth chattering slightly as she spoke. Glancing over, I saw that she was rubbing her arms through her down jacket.

'Are you OK?' I said.

Reaching for her zipper, she pulled it up so the collar fitted more snugly under her chin. 'Just a bit cold. I'll be fine once we start walking again.'

Alexander placed a protective hand on her shoulder. 'Can we get moving now?' he said to Bruno. 'I expect Mr Wolff will be wondering where we are.'

'Of course,' our guide said with a deferential bow of the head.

Fifteen minutes later, we emerged from the tree canopy into a large grassed area, pitted with tyre impressions. Two vehicles occupied the space – a black Jeep Wrangler that looked fresh out of the showroom and a much older blue pickup. On the left of this makeshift car park lay the river, on the right was a wide track.

'Why didn't our drivers use that route?' asked Frederik, pointing to the track.

'It would've been a smoother ride, that's for sure,' said Nathan.

Bruno looked faintly amused. 'Mr Wolff thought you'd prefer the scenic route.'

Saskia, who was busy cleaning off her trainers with a handful of dock leaves, snapped her tongue against the roof of her mouth. 'It's just a pity we weren't offered the choice.'

'Look!' said Gabrielle suddenly. She pointed to the Jeep. The driver's door had opened and a figure was emerging from the vehicle. A man in his mid-forties. Below average height, with a slender physique, strawberry blond hair and a smattering of sandy-coloured stubble around his jaw.

Lukas Wolff. In the flesh.

6

As he started walking towards us, all the tiny hairs on the back of my neck stood on end. I had an overwhelming sense that this was a huge moment; a moment that could very well change the trajectory of my entire life.

'He's smaller than he looks on TV,' Flora whispered.

She was right and yet, even from this distance, Lukas Wolff had an unmistakeable presence. An air of strength and curt efficiency; nothing wasted in his movements.

He went over to Bruno and stood beside him. The two men were dressed very similarly, except Lukas's jacket was blue.

'Good morning and welcome to Bavaria,' he said, regarding us with a cool directness. 'It is, as I'm sure you'll agree, a beautiful part of the world.' His English was flawless but heavily accented, the vowels short and sharp.

Saskia gave a simpering smile. 'Your homeland is absolutely *stunning*, Mr Wolff. And can I just take this opportunity to thank you from the bottom of my heart for inviting us here.'

Melissa, standing beside me, made a noise in the back of her throat, as if she was annoyed with herself for not beating Saskia to the punch.

I wished I could think of something smart or witty to say, but I was so in awe of the man standing before me, my brain was flailing around as feebly as a slow-worm.

'You're most welcome,' Lukas replied. 'I'm sorry I wasn't at Schloss Eis to greet you yesterday, but I trust you have everything you need. If any of you do have additional requirements at any point during your stay, please speak with Annett, who will do her best to accommodate you.' He exhaled: a long and measured breath. 'I expect you're wondering why I've brought you here.'

'We are indeed,' said Alexander, although the question was clearly rhetorical.

'Our training proper will begin tomorrow, but before we get down to the serious stuff, I thought it would be nice to have some fun together.'

The words chafed. I didn't claim to be an expert on our host, but I'd done my homework. Although Lukas Wolff didn't have an official website, or any social media presence to speak of, I had found a ton of other useful stuff – YouTube videos, newspaper articles, critiques by pundits and competition judges. I'd watched his gold medal-winning performance in Beijing over and over again. Analysing the footage frame by frame, marvelling at the complexity of his routine and the flawless way all the elements fitted together. Everything about it was perfect – and not just the routine itself, but Lukas's amazing costume, with its cowl-like hood that he flipped up over his head seconds before launching himself into the Grim

Reaper. And all of it set against the heady backdrop of Prokofiev's 'Dance of the Knights' from *Romeo and Juliet*. I'd come across several TV interviews with the great man and pored over them, trying to discover what made Lukas tick. I sensed he was a person overloaded by the weight of his own ambition. Not unhappy exactly, but never satisfied. Always striving to jump higher, spin faster, do things the human body was never meant to do. And it wasn't just about him; it was about his audience too. Connecting with them wasn't enough; the way he described it, it was almost as if he wanted to commune with them on a transcendental level.

All of it had led me to one conclusion: that the Wolff Man, as he was affectionately known by his fans, was never anything less than deadly serious. In all the material I'd unearthed, there was no indication, not even the vaguest hint, that the word 'fun' figured anywhere in his personal lexicon. Still, I told myself as I tuned back in to his voice, perhaps age had mellowed the former champion.

'I've devised today's team-building event in collaboration with my dear friend, Bruno Frerich,' Lukas went on. 'Come this way, please, and I will elaborate further.'

He started walking towards the river, chin jutting out from his neck in an attitude of stern authority. There was a palpable air of excitement among the skaters as we followed obediently in his wake. But for some reason, probably because I was feeling so far out of my comfort zone, I just wasn't feeling it.

A series of huge boulders obscured our view of the river. But when we walked around them, Lukas's intentions immediately became clear.

Bobbing on the surface of the fast-flowing water was a rigid inflatable boat, its tether looped around one of the boulders. On the bank beside it was a pile of paddles and sundry safety equipment. I'd never tried rafting before, but I thought I was reasonably well equipped for it. Like most skaters, I had a love of speed, coupled with excellent balance and coordination. Perhaps the team-building activity wouldn't be too excruciating after all.

I studied the others, trying to gauge their reactions. Alexander and Gerhard were busy high-fiving each other, clearly stoked. Gabrielle's eyes were big and round; she seemed up for it too. The others were harder to read.

My gaze switched to Lukas. His face was expressionless; it gave nothing away.

He cleared his throat, demanding our attention. 'As I'm sure you've guessed, today we're going to be experiencing the thrill of whitewater rafting, under Bruno's expert guidance. He's highly experienced in the sport and knows this river like the back of his hand. The two of us are also keen fishermen and we've spent many happy hours together fishing these waters.' He smiled at the other man. 'Over to you, my friend.'

Bruno stepped into the centre of the group. 'Have any of you tried rafting before?'

Nathan raised his hand. 'I shot the rapids in Utah last year, on a bucks' weekend.'

'Did you enjoy it?'

'You bet! The second it was over, I wanted to do it all over again.'

'Glad to hear it,' Bruno said, nodding in approval. 'Anyone else?'

We all shook our heads.

'That's absolutely fine, no experience is required. I have to say this is a great spot for your first rafting adventure. Several outdoor adventure companies operate from this location. I used to be employed by one of them, but I'm freelance now.' He swept a lock of hair off his forehead in an oddly flamboyant gesture. 'I appreciate that some of you may be feeling a little nervous right now and, while it's true that rafting does involve an element of risk, it's no more dangerous than many other daily activities. Just like swimming in the ocean or driving a car, so long as you stay alert, you have nothing to fear. The other thing I need to stress is that every one of you must pull your weight; there are no passengers on this trip.'

Pep talk over, Bruno spent the next fifteen minutes talking us through the anatomy of the boat, teaching us about thwarts and carabiners, paddling technique and seating position. Then it was time to don our helmets and life jackets. Only once we were kitted up did he broach the subject of what to do if one of us was unlucky enough to fall out of the boat.

'If you can, grab the safety rope on the side of the raft and we'll pull you back on board the first chance we get,' he told us. 'If you find yourself drifting away from the boat, you need to roll onto your back and bring your legs up towards your chest, so your toes are above the surface of the water. Don't try to swim, just stay in this position; your life jacket will keep you afloat. Remember that every rapid is followed by a calm section of water. When you reach one of those calm sections, you'll have the chance to swim to the bank and await recovery by your teammates.' A warning note crept into his voice. 'One thing you mustn't do is panic. It'll disrupt your breathing pattern and cloud your judgement. Try to stay calm, regulate your breathing and maintain focus.'

By this point, I was starting to experience information overload. I was usually a quick learner, but there was an awful lot to absorb in a short amount of time, especially with regard to the safety protocols. For the first time, I began to feel uncomfortable about what we were being asked to do.

Bruno was still issuing last-minute instructions as he ushered us all onto the raft. 'Don't forget, we need to steer *into* the current, not away from it, even though it seems counterintuitive,' he said, as he helped Gabrielle on board. 'When we get to the witch's cauldron, we'll be utilising a slightly different technique, but I'll tell you what to do when we get there.'

At the mention of the witch's cauldron, there was a brief, stunned silence before Alexander jabbed his paddle in the air and cried, 'Oh yessss! Bring it on, baby!'

A hot, kinetic tremor radiated out from the base of my spine. I had naturally assumed that, as novices, we'd be travelling down the calmer tributary – the one on the other side of the island.

Saskia clearly shared my concerns. 'You can't be serious,' she said. 'Did you see how fast that whirlpool was moving? We'll never be able to get across it. It'll swallow the raft up – and us with it.'

'No, it won't,' said Bruno. 'I know what I'm doing. Just trust me, OK?'

'What about the other tributary?' I said. 'Can't we raft down that one instead?'

Bruno looked faintly disgusted. 'C'mon, guys, where's the fun in that? Today is all about teamwork, remember? Tackling the witch's cauldron is the perfect way to show what we can accomplish when we all pull together.'

'Bruno's right,' said Lukas as he squeezed himself in between Gerhard and Alexander at the rear of the raft. I noticed that the extra weight made that end of the boat sit much lower than the prow, which I wouldn't have thought was advisable. But what did I know?

'Personally, I'm really looking forward to the challenge,' Lukas added. 'I thought you would be too. It's part of the reason I chose you all – I believed you had courage; determination.'

It was true that I enjoyed pushing myself to the limit. It was also fair to say that, after everything I'd been through with Mum, there wasn't much in the physical world that scared me. But by the same token I wasn't someone who threw caution to the wind, on the basis that things thrown into the wind had a tendency to blow back in your face. Nor was I deluded and, from where I was standing, a bunch of beginners taking on the witch's cauldron was nothing short of madness.

Bruno, who was still standing on the riverbank, legs aggressively akimbo, clearly thought otherwise. 'I appreciate how scary it looks, but I've done this four or five times before without any issues. The trick is to use the whirlpool's energy to our advantage. If we paddle into the correct part of it, we'll get a free ride with hardly any effort on our part. Honestly, we'll be over that motherfucker before you know it.'

I stuck out my lip, still not convinced. 'And what *is* the correct part of it?' I asked him. 'Or is that a trade secret?'

He sighed, the irritation coming off him in waves. 'We paddle into the side of the whirlpool, rather than the centre – into the part of the current that's moving downstream, in other words. That way, we'll be able to slingshot the raft around and out the other side.'

'But what if something goes wrong and we do find ourselves in the centre?' asked Flora. 'What if one of us gets thrown into the water? What are we supposed to do then?'

'That scenario is highly unlikely, but if it does happen, the drill's the same. You float on your back with your legs up, just like I told you before. Eventually, the whirlpool will spit you out and carry you downstream, where the rest of us will be waiting to recover you.' He adjusted the chin strap on his helmet. 'Are there any more questions?'

No one spoke. I looked down at my lap, not wanting the others to see the fear in my eyes. Especially not Lukas.

'If anyone's not prepared to give this a hundred per cent, they should say so now,' said Bruno. 'What's that English phrase? Go hard or go home.'

Still no one spoke.

My life jacket felt uncomfortably tight around my chest and I could taste the rye bread I ate at breakfast at the back of my throat. Was I the only one who wasn't buying into this macho bullshit?

'Good,' said Lukas. 'We're all happy then.'

I wasn't happy. Not in the slightest. But instead of voicing my feelings, I watched, rabbit-in-the-headlights, as Bruno started to unhook the raft's tether from the boulder.

This all felt too rushed. The training was minimal; the safety briefing inadequate. He hadn't even asked if everyone could swim. It was all very well Bruno boasting that he had conquered the witch's cauldron a handful of times before, but on this occasion he was going to be responsible for ten other people. And what about the stronger-than-usual current he mentioned earlier – a consequence of the recent heavy rainfall? Had he factored that into his calculations?

I couldn't help feeling Bruno was being overconfident. Arrogant, almost. He seemed to be ignoring the fact we were dealing with nature here: wild, unpredictable, impossible to second-guess. Did he know for a *fact* that anyone falling into the witch's cauldron would eventually wash up downstream, or was it just an educated guess? And even if that assumption were correct, surely there was a high chance of injury while one was being tossed around and around in that seething vortex, like a sock in a washing machine. Wouldn't it be the easiest thing in the world to get struck on the head by a piece of flotsam – a rock or a tree branch – and be knocked unconscious? Then there was the question of what would happen if the raft capsized and all of us ended up in the water. Who would come to our rescue then? Yes, some of us might be able to swim to shore, but I'd seen with my own eyes that the banks flanking the river were high and slippery with moss. My upper body strength was pretty good, but I seriously doubted I'd be able to get out of the water under my own steam.

Something else was bothering me too. Why were we the only people here on a weekend? If this was such a popular rafting spot, how come there were only two vehicles in the car park? One of them belonged to Lukas, and the pickup, with its generous flatbed, perfect for transporting an inflatable, must surely be Bruno's.

Unease flexed inside me like a cramp. So much about the situation didn't feel right. And I had mere seconds to get myself out of it.

'I'm sorry,' I heard myself say. 'I don't think I can do this.'

Bruno froze, the rope tether still in his hands. 'You want to back out?' he said in a hostile tone.

Suddenly, my cheeks were burning hot. 'I just have a

few concerns.' I took a quick swallow. 'About my personal safety.'

I looked at Lukas. Disappointment was written all over his face.

'But Bruno is one of the best whitewater guides in Bavaria,' he said. 'He's not about to risk his reputation by letting anything happen to you.'

'I appreciate that, it's just . . .' My breath caught. There was a long silence; it became a vacuum that sucked all the air out of my lungs.

Lukas looked at me with undistilled contempt. 'Let me put it another way. Do you really think *I'd* be doing this, if I thought there was any real danger? I'm not an idiot, you know.'

I felt something inside me crumble and turn to dust. Now I'd managed to insult him; ruined our relationship before it had even begun. 'No, of course not,' I said quickly. 'I wasn't suggesting you were.'

As I was talking my mind was working overtime. Was I making the right call, or was this a wilful act of self-sabotage? What made me think I knew better than everyone else here? Shouldn't I just get over myself?

Nathan caught my eye. He smiled encouragingly and mouthed the words, *It's OK*.

'You need to make up your mind,' said Lukas. 'Are you coming with us, or not?'

'Not,' I said softly.

He cupped a hand behind his ear. It felt very much like mockery. 'I'm sorry, I can't hear you.'

'No, Mr Wolff,' I said in a louder voice, so there could be no mistaking my intentions. 'I won't be coming with you.'

His face remained darkly immobile, but there was a shift in his voice, like the drop in temperature when afternoon turned to evening. 'In that case, it seems I have misjudged you.'

Embarrassment soaked into my clothes, stained my skin, seeped beneath my fingernails.

'Please don't delay us any further, Miss Allen,' he said. 'Kindly step out of the raft.'

I felt the weight of ten pairs of eyes on me as I stood up and took a lurching step over the rim of the boat onto the bank. It was as if the ground beneath me was beginning to open, revealing a trapdoor that had been there the whole time. I should never have come to Bavaria; I was clearly punching above my weight.

'What about the rest of you?' said Lukas. 'Is anyone else having second thoughts?'

'Not me,' declared Saskia. 'I've never been a quitter and I'm not about to start now.'

I looked down at the ground, my humiliation complete.

'Excellent,' Bruno said when no one else demurred. 'Looks like we're ready to launch then.'

'Wait!'

I looked up. At first I wasn't sure who had spoken, but then I saw Frederik getting to his feet.

'I don't want to do this either,' he said in a low voice.

Lukas pinched the bridge of his nose, as if he couldn't quite believe this second act of mutiny. 'God give me strength,' he said. His voice was low, the blade of his anger still half-sheathed. 'Off the boat,' he ordered Frederik, jabbing a finger towards the bank.

Frederik did as he was told, almost falling over in his haste to reach terra firma. As he came to stand next to me, his hand brushed against mine. The contact felt intentional – a sign of solidarity. I appreciated the gesture, it felt good to know I wasn't alone.

Lukas reached into the waterproof pouch that hung around his neck on a cord and withdrew a set of car keys. 'Wait in my vehicle,' he said, tossing the keys onto the grass in front of us. 'You might want to spend the time thinking about what you've just thrown away.' He turned to Bruno. 'We've wasted enough time; let's go.'

As I unbuckled my helmet, I had the sense that my time in Bavaria had come to an end. I recalled what Annett had said earlier – about the punishment for 'non-participation in scheduled activities'. I had no doubt that Frederik and I would be heading to the airport first thing in the morning, if not sooner.

7

Frederik bent down to pick up the keys. 'Let's get out of the cold, shall we?' he said. 'We might be in for a long wait.'

Turning our backs on the river, we made our way towards the Jeep. We were almost there when I heard a shout. Turning round, I saw that it was Bruno.

'Guys, can you come back over here, please?'

Frederik looked at me. 'What do you think he wants?'

I stared back at him. 'No idea,' I replied, desperately hoping we weren't in for a second round of mortification.

We started walking back to the boat. By the time we got there, all the other skaters had disembarked and were huddled together on the riverbank, still wearing their life jackets. They looked every bit as confused as I felt.

'Bravo!' Lukas said as Frederik and I approached. I couldn't tell if he was being sarcastic.

He directed us to stand on his left-hand side, so that now we were facing the other skaters. It felt a bit weird; a bit confrontational. I still had no idea what was going on.

Lukas cracked the knuckles of first one hand and then the other. It seemed terribly theatrical and I had to resist a horrible, nervous urge to laugh.

'Strip it down to its bare bones and competitive skating is all about survival of the fittest,' he said. 'It's the same with any sport.' He tipped his head towards Frederik and me. 'These two are survivors. As for the rest of you . . .' He paused; shook his head. 'Some of you would almost certainly have lost your lives if this rafting expedition had gone ahead.'

'What do you mean?' said Alexander, his smooth pink skin now flushed a hectic mauve.

'What I mean, my dear young friend, is that at this time of year the water temperature is approximately four degrees Celsius and none of you are wearing wetsuits. If you were unlucky enough to fall into the river, several things would happen. For the first few minutes, you'll be hyperventilating – breathing uncontrollably, very fast and very deep. If your head goes under the water during this critical stage, you'll end up gulping water into your lungs, in which case drowning will probably be instantaneous.'

My diaphragm contracted. I had no doubt Lukas was telling the truth, but what twisted game was he playing here?

'For the sake of argument, let's say you manage to keep your head above the surface. Within the next ten minutes, your muscles will start to weaken and your coordination and strength will fade. It's a sign that blood is moving away from the extremities and towards the centre of the body. Shortly afterwards, you'll start to feel disoriented. If you try to speak, your words will be slurred. As the flow of blood around your body slows, so will your heart rate. If you're still in the water ninety minutes after entering it, you won't be conscious. Drowning is unavoidable.'

Gabrielle's mouth had opened and closed several times during this deeply unsettling monologue and finally she managed to squeeze out some words. 'But I thought the risk of anyone falling overboard was minimal; at least that's the impression I was given.'

'You were indeed given that impression,' said Lukas. 'But you're an intelligent woman, are you not, Gabrielle?'

'*Oui*,' she replied, reverting to her native language in her confusion.

'And you saw the whirlpool with your own eyes, Gabrielle; how fast and treacherous it was.'

'Yes, but . . .' Her voice faded away.

Gerhard took up the argument. 'But Bruno insisted it was within our capabilities. He said all we had to do was hit the right spot.'

Our instructor stepped forward. 'I lied; I've never even attempted to raft the witch's cauldron. To the best of my knowledge, only one person has – and he was an international wild-water canoeing champion, who had a fully equipped safety crew watching his every paddle stroke.'

'It's actually no longer possible to access the witch's cauldron, is it, Bruno?' said Lukas.

'Correct. There are metal barriers in place at the point where the river splits in two; it's been that way for the last fifteen years. The last thing the Bavarian tourist board wants is a load of adrenaline junkies taking stupid risks.

Now, all river traffic is diverted down the much safer alternate tributary.'

Melissa's eyes tracked Bruno as he went to the bank and started to pull the raft out of the water. 'So, basically, Bruno, you duped us.' Her tone was light, but Lukas didn't seem to take her comment the way it was intended.

He threw her a sharp look. '*I* devised this task; Bruno was simply following my instructions. As for duping you . . . if you had a shred of common sense, you would consider this part of your personal development.'

Melissa looked crushed. 'I'm sorry. I didn't mean to sound ungrateful.'

'Apology accepted,' Lukas said briskly. 'But in future please keep your jokes to yourself. There is no room for humour on this training programme.' He folded his arms across his chest. 'Figure skating is as much about mental agility as physical. We take risks in training; of course we do, otherwise we'd never progress – but they need to be calculated risks. The ice is unforgiving; it's no place for reckless behaviour. Sustain an injury and you could be out of competition for months. A bad one could even end your skating career.

'As children, we do what we're told without question, trusting grown-ups to make the important decisions for us. But everyone here is an adult with free will. It was clear to me that nearly all of you had serious misgivings about our trip, and yet you were prepared to go along with it. I'm not saying you should ignore the advice of your coaches and other authority figures, but don't ever let anyone convince you to do something you know you're not ready for. Trust your instincts; if something feels wrong to you, then it probably is.' He paused, looked around the group, cocked an amused eyebrow.

'It's not as if Bruno and I were being particularly subtle. There were numerous red flags: the lack of wetsuits, the sketchy safety briefing, the failure to ask if any of you were non-swimmers. Then there's the complete absence of any other rafting activity. There's a simple reason for that – no reputable company would dream of bringing their clients to this particular stretch of river following a prolonged period of heavy rainfall like the one I know Bruno told you about. The water level's too high and the currents are too powerful for beginners, no matter how skilled their instructor. There's also the small matter of our overloaded craft. I would've thought it was obvious it was never designed to carry eleven people – or anywhere near that number. For your information, this boat can safely accommodate a maximum of six.'

He hesitated just long enough for Bruno to drag the offending inflatable the final few inches onto the back of the pickup.

'I'm a little surprised that only two of you had the ability to not only identify the potential dangers, but also to stand firm in the face of considerable psychological pressure from Bruno and me. That takes real strength of character – and, let's be honest, the stakes were high.' His Arctic blue eyes fixed on me. 'Tell me, Libby, what did you believe was going to happen to you on your return to Schloss Eis?'

I shifted my weight from one foot to the other. I hated being in the spotlight like this. 'Erm . . .' I began hesitantly. 'Annett warned us about the consequences of non-compliance. I guess I thought Frederik and I would be on the first flight out of Munich in the morning.'

Frederik nodded in agreement.

The corners of Lukas's mouth twitched. 'You see . . .' he said, turning to the other skaters. 'They were willing to sacrifice their place on the training programme because they knew there was a prize much more precious at stake – their lives.' He jerked his thumb towards the car park. 'I see your ride back's arrived.' The two vehicles that had brought us here were in the process of parking up beside Bruno's truck. 'The rest of the day is yours to spend as you please.' He went over to Frederik and held his hand out. 'My keys, please.'

The Dutch skater fumbled awkwardly in his jacket pocket for a few moments before offering up the keys to the Jeep.

'I'll see you all tomorrow morning,' Lukas called out as he started walking towards his vehicle. 'Please refer to your schedules for the timings, and bear in mind that I have a very low tolerance for tardiness.'

The grumbling began as soon as we were out of Bruno's earshot.

'What a joke,' Saskia fumed. 'Today's been a complete

waste of time. I didn't come here to be humiliated; I came here to skate. Honestly, I've a good mind to throw in the towel.'

Nathan gave her a withering look. 'I thought you said you weren't a quitter.'

She made an exasperated noise and stormed off in the direction of the 4×4s.

Flora winced. 'Sorry, guys, Sas can be a bit of a drama queen at times. You'll get used to it.'

'She does have a point though,' said Alexander, who looked utterly deflated. 'I appreciate the lesson Lukas was trying to teach us, but we're only here for a few weeks. Wouldn't the time have been better spent on the ice? That's why we're all here, isn't it?'

'It felt like Lukas was playing a game with us,' said Melissa. 'My agent would have a fit if he knew what had happened.'

Frederik gave a one-shouldered shrug. 'Then don't tell him.'

As we made our way to the car park, he fell into step beside me.

'Thanks, Libby,' he said in a voice too quiet for the others to hear.

I angled my head towards him. 'What for?'

'I was crapping myself at the thought of going over the witch's cauldron, but I wouldn't have had the guts to back out if you hadn't spoken up first.'

I smiled at him. 'You still did it though, didn't you, Frederik, and that's all that matters.'

He smiled back at me. 'You should call me Fred; all my friends do.'

On the drive back to Schloss Eis, there was plenty of speculation about what other little surprises Lukas might have planned for us. I didn't contribute much to the conversation, cocooned as I was in my own private thoughts. There was so much to process, so many observations to work over in my mind. I found it very telling, for example, that none of us had introduced ourselves by name and yet Lukas was able to match names to faces. It meant he'd done more than just study our competition stats. He must have watched video footage of our performances, perhaps even checked out our social media. It seemed I wasn't the only one who'd done their homework.

I was glad I had acquitted myself well, but I wasn't about to rest on my laurels. The day had demonstrated that Lukas Wolff was a highly unconventional coach and also, perhaps, a little manipulative. I had lost none of my admiration for him, but I knew that in order to survive at Schloss Eis, in order to keep performing well, I needed to be on my guard. I had to be focused and watchful, never taking anything at face value.

8

I checked my bag for what felt like the millionth time. Skates, blade guards, warm-up jacket, gloves, two pairs of spare laces, microfibre towel, water bottle, tissues, notebook and pen. Satisfied that I hadn't forgotten anything, I hoisted the bag over my shoulder and set off to meet the others.

Downstairs, Fred, Melissa and Gerhard were already waiting patiently in the entrance hall for the arrival of the transport that was going to take us to the ice rink. The atmosphere was subdued, just as it had been at breakfast. I think we were all feeling a little anxious about our first day of training. Meanwhile, the awkwardness of the previous day still lingered.

One by one, the others drifted in. Alexander and Gabrielle arrived together. They seemed to have given up any pretence of trying to hide their romance. Gabrielle's cheeks were flushed and Alexander looked like he'd been up half the night, which, to be fair, he probably had.

Last to arrive was Saskia. She'd barely said a word at dinner last night, apparently still smarting from the 'team-building farce', as she put it. As soon as the meal was over, she had excused herself, claiming to be exhausted. When she was a no-show at breakfast, I wondered if she'd made good on her threat and was already en route to the airport. In some ways, I hoped she was.

But here she was, kitbag in hand, apparently having had second thoughts. In contrast to yesterday, she actually seemed quite chipper. Perhaps conscious of the need to make up for her abruptness yesterday, she embarked on a charm offensive, complimenting Melissa on her tennis bracelet and asking Gabrielle where she got her 'adorable' knitted leg warmers. As she produced a tissue from her bag to tend to a shaving cut she'd spotted on Fred's neck, Nathan and I exchanged an amused look over the top of her head – a look that said Saskia hadn't fooled him either.

On the stroke of ten, Annett materialised. She reminded me of one of those wooden cuckoos that spring from a clock. I almost fancied that if I put my head to her chest, I would hear the whir and click of a hidden motor. I still had no idea whereabouts in the castle she ate, or slept, or worked. I'd made a casual enquiry about her living arrangements the previous night, as she'd served up lamb stew from the trolley. Her answer had been vague – deliberately so, I felt. 'I'm in the west wing, with Lukas,' she'd explained. 'But if you need me, don't come looking; just call my mobile.'

That was fine in theory, but, as I had already discovered, the phone signal inside the castle was patchy – as was the Wi-Fi – and it often took several attempts to send a simple text.

'There's still no sign of our transport,' said Gerhard, who'd been standing sentry at the window for the past ten minutes.

'We won't be needing it today,' Annett told him.

Gabrielle's face fell. 'Don't say our training's been cancelled.'

'Certainly not. Please, follow me.'

Without further explanation, she turned on her heel and led the way along a windowless corridor giving off the hall, one of many I had yet to explore.

We set off after her, like a flock of ducklings following their mother. I'd been anticipating lots of twists and turns, but on this occasion we proceeded in a straight line, heading into what felt like the very heart of the building. The corridor ended abruptly at a huge set of double doors, regally decorated with gold filigree. Annett flung them open and waved us in.

What I saw when I entered the room rendered me temporarily speechless. All of us had assumed our coaching sessions would take place either at the nearest public rink, or at a local ice hockey club with a private facility for hire. None of us had even considered the possibility that Lukas might have his own rink, right here in the castle.

The room we found ourselves in was vast; forty to forty-five metres long. Dominating it was a rectangular ice rink. Unlike most public rinks, there was no barrier. Three sides of the ice ran flush with the rubber matting that had been laid across the parquet floor, while the fourth side faced onto a huge, mirrored wall. Equally impressive was the dome-shaped roof lantern above our heads that flooded the space with natural light.

'I wasn't expecting this,' said Nathan as he walked towards the ice.

'Not bad, is it?'

Lukas Wolff waved to us from a row of tiered seating. I'd been so transfixed by the rink I hadn't seen him sitting there.

'This used to be the ballroom,' he told us. 'But I've never been much of a quick-stepper, so when I bought Schloss Eis I had it repurposed.'

'It's incredible,' said Flora breathily. Her gaze drifted up to the lantern. Weak winter sunlight filtered through the glass, casting flickering patterns on the ice. 'How do you control the temperature in here? Doesn't the ice melt as soon as the sun hits it?'

Lukas rose to his feet and walked towards us. 'Temperature isn't an issue. This ice isn't made from frozen water.'

'No?' said Melissa in surprise. 'What *is* it made from?'

'Self-lubricating, ultra-high molecular weight polyethylene.'

Fred gawped at him. 'Say that again.'

'Otherwise known as synthetic ice. The blades of a skate cut open molecules in its surface. This action releases a lubricant that reproduces the gliding effect you get on regular ice. But, unlike regular ice, there's no need for coolants, condensers, resurfacers or noisy generators. The only maintenance it requires is a weekly vacuum and polish. And the fact it consumes zero energy makes it environmentally friendly too.'

Nathan let his kitbag slide off his shoulder and drop to the floor. 'Does it come in one piece?'

'No, it's made up of interlocking panels.'

'Like a jigsaw puzzle?' said Saskia.

'Yes, except there's no danger of it breaking apart. Each piece is attached to the next one with a series of small plugs. As you can see, the joins are practically invisible.'

Gerhard went over to the rink and stared down at the ice. 'I've skated on this stuff before. It's OK, but it's a bit slower than the real thing, isn't it?'

'Marginally,' said Lukas. '*This* synthetic ice uses the very latest technology. The glide effect is only two per cent slower than traditional ice, which, for training purposes, I actually think is preferable.'

Gerhard rolled out his bottom lip. 'How so?'

'The added friction makes it easier to feel the blade under your foot, helping to isolate specific movements and build muscle strength, which in turn results in faster, more controlled spins. Furthermore, it encourages you to press harder into jumps, resulting in more height. It also means that, when the time comes to transfer your newly acquired skills to a conventional rink, everything feels just that little bit easier.' Lukas's mouth twitched in an approximation of a smile. 'And, of course, it doesn't feel cold when you fall over.' He pushed the sleeves of his thin sweater up to his elbows. 'I hope you all enjoyed a hearty breakfast because you're going to be expending a great deal of energy over the next few hours. Before we begin, does anyone have any questions? If so, please unburden yourself now. I don't want any distractions once we get onto the ice.'

'Uh, yeah, I do,' said Nathan. 'It's about the selection process.' He paused, as if waiting for the go-ahead to proceed.

'I'm listening,' said Lukas.

'I know you said that stuff yesterday about choosing us because we had courage and whatnot, but there's got to be more to it than that. There are so many other skaters you could've picked; why us?'

I was pleased he'd asked the question. It was something all of us had been wondering.

Lukas made a fist of one hand and cupped it with the other hand, grinding his fist against it. 'I can't go into specifics; it's an issue of confidentiality, as I'm sure you'll appreciate. But I'd be happy to make some general comments if people feel that would be useful.'

A series of *yes, please*s rang out, mine among them.

Lukas gave a nod of acceptance. 'I should preface my answer by saying that my research took several months, although I'm not willing to go into detail about my methodology. Suffice to say, some of my techniques were rather unorthodox – though not, I must stress, illegal.'

Interesting.

'I was looking for a certain type of skater, one with a specific set of physical attributes, as well as the technical skill required for the particular project I had in mind. A fearless and fiercely ambitious skater; the kind of skater who views failure not as a reason to give up, but as fuel to ignite their ambition and make them try harder the next time.' He started pacing up and down beside the rink. 'I'm very aware that all of you have experienced struggles in your career in one form or another – injury, bereavement, financial hardship, an uphill battle to step out of the shadow of your illustrious forebears . . .'

I sneaked a sideways glance at Saskia. No prizes for guessing who he was referring to with that last one.

'It would've been the easiest thing in the world to throw in the towel. But none of you did.'

My cheeks grew warm. Lukas's research clearly hadn't revealed I'd been on the verge of quitting skating to work in an office. I sent up a silent prayer that I hadn't publicised my new job on my socials.

He stopped pacing and looked at Gerhard. His pupils didn't move, their fix on the German boy almost disturbing in their focus. 'You look sceptical, Gerhard.'

'It's not that; I was just thinking that there must be lots of better skaters than us who possess those qualities. I don't wish to insult anyone here, but let's be honest, none of us are Olympic contenders. Why didn't you set your sights a bit higher?'

'Because that would've been too easy.' Lukas reached a hand to his neck and tugged on the skin around his Adam's apple. 'As you're probably aware, I stepped back from coaching several years ago. I became disillusioned with the sport for a variety of reasons, although I don't feel this is an appropriate forum to air my grievances. Suddenly, I had a lot of time on my hands and I spent it thinking very hard about what I should do with my life going forward. Part of me was bored of pro skating and all the petty rules and regulations that govern it, but the other part was unwilling to let it go. Eventually, I reached a compromise with myself. I decided that I would sever all ties with the sport, but before I did I would set myself one last coaching challenge – a challenge that would push me to the very edges of my capabilities. And in order to do that I needed enthusiastic amateurs like yourselves, not professionals.'

Ah, now I understood. This wasn't about us at all; it was about *him*.

His pale blue eyes swivelled in my direction. 'What's on your mind, Libby? You seem troubled.'

He did this a lot, I'd noticed. Tried to get inside people's heads. Move things around. Perhaps he thought that by encouraging us to talk about our feelings, he was helping us. But my private thoughts were precisely that: *private*.

With some difficulty, I met his gaze head-on. 'I'm not troubled at all,' I lied. 'I'm just intrigued. I'd love to hear more about this challenge you've devised.'

His tongue flickered out to moisten his lips, a reptilian little tic. 'I think perhaps it would be easier to show you.'

He lifted his right foot and rested it on his left thigh. It was only then that I saw he was wearing ice skates.

'I need to warm up first,' he said as he removed first one blade guard and then the other. 'It shouldn't take long; I was practising just before you got here.'

Lukas Wolff's warm-up was a footwork masterclass – his backward crossovers sublime, his Russian stroking poetry in motion. Even though this wasn't a performance in the traditional sense, his natural showmanship shone through. The commanding presence, the confident posture, the electric energy that emanated from him like static, lifting the ends of my hair. As he embarked on a series of seemingly effortless edge pulls, Nathan leaned in to me.

'This is such a privilege,' he whispered. His breath felt hot against the side of my face and I could smell his cologne, woody and clean. 'I wouldn't swap places with anyone in the world right now.'

'Nor would I,' I whispered back, unable to tear my eyes away from Lukas, not even for a second.

I could have watched him forever, but all too soon his warm-up was complete and he was skating back over to us.

'Pay close attention, my friends,' he said as he came to a halt on the ice. 'I will demonstrate this only once.'

He took a deep breath and looked up at the roof lantern, as though summoning his thoughts to an internal muster station. A moment later, he was propelling himself into the centre of the rink with astonishing speed.

For the next twenty seconds or so, I watched, utterly transfixed, as Lukas performed a spectacular and cardiac arrest-inducing series of jumps, spins, loops and flips that seemed to defy the laws of physics and stretch the limits of human physiology to breaking point. It stirred something deep inside me, making me almost tearful. It wasn't figure skating in the traditional sense. It was freestyle, mixed with parkour, with a dash of martial arts and pinch of classical ballet – all the disparate parts melding together perfectly to form a single, heartbreaking whole.

But this thing of great beauty had a very ugly name. They called it the Grim Reaper.

9

There was a brief stunned silence, before Flora said out of the corner of her mouth, 'Is this a joke?'

Alexander gave a stunned cough. 'He looks pretty serious to me.'

Lukas came towards us. As he got closer, I could see the vein pulsing in his neck, the sweat coating his top lip. I wasn't surprised he was breathing so heavily. Frankly, I was amazed a man in his forties was still able to execute such a complex and demanding sequence.

'Well?' he said hoarsely. 'Are you up for the challenge?'

Melissa wrinkled her nose. 'I'm not sure I fully understand the terms and conditions.'

'Then let me spell it out for you.'

He waited a few beats. Whether this was an attempt to keep us in suspense or give him a chance to catch his breath, it was impossible to say.

'Eight weeks,' he said. 'You have eight weeks to learn the Grim Reaper.' His shoulders quivered. 'I've always hated that name, but I suppose it's too late to change it now.'

Gerhard gave a little shake of the head. 'I'm sorry, but I don't think that's realistic.'

'Admitting defeat already?' said Lukas, his pale eyes

steady and shrewd. 'Just like you did at the Baden-Württemberg Championships in 2022, when you quit before you'd even set foot on the ice.'

A look of pain collected on Gerhard's face. 'I had a stomach upset. I thought I would be OK to compete, but I was wrong. As soon as I started the warm-up, I knew it would be too much for me and so I decided to withdraw.'

'If you want your career to progress, perhaps you should take a page from Nathan's playbook.'

Gerhard looked at him blankly.

'I'm referring to his performance at the Nashville Invitational in the same year. He came fifth in his category. That's right, isn't it, Mr Carter?'

Nathan dipped his head in acknowledgement.

'Fifth?' Gerhard sneered. 'That's not very impressive.'

'Actually, it was a magnificent achievement when you consider that the evening after completing his short programme, Nathan was struck down with food poisoning after eating a meal containing shellfish at his hotel. He spent most of the night vomiting – and yet he still managed to get on the ice the following morning for his free skate. Now, *that*, in my opinion, shows true strength of character.'

Nathan looked at him in amazement. 'How did you know that? I never made that information public.'

'I have my sources,' Lukas replied enigmatically.

'Your advice is duly noted,' said Gerhard, puffing his chest out. 'And I'm more than willing to accept any challenge you throw at us, but the fact remains that no other skater has ever conquered the Grim Reaper. Plenty have tried, and all of them more accomplished than us.'

'Ah, but *you* have something none of those others had.'

Gerhard raised a questioning eyebrow.

'Me,' said Lukas. 'I invented the Grim Reaper and I alone possess the necessary skills to teach it to another.'

It was a bold claim – and one I wasn't convinced was accurate – but I wasn't about to risk his wrath by disagreeing with him.

'Have you tried to teach it to anyone else before?' asked Saskia. 'Tania Jurkovic, for example. You coached her for three years, didn't you? As Croatian national champion, I would've thought she had the necessary ability.'

'Never,' Lukas fired back. 'Until this moment, I wasn't ready to share the knowledge.'

Saskia cocked her head to the side. 'So this is an experiment then?'

'Yes, in a manner of speaking. I assume you have no objection to being my guinea pig?'

She thrust her chin out. 'Not at all, Mr Wolff.'

'Please, enough of the formalities, it's just Lukas.' He looked around the group. 'As for the rest of you, it's not too late to back out. If anyone wishes to withdraw from the training programme, they should say so now. Oh . . .' He raised a finger in the air. 'But before you make up your minds, there *is* one more thing you should know.'

I had a sudden sense of déjà vu. It was the same feeling I had yesterday: that this was a performance, everything planned and rehearsed in advance. Except Lukas was the only one with the script.

'Unfortunately, not all of you will be here for the entire eight weeks. Each week, someone will be going home, until only one of you is left.' He delivered this blow like a poker player, facial features impassive.

'Like in a reality show, you mean?' said Melissa.

'Not quite. There will be no cameras or public vote; I alone will decide who leaves.'

Nathan let out a long, low whistle. 'And you'll base your decision on how well we've performed in the previous week?'

'Correct. Just to clarify, this means that only one of you will have the chance to learn the Grim Reaper in its entirety. For any skaters returning home early, I shall, of course, reimburse you for any additional costs incurred in amending your travel arrangements.'

I ground my rear molars together. I was fast learning that with Lukas Wolff, nothing was quite what it seemed. Would I have burned my bridges with the council if I'd known the full rules of engagement? Absolutely. Despite Lukas's latest bombshell, this still represented an amazing opportunity. Any skater who managed to pull off the Grim Reaper in competition would receive heaps of publicity, that would in turn lead to lucrative sponsorship deals. For the first time in my life, I wouldn't have to worry about paying for skates, or costumes, or travel expenses. I might even be able to turn professional.

Even if I only managed to eke out a couple of weeks here, I was certain to pick up lots of new skills that I could incorporate into my routines – and just being able to say I was part of this experience would probably raise my profile and might attract interest from sponsors. I had no idea if it was possible for mid-level skaters like us to learn the Grim Reaper in the short amount of time available, but I was certainly going to throw everything I had at it. This was, I knew, the only chance I had of resurrecting my skating career.

'So?' Lukas said. 'Does anyone wish to leave?'

Unsurprisingly, there were no takers.

'Good,' he said. 'You have twenty minutes to warm up.'

It was the first time I had skated on synthetic ice and my initial impressions were favourable. Its surface was super smooth, almost freakishly so, and I saw right away how it would come into its own for complex jumps and intricate choreography. And since it had none of the minor imperfections you get on real ice, the risk of falls was vastly reduced. It was true that a little more effort was required to glide and maintain speed, but, as Lukas had pointed out, for training purposes that wasn't necessarily a bad thing.

Once I felt comfortable in this new environment, I began my warm-up with a serpentine stroking sequence, before moving on to leg extensions, forward and backward crossovers, lunges, mohawks and edge pulls. With the basics out of the way, I trialled some simple twizzles and waltz jumps. As I set off on a lap around the rink, I saw Saskia execute a flawless split jump. It wasn't the sort of thing one would normally include in a warm-up, but maybe she was right to come out all guns blazing. This was a competition, after all.

Feeling under pressure to prove myself, I arched my back, dropping my head and shoulders towards the ice, arms positioned above my torso in a C-shape. Extending one leg behind me, I began to spin on my supporting skate, quickly building momentum until I felt a wonderful light-headedness that seemed to lift me from the solidity of the ice into thin air. As if the top of my head had opened and all the anxieties of the past two days were pouring out of it.

'Nice layback, Libby,' I heard a male voice say.

I spread my arms out, decreasing my speed, and the blurred shapes around me morphed into people. Only then did I realise that the praise had come from Lukas. The last time I saw him, he was critiquing Fred's spread eagles. Now he was standing less than six feet away from me.

'Oh,' I said, genuinely surprised by the compliment. 'Thank you very much.'

The smile on his face congealed. 'Next time, try to go into the spin with a little more power. It'll help you find the sweet spot quicker and make your rotation speed more consistent.'

Before I could reply, he turned his back on me.

'Warm-up's over,' he said, clapping his hands together. 'Time to get down to business.'

Immediately, everyone stopped what they were doing and skated towards Lukas, forming a tight semicircle around him.

'This week, we will be focusing on a single element of the Grim Reaper – the triple Salchow,' he announced without flourish or emphasis.

He was referring to a jump. In terms of difficulty, it ranked in the middle of the spectrum – harder than a toe-loop, but not as hard as an Axel. Named after its inventor, ten-time World Champion Ulrich Salchow, a standard Salchow involved a single rotation in the air, a double two rotations, and so on. I had a pretty solid double, but as of right now, a triple was only a distant dream.

'Have any of you successfully landed a triple?' asked Lukas.

'I have, a handful of times,' said Melissa. 'But only in training.'

On hearing this, Saskia moved her head towards the Chinese girl like an animal following the motions of its prey. I could only imagine the jealous thoughts that were raging through her mind.

'Very good, Melissa,' said Lukas. 'But that doesn't mean you can relax. I want you to spend the next few days polishing your technique – and if I don't see any signs of improvement, you could still be going home this week.'

'Got it,' she snapped back.

'When it comes to perfecting jump technique, it's all about the science,' Lukas said. 'Jumps demonstrate perfectly the vital part played by physics in our sport. We take off from the ice and sail through the air in a parabolic curve, spinning as we go. That trade-off between the energy used for sailing and the energy used for spinning is what makes jumps such a difficult and compelling part of any skater's routine.'

He ran a hand over his forehead, as if to rub away the tension there.

'Most of the skaters I've worked with have had no problem producing the necessary momentum as they leave the ice. The difficulty lies in getting enough rotational speed to complete the jump. The good news is that, according to the science, a change in arm position by just three or four degrees can increase your spin rate and should make three full rotations achievable for all of you.'

He pursed his lips. 'However, in addition to the physical challenges, there are also significant psychological hurdles to overcome. Scientists have proven that humans have a hardwired maximum speed limit, which varies from person to person. It can take months for a skater to break that mindset and spin faster than their natural comfort zone allows. But as you know, we don't have months; we have one week. One week to land a triple Salchow. Anyone who fails to do so runs the risk of an early departure from Schloss Eis.'

Gabrielle saucered her eyes. 'But I thought you said only one person would be leaving.'

'My apologies, I should have been more precise. What I meant was *at least* one person.'

I took a metaphorical gulp. A week. I didn't think it was possible – not for me, anyway.

Lukas eyed us closely. 'Are any of you familiar with Newton's First Law of Motion?'

He was met with blank looks and head shakes.

'Put simply, it states that an object will remain at rest unless an external force acts upon it. The degree to which an object resists the influence of such a force is known as the moment of inertia. In figure skating, this is the measurement of the distance the skater's mass extends outward from the axis on which he or she is spinning. A higher moment of inertia corresponds to a lower rotational speed, and a lower moment of inertia to a higher speed. It's the reason we control our spins by pulling our arms in when we want to turn faster, and spreading them out when we want to slow down.' He paused. 'Is everybody still with me?'

Barely, I thought, forcing a nod.

'Jumps are all about controlling that moment of inertia. Even a tiny bend in the hips and knees can allow the skater to land with a lower centre of mass than they started with, thereby squeezing out a few precious degrees of rotation and a better body position for landing. It stands to reason then that if we can artificially trigger a bigger change in the moment of inertia, it will give our rotational speed a boost.'

Alexander, who was clearly struggling to grasp the concept, sniggered. 'I guess we'll have to take your word for it.'

The look on Lukas's face suggested he was not amused. 'Thank you, Mr Nowak,' he said tightly.

Alexander frowned. 'What for?'

'For volunteering to demonstrate.'

Without further explanation, Lukas skated to the edge of the rink, where a large plastic storage box was sitting on the rubber matting. As he bent down to flip its lid open, I saw him wince and put a hand to his stomach. Maybe the Grim Reaper had taken more out of him than he cared to admit. He reached into the box and removed a couple of items before skating back to the group. As he got closer, I realised he was carrying a small pair of dumbbells.

'Take these, one in each hand,' he said, thrusting them at a bewildered Alexander. He pointed to the centre of the rink. 'Now, get out there and give us your best double Salchow.'

Alexander looked down at the weights. 'What am I supposed to do with these?'

'Keep holding them. Use your hands and arms exactly as you would normally and just pretend the dumbbells aren't there.'

I ran my tongue under my upper teeth. What was Lukas up to now? Jumps called for controlled arm movements and the hand weights would be a massive hindrance. I hoped this wasn't another one of his mind games; a way of humiliating Alexander, bringing him down to size.

Unzipping a pocket in his jacket, Lukas produced a mobile phone – a small, basic model. Combined with his lack of socials, it hinted at the fact he wasn't the world's most prolific communicator. 'I'm going to record you,' he said, swiping the screen. 'And afterwards we will analyse your performance.'

Alexander flopped his shoulders, a gesture of resignation. Cocky as he was, I couldn't help feeling sorry for him. Even for seasoned skaters, it was hard to jump on demand – especially with everyone watching, and Lukas filming. However, with an elimination looming in a few days' time, Alexander couldn't afford to refuse. All he could do was try to come out of it with his dignity intact.

He straightened his spine and pushed off the ice, dumbbells clutched to his chest. Instead of rushing into the jump straight away, he set off on a lap of the rink, giving him time to build his composure. It was a smart move and, if Lukas was irritated by the delay, he didn't show it.

As Alexander completed his lap, he went into a mohawk turn, which was my own preferred mode of entry into the Salchow. It was the signal for Lukas to start filming.

Given the pressure and the added encumbrance of the weights, Alexander performed better than I'd anticipated.

Much better, in fact. Not only did he achieve a reasonable height, he managed to keep his form throughout the entire jump and land it cleanly.

'So,' said Lukas as Alexander skated over to us. 'How did that feel?'

'Strange,' he replied. 'But in a good way. I thought the dumbbells would weigh me down, but when I was in the air, it actually felt as if I was spinning quicker than I normally do.'

'That's because you were. From where I was standing, it looked as if you managed two and a quarter rotations. But let's see what the video shows.'

Lukas looked down at his phone, eyebrows knitted together as he watched the replay.

'Yes, I'm right. Take a look for yourselves.'

He turned the screen towards us and played the video again – once at normal speed and then again in slow motion.

There was no doubt about it. Alexander had managed two and a quarter rotations.

'Wow,' said Alexander, who was grinning from ear to ear. 'I've never managed more than two rotations before.'

'You made it look so easy,' gushed Saskia, treating the Polish man to a megawatt smile. 'It was incredible to watch.'

'Not incredible,' said Lukas brusquely. 'Just physics in action. When you brought your arms in close to your body, the increased weight in your hands meant there was a bigger change in the moment of inertia, which naturally accelerated your rotational speed. If you managed an extra quarter rotation on your first attempt, just imagine what you could achieve in the coming days if you keep practising with the weights.'

'Yes,' said Alexander, nodding enthusiastically. 'It all makes perfect sense now.'

Lukas pointed to the storage box. 'There are enough dumbbells for all of you. Please take a set and experience Newton's First Law for yourselves.'

10

It was day five of the programme and I was relaxing in the library after a long day on the ice. I was exhausted, but at the same time exhilarated. It was as if a spark had been lit inside me and every day I woke up and found myself still here, the flames burned higher and brighter.

I had learned more about skating in the short time I'd been at Schloss Eis than I had in a whole year with Eva. Not that she was a bad coach; far from it. Her reputation was excellent, so much so that she had a waiting list of clients. But Lukas wasn't just in another league, he was in another stratosphere.

He was a master at breaking down a jump into its constituent parts, showing you how to perfect each one and then helping you put all of the pieces back together again. His approach was meticulous and he was a stickler for detail – the kind of detail that separated a superb skater from a merely good one. He had already highlighted several weaknesses in my jump technique, which nobody had ever pulled me up on before. It was like suddenly realising that, though you believed you'd been running in a race, you'd actually been on a treadmill the whole time.

The Wolff Man was also a genius when it came to the aesthetic aspect of figure skating. Traditionally, not much training time was devoted to artistic development. There tended to be an assumption that either you had it or you didn't. But Lukas had turned all that on its head. He'd made me understand how the non-technical aspects of skating – qualities like grace and fluidity, as well as subtle hand movements and nuanced footwork – could add depth and authenticity to my performances. In training today, he'd made us all stand in front of the ballroom's mirrored wall for half an hour – not skating, just prac-tising different facial expressions and trying to work out which ones would help us establish an emotional connec-tion with judges and audience alike.

I'd made another interesting observation too. Despite his reputation as a daredevil, I'd come to realise that Lukas was actually very cautious. In yesterday's session, he'd spent several hours educating us in the mechanics of landing jumps, so that our bodies were in proper alignment and we wouldn't cause any unnecessary strain on our joints. He'd also encouraged us to make full use of the castle's tennis court as he believed that playing different sports helped skaters develop the coordination and flexibility that was critical to preventing injury. I was pretty bad at tennis, but Flora and I had enjoyed a few early-morning knockabouts. Lukas had also directed us to make full use of the castle's gymnasium, hydrotherapy pool and sauna – advice which I had fully embraced. Even though my chances of making it through to the final week were slim to non-existent, I was determined to squeeze every drop I could out of this experience.

At the same time, one question kept nudging at me with an unnerving insistence: why was Lukas doing this? He claimed he wanted one last challenge before he quit skating for good, but surely there was another goal he could've set himself – one that wouldn't have required quite so much time and effort on his part, not to mention the expense and inconvenience of hosting a group of strangers in his home.

I kept telling myself not to over-analyse. Sometimes it was better not to think; to hunt for hidden meanings that might not even be there. If I wanted to do well in the programme, I couldn't afford any distractions, which meant pushing any concerns I had about Lukas's motivations to the back of my mind.

I looked down at my phone, reading through the message I was busy composing for the family group chat. I'd been posting regular updates for Mum and Gran, and today I was sharing the very exciting news that I'd landed my first ever triple Salchow. True to form, Lukas's praise had been sparing. He had congratulated me – but then, in the same breath, told me I had 'all the grace of a pregnant hippopotamus'. The barb stung, but I took it on the chin, just relieved my chances of going home in two days' time were now much reduced. I hadn't relayed this fact in the message to Mum and Gran; they still didn't know I was in competition with a bunch of other skaters. I'm not sure why I hadn't told them; I guess I didn't want to ruin the fantasy for them.

'Libby?'

I looked up from my phone to see Flora holding a teabag aloft. She was standing at the hostess trolley that Annett had just wheeled into the library. On it sat a thermos flask of hot water, a wooden box containing a selection of herbal teabags and a plate of rustic-looking biscuits – a little something to keep us going until dinner time.

I sent the message and let the phone fall into my lap. 'Sorry, Flora, I'll have peppermint, thanks. Actually, no . . . make that chamomile; it'll help me to unwind.'

Training had finished a couple of hours ago, but I was still coiled tight as a spring. I had considered heading to the hydrotherapy pool with Alexander, Gabrielle and Saskia. Ever since we'd got here, the three of them had been thick as thieves. Obviously, Alexander and Gabrielle were a couple of sorts, but I wasn't sure what had drawn the pair of them to Saskia. Perhaps it was her single-mindedness; certainly, all of them were fiercely competitive, although Saskia was definitely the worst. In training, she was utterly shameless; forever grandstanding, doing anything she could to grab Lukas's attention. To our mentor's credit, he distributed his time equally between us. No doubt this was a vital part of his methodology as he carried out his self-styled experiment.

Fearing my presence might be unwelcome at the pool, I'd decided to chill in the library with Flora and Nathan instead. The three of us had naturally gravitated towards one another and I found them both warm, open and incredibly easy to get along with. The fact I fancied the pants off Nathan helped of course, but I was trying not to let that get in the way.

I was surprised at how quickly allegiances were forming. I put it down to the castle's slightly claustrophobic atmosphere and the fact we were spending twelve or thirteen hours a day in each other's company.

'Thanks,' I said as Flora handed me a mug. The tea was too hot to drink, but its warmth was welcome. Although the castle had undergone an extensive programme of modernisation, its high ceilings and stone floors presented a challenge to the central heating system, especially in the evenings when the temperature outside dropped like a stone. The full-length curtains were tightly drawn against the cold, but the wind was picking up. I could hear it buffeting the trees in spiteful gusts, shoving and jostling, flexing its muscles. 'What do you think Lukas is doing right now?' I asked as Flora handed Nathan his rooibos.

'Devising new ways to torture us, probably,' she replied. She set her own drink down on a side table before joining Nathan on the sofa. 'Those single-leg squats he made us do earlier have given me shocking shin splints.'

'His methods are effective though, aren't they?' said Nathan. 'You almost nailed your triple today. Another quarter rotation and you'll be there.'

'You're right,' she conceded. 'I feel like an hour with Lukas is worth a week with any other coach.'

I blew on the surface of my tea. 'Do you think there's a chance he might change his mind about retiring from coaching once the programme's finished?'

Flora shrugged. 'Who knows what goes on inside Lukas Wolff's head? The man's a total enigma.'

'A total sociopath, more like,' said Nathan.

I regarded him over the top of my mug. 'That's a bit harsh.'

'Not really. Let's look at the evidence. Lacks empathy: check. Exhibits controlling behaviour: check. Exploits others for personal gain: check.'

'I don't think he's exploiting us,' said Flora. 'We're getting just as much out of this experience as him – probably more.' She reached across Nathan for her tea. 'Do you think Lukas has a significant other? There's certainly no indication that anyone apart from Annett is living here with him.'

I thought back to all the research I'd done online before coming here. 'If he has, they haven't gone public with their relationship.'

Flora pulled a pink mohair throw off the back of the sofa and draped it over her legs.

'He dated that French skater for a while, didn't he?' she said. 'The one with the to-die-for sit spin.'

I nodded. 'Léa Molyneux.'

'Yeah, that's her. I remember seeing photos of them together at Paris Fashion Week.'

'Lukas showed up to Fashion Week?' Nathan said, sounding surprised. 'That doesn't sound like him. Even at the height of his fame, he always went out of his way to avoid publicity.'

'Léa was appearing on the runway for one of the big-name French designers,' I told him. 'I don't remember his name, but he used a whole load of female athletes in his show. I guess Lukas went along to support her. I have to say, he looked pretty uncomfortable in the photos.'

'How long were they together?'

'Two or three years, I think.'

Nathan put his mug down on the floor and rested his hands on his thighs. He had beautiful hands, strong and clean as a surgeon's; the sort of hands you could rely on.

'I'm amazed Léa lasted so long,' he said. 'I think I'd rather donate a kidney than spend an evening socialising with Lukas Wolff. I've met morticians with better senses of humour.'

A giggle rose in my chest. 'Aww, he's not that bad.'

'He is – and you know it,' Nathan said, half joking, half serious.

'Annett's not much better,' said Flora. 'She's so uptight. She must get lonely sometimes; you'd think she'd be glad to have an actual conversation with someone, but whenever I try to make small talk with her, she always shuts me down.'

'It would be nice if she ate dinner with us occasionally,' I said. 'Lukas too. At the moment, it feels very much like them and us.'

Nathan got up and went to retrieve the biscuits from the trolley. He offered the plate to each of us in turn, before he sat back down and rested the plate on his lap. 'It's strange to think one of us will be going home on

Friday,' he said, helping himself to a shortbread round. 'Who do you think it's going to be?'

I was reluctant to voice my opinion. It was obvious who was excelling, who was struggling and who was somewhere in the middle (I counted myself in this last subset). I just wasn't comfortable critiquing people behind their backs; it didn't seem very sportsmanlike somehow. Or maybe I just felt that way because the thought of having my own sporting odds discussed by the others made me cringe.

Flora had no such compunction. 'I reckon anyone who already has their triple Salchow is safe,' she said. 'That just leaves me, Fred, Saskia and Gerhard – and the smart money's on Fred.'

'Yeah, he's definitely the weakest skater here,' said Nathan, as he broke off a chunk of shortbread and stuffed it in his mouth. 'Although I wouldn't be crying into my pillow if Saskia went.' He turned to look at Flora. 'Sorry, I know y'all are family.'

She flipped her hand, batting away his concerns. 'It's fine, I know Saskia can be a bit difficult at times. She has very high standards; she gets frustrated when things – or people – fall short of her expectations. Unfortunately, she has one of those faces that can't hide what she's thinking. Honestly, I don't think she knows she's doing it half the time.'

Flora's interpretation was a generous one. Personally, I didn't trust Saskia – and I suspected the feeling was mutual. Underneath the smiles and the chit-chat, there was an undercurrent of suspicion between us. No matter what she asked me, I could hear the sub-textual rip-tide of what she really wanted to say. *Why are you here? What could a girl like you – a girl who's never competed on the international circuit and who is quite clearly from the wrong side of the tracks – possibly bring to Lukas Wolff's party?*

As usual, I kept my feelings to myself. I felt the same way I did as a child, when I stayed tight-lipped about my home situation, terrified I might inadvertently reveal the truth and that all my rotten secrets would come spilling out like maggots.

'Do you and Saskia see much of each other back home?' I asked Flora.

'Not really; we live in different countries, don't forget. The only time we get to catch up is at competitions.'

Nathan took another biscuit from the plate. 'Do you think she's pissed that you spend more time hanging out with us than her?'

'God, no. Saskia always does her own thing; she won't have given it a second thought.'

She broke off as the door opened and Fred appeared, followed by Gerhard and Melissa. It was the first time I'd seen any of them since training had finished.

I said hi to Fred as he passed within inches of my armchair, but he didn't reply. His eyes were glazed and he seemed a little unsteady on his feet. He took a circuitous route across the room, almost tripping over a standard lamp, before finally collapsing onto a green velvet chaise.

'Are you all right, Fred?' asked Flora.

'No, he isn't,' said Melissa. 'He's drunk.'

'Lucky him. Where did he get the booze from?'

'No idea,' she replied. 'Gerhard and I were coming back from the sauna and we found him in the entrance hall, swigging from a bottle of Jägermeister and singing at the top of his lungs. We were terrified Annett would hear him, so we tried to persuade him to go back to his room.'

Gerhard gave an exaggerated eye roll. 'We managed to get him halfway up the stairs, but then he changed his mind and decided to come charging in here instead.'

'So where's the Jäger now?' asked Nathan hopefully.

'I took it off him and hid it behind the console table in the entrance hall,' said Melissa. 'Don't get excited; it was almost empty.' She sighed. 'Shall we have another go at trying to get him upstairs, Gerhard?'

I looked over at Fred. He was lying on his side with his eyes closed.

'I'd leave him where he is, if I were you. I doubt Annett will show her face – and if she does, we'll just say Fred's taking a nap.' I glanced at the carriage clock on the mantelpiece. 'There's still a couple of hours before dinner. He should have sobered up a bit by then.'

'Good plan,' said Flora. She got up and took the mohair throw over to the chaise, laying it carefully over Fred, who was making soft guttural snorts.

'We need to wedge something behind him,' I told her. 'We don't want him rolling onto his back, just in case he's sick.'

Setting aside the plate of biscuits, Nathan scooped up an armful of sofa cushions and carried them over to the chaise. Fred barely stirred as Nathan stuffed two of the cushions behind his back and another one underneath his head.

'Do you think that'll be enough?' he said.

'Should be,' I replied. 'But let's keep an eye on him, just in case.'

I found Fred's behaviour worrying. He seemed like such a quiet, sensible man; not the sort of person who'd get blind drunk on his own. I wondered where he'd got the booze from. He'd either found a secret stash somewhere in the castle or he'd brought it with him in his luggage. Either way, if word of his infraction got back to Lukas, I had no doubt the consequences would be severe.

Flora busied herself making tea for the new arrivals, while Gerhard pulled up an ottoman for him and Melissa to sit on. Outside, the gale showed no sign of abating. It was raining now; I could hear heavy droplets ricocheting off the windowpanes.

'I'm sorry for the intrusion,' said Melissa. 'We can take our tea back to our rooms, if you'd prefer.'

'Don't be silly,' said Flora as she poured hot water into two mugs.

Nathan passed the plate of biscuits to Melissa. 'It looks like the pressure's really getting to Fred, huh?'

'He's probably crapping himself because he still hasn't got his triple Salchow,' she said as she took a heart-shaped cookie and passed the plate to Gerhard.

'Neither have I,' said Gerhard. 'But you don't see me getting wasted and making a fool of myself.'

Nathan looked at Fred, who was now snoring full throttle. 'Lukas was quite tough on him today. If I were Fred, I'd be feeling pretty shitty right now. Maybe he just wanted to kick back.'

It was a good point. We'd all witnessed Lukas laying into Fred after he kept making the same mistake as we practised our take-offs. Time after time, Fred had allowed the blade of his skate to turn forward just before his foot left the ice. It was a cardinal sin in competition skating and meant the judges would deem the jump 'cheated' and therefore invalid. Lukas hadn't raised his voice, but his tone was so savage, Fred had physically reared back as if he'd been slapped. He told Fred he'd never worked with such an untalented skater and claimed he was beginning to regret his decision to include him in the programme.

By the end of Lukas's tirade, Fred had looked utterly cowed. Although we were competing against each other, I took no pleasure from the collapse of his facial muscles, the scorch of pain in his eyes. If it had been any other rink in any other place, I'd have gone over and put my arms around him.

Fred had apologised profusely to Lukas, promising he'd try harder next time. But by then Lukas seemed to have given up on him. For the remainder of the session, he basically ignored him. I understood that coaches had to be tough in order to get results, but to me, Lukas's behaviour verged on bullying. I still thought Nathan was wide of the mark when he suggested our mentor had a personality disorder, but his interpersonal skills could definitely use some work.

'I can see why Lukas was angry though,' said Gerhard, as Flora handed him his tea. 'He pointed out where Fred was going wrong numerous times, but Fred refused to listen.'

'I don't think it was a case of him *refusing*,' said Melissa. 'Have *you* never had an off day, where you couldn't get something right, no matter how hard you tried?'

Gerhard gave a hard laugh. 'Yeah, but every day's an off day for Fred.'

'That's a bit unkind,' said Flora.

'Oh, come on, we all know Fred's the worst skater here. The truth is, he doesn't deserve to be at Schloss Eis. If I were Lukas, I'd stop trying to correct his fuck-ups and send him home today. At least then he'd have more time to devote to the rest of us.'

Melissa turned to him, aghast. 'That's a vile thing to say. Of course Fred deserves to be here; he probably needs this more than any of us.'

'How do you know that?' Gerhard retorted. 'I'm sure we all want this just as badly as he does.'

Melissa's eyes blazed. 'Yes, but your family member's future well-being doesn't depend on it, does it?'

Flora looked at her. 'What are you talking about?'

Melissa glanced at the chaise, checking to see that Fred was still asleep.

'Have you heard of Pieter Jansen?' she said.

Most of us had, with Flora being the only exception.

'He was a Dutch ice dancer,' Nathan told her. 'An outstanding one, with a ton of senior titles, but his career was cut short when he was involved in a car smash.'

'Actually, he was on a bike,' Melissa corrected him. 'Cycling to his local ice rink, very early one morning. A lorry hit him; the driver said he never even saw Pieter. Unaware there'd been a collision, he dragged the bike, with Pieter still on it, down the road for nearly fifty metres. He only stopped when a passing pedestrian flagged him down.'

Flora's hand flew to her mouth. 'That's awful. Did he die?'

'No, but he was left paralysed from the waist down. He'll never skate again.'

A silvery chill snaked down my back. I was too young to remember the news coverage of the accident, but it had passed into skating folklore: the prince of ice dance who had his dream snatched away in the cruellest way imaginable.

'So what's this got to do with Fred?' asked Gerhard.

'Pieter is Fred's older brother.'

All our jaws hit the floor at once. 'Seriously?' I said. Melissa nodded.

'So why the different surnames?' asked Gerhard.

'Same mother, different father. Fred's a lot younger than Pieter; there must be at least a decade between them.'

'How do you know all this?' asked Nathan.

'I googled you all, right after our first training session,' Melissa said, looking slightly bashful. 'I wanted to see what I was up against. When I searched for Frederik Bakker, I came across an interview his mother had given to one of the skating websites last year. She said the family was hoping to send Pieter to Switzerland for a pioneering new treatment that could help him walk again; something to do with implanting electrodes in the spinal cord. It's still in the research phase, but the initial results look promising.'

'Sounds amazing,' I said. 'Pieter must be so excited.'

'I'm sure he would be – *if* his family could afford to pay for the surgery. Right now, the treatment's only available privately and it's incredibly expensive – the equivalent of a hundred and fifty thousand dollars, I think it said in the article. The family has done a few fundraisers and one of Pieter's friends has set up a GoFundMe, but they're still a long way from their target.'

'That's a shame,' said Flora. 'Was Fred quoted in the interview?'

'No, but Mrs Bakker said how proud she was that her younger son shared Pieter's skating talent. There was a photo of Fred, receiving his runner-up medal at some skating competition in Holland; that's how I knew it was the same Frederik Bakker. Apparently he donated all the prize money to Pieter's GoFundMe. His mum also mentioned an upcoming audition he had with a touring ice dance company. She said that if he got the job, he was planning to donate a big chunk of his monthly wage to the fund.' She put her thumb to her mouth and chewed on the nail. 'I could be wrong, but I really get the impression the family is relying on Fred to make Pieter's surgery happen.'

'They'll be waiting a long time then,' said Nathan. 'It'll take him years and years to make the sort of money you're talking about.'

Gerhard looked at Melissa. 'Is that what you meant when you said Fred needed this more than the rest of us?'

'Yes,' she replied. 'We all know how big an opportunity this is. Any skater who can replicate the Grim Reaper will have sponsors queuing up to sign them.'

Nathan looked slightly unnerved. 'I hope you're not suggesting the rest of us throw the competition. I have a lot of sympathy for Fred and his family, but my folks aren't wealthy either. They've made huge financial sacrifices for my skating career; I feel like I'd be throwing it back in their face if I didn't even try to make it through to the final week.'

'Absolutely not,' Melissa said staunchly. 'I'd never ask any of you to do that. I'm just trying to explain why Fred might be crumbling under a huge weight of responsibility right now. I think it's important we do what we can to support him and show him we care.'

I realised in that moment I'd misjudged Melissa. I had assumed she was a spoiled little rich girl, who was used to getting everything on a silver platter. But now I realised what a sweet and thoughtful person she was. Strange as it sounded, you could actually see it when she was on the ice. Even though her technique wasn't always perfect, her skating had a wonderful expressiveness – a warmth and a dignity that seemed to come straight from the heart.

Just then, the windowpanes rattled in a sudden gust, making me jump. It sounded as if a storm might be brewing; I could almost sense the drop in barometric pressure.

I got up from my armchair. 'I'm just going to check on Fred.'

'Oh, stop fussing over him,' said Gerhard. 'I'm sure he's fine – and if he isn't, then he's only got himself to blame.'

Ignoring him, I padded over to the chaise. The wooden floor felt cold beneath my stockinged feet. One of Fred's arms was hanging over the edge of the chaise, his fingers grazing the expensive-looking rug. He looked almost angelic, with his pale skin and the long, dark eyelashes that kissed his cheekbones. I watched him for a few moments, making sure he was still breathing. I knew I was being overly cautious, but after everything I'd gone through with Mum, it was hardwired in me now.

Satisfied that all was well, I walked over to the window and parted the curtains, pressing my nose against the glass as I stared out across the gardens. Dusk had fallen and I could see the shapes of shrubs and bushes squatting darkly on the lawn, and beyond them the branches of the trees swaying in the wind. I hated storms at the best of times, but the thought of experiencing one here was particularly unsettling. My bedroom was up in the eaves and the only thing between it and the devastating weight

of a fallen tree was a thin layer of tiles. As I used the
sleeve of my sweatshirt to wipe away the condensation
left by my breath, I made a mental note to ask Annett
if extreme weather was common in Bavaria at this time
of year.

'Everything OK, Libby?' I heard Nathan say.

I drew the curtains and turned around. 'I think so.'

11

You could cut the atmosphere on the rink with an ice pick. After one of the most intense weeks of my life, it was finally here: elimination day. Everyone was jittery, especially Flora. She was one of only two skaters who still hadn't nailed the triple Salchow, despite coming agonisingly close on several occasions. The other was Fred – but, unlike Flora, he was still a long way off. He hadn't done himself any favours by getting drunk the other day; training when you were hung-over was never a good idea. I wasn't sure if Lukas had registered his sub-par performance; if he had, he didn't say anything. Fred had at least apologised to the rest of us for his behaviour. It turned out he'd bought the Jägermeister from duty-free at Schiphol Airport. He claimed that back home he was practically tee-total. I wasn't sure I believed him. Why buy a bottle of booze in the first place if you hardly ever touched the stuff? Still, I wasn't going to judge him. This was a high-pressure environment and all of us were dealing with it in our own way. Anyway, if the other skaters' prediction was correct, Fred wouldn't be here for much longer.

When we arrived in the ballroom at the scheduled time, Lukas was nowhere to be seen. Some of the group wanted to wait for him, while others thought we should start warming up. When he still hadn't appeared fifteen minutes later, a unanimous decision was made to don our skates.

As I began my warm-up, my thoughts turned to the upcoming elimination. The prospect of leaving Schloss Eis filled me with dread. When I'd touched down in Bavaria seven days ago, it was as if a new map of the world had unfurled before my eyes – one I was reluctant to fold away just yet. With my triple Salchow already in the bag, I knew I was in a better position than some of the others, but I would be stupid to assume I was safe.

It was another twenty minutes before Lukas finally showed up. He offered no greeting, much less an apology, and walked directly to the seating area. I wondered if his tardiness was deliberate; if it was another one of his tests – a way to see what we would do in his absence. But then I noticed how gingerly he lowered himself into a sitting position, gripping the back of the seat in front for support. Perhaps he'd pulled a muscle in training yesterday; perhaps that was the reason he was late.

'I'm pleased to see you've been using your time constructively,' he said. 'Has everyone completed their warm-up?'

Everyone said that they had.

Lukas sat very straight-backed, hands resting on his thighs. 'As you know, one of you will be leaving the programme today. But first, I want to teach you another element of the Grim Reaper. I haven't yet made up my mind which one of you will be going home and your performances today will help me decide.'

My heart boomed in my chest. Naturally, I was pleased to have another chance to prove myself, but at the same time, the suspense was killing me. We'd been building up to this moment all week and now that elimination day had finally arrived, I just wanted it to be over.

'We'll be working on the interlinking footwork sequence that follows the triple Salchow,' Lukas continued. 'It's not particularly difficult, but it needs to be executed perfectly to ensure you're in the correct position for the flying spin that follows.'

He reached into his back pocket and pulled something out. I thought at first it was his phone, but then, as a projector screen began to descend from the ceiling above the mirrored wall, I realised it was a remote control.

'Forgive me if I don't join you on the ice today, but my joints are feeling a little stiff.' He gave a peculiar twisted smile. 'One of the side effects of getting older – and this cold weather doesn't help.'

Glancing behind me, I spotted some AV equipment mounted on a high shelf at the back of the room that I'd never even noticed before.

'But I have the next best thing.' He pressed the remote control again and the screen flickered into life. 'I advise you to pay close attention.'

I knew what it was immediately. I'd watched it so many times, I knew it almost off by heart. Beijing 2008. Lukas's Olympic gold medal-winning performance. The video had been cued up to the halfway point of the routine.

There was no audio, just visuals, and the footage was in super-slow motion.

I felt a familiar tingle in my fingertips as I saw my childhood hero flip the hood of his custom-made skating jersey and launch himself into what was to become one of the most iconic sequences in figure skating history. First, the triple Salchow. Yet again, I marvelled at the precision of Lukas's technique, the height he managed to achieve, the smoothness of his landing. As I watched him, a ball of longing unravelled inside me. It must be an amazing feeling to represent one's country at the Olympics. If Lukas's younger self were pitted against today's Olympians, he probably wouldn't even make the podium, but back then he was a trailblazer, with a style and a daring that were utterly unique.

After the Salchow came the short footwork sequence Lukas had just referenced. Although I was already familiar with it, seeing it in slow-mo gave me a greater understanding of its subtle and unshowy sophistication.

As Lukas entered the flying spin, he paused the clip.

'I'm sure you all know the individual steps you've just seen; the real skill comes from melding them together so the transitions are utterly seamless. It's all about utilising the entire surface of the ice to showcase your creativity, and using changes of direction and rotation to keep the sequence dynamic and engaging. It's not just my feet you need to watch, it's my hand placement, my head position, my facial expression. Every single movement should be intentional and executed with precision.'

Suddenly, he stopped talking, his eyes locked on Saskia. She didn't notice at first; she was too busy staring at the fitness tracker on her wrist.

'Is that gadget really more important than listening to me right now?'

Saskia's head jerked up. 'Sorry, Lukas, I was just resetting my heart rate monitor.'

He shook his head slowly from side to side. 'Ridiculous girl.'

'I beg your pardon,' she said, unable to keep the indignation out of her voice.

'How your generation worship your devices, your social media, your number of followers,' he said scathingly. 'To you, these things signify wealth, success, virtue. They make you believe you're so important, you must be connected to them every second of the day. But I see them for what they are – the tools of corporations to keep you wanting, buying, unable to be present in the moment. It's a con, a scam, and you, Miss Blair, have become totally enslaved. You're just too stupid to see it.'

Saskia's mouth was frozen in a haughty expression. '*Enslaved?* I resent that accusation.'

'Resent it all you like, but while you're in *my* home, you'll play by *my* rules.' He inclined his head to the side. He had the look of a hawk about to strike. 'Or perhaps you think that because your mother is a former national champion, you're exempt.'

Saskia looked as if she was about to retaliate, but then she seemed to check herself. 'No, of course I don't think that.' She unfastened the device from her wrist and skated over to Lukas. 'Here,' she said, holding it out to him. 'You can have it. Nothing's more important to me than being in this room with you now; I want you to know that.'

Lukas remained stubbornly seated. 'Just put it down on the floor there,' he said, pointing to the rubber matting. 'You can collect it at the end of the session – and if I witness any further lapses in focus, make no mistake: you *will* be going home today.'

Saskia stared down at the ice, chastened. 'Understood.'

'Good. Then let's stop wasting time and get to work.'

Any thoughts we might have had that this was a two-horse race between Flora and Fred had just evaporated. Lukas had made it perfectly clear that every single one of us was in jeopardy.

We practised the sequence over and over again as the Beijing clip played on repeat, reminding us of the impossibly high standard we were reaching for.

Lukas didn't leave his seat once, but he kept us under close surveillance, barking out commands like a drill sergeant. He seemed in a permanent state of fury, and his dark mood didn't improve when Fred kept messing up the transition between the chassé and the three-turn.

'No, no, no!' Lukas shouted, the words spraying out of his mouth like bullets from a semi-automatic. 'Your timing's all wrong. You need to slow down; how many times do I have to tell you?'

I flinched. My childhood experiences had made me resilient; I could handle Lukas's abrasive style. But at the same time, I knew that, when targeted at a more delicate personality, it could be very damaging. And Fred, I sensed, was the most fragile of all of us.

And Lukas wasn't done with him yet. 'You're not just letting yourself down,' he raged. 'You're letting down your entire family. What would your brother make of your performance today, I wonder? Do you think he would be proud?'

There was no doubt in my mind that Lukas knew precisely who Fred's brother was, and what had happened to him. Like so many of Lukas's putdowns, it was targeted. *Personal.* Designed to land like a poison-tipped arrow in the softest, most vulnerable part of one's body. Judging by the way Fred didn't reply, just hung his head in shame, the arrow had hit its mark.

I didn't know what was eating Lukas, but I was glad when the session came to an end. I had done my best with the footwork sequence and now I was about to discover my fate.

But I was wrong. Lukas had other plans.

'Stop!' he ordered as Gabrielle skated to the side of the rink and started to unlace her boots. 'We haven't finished skating.' His eyes gleamed. 'I'm going to give you one last chance to prove yourselves.'

It was a struggle to keep my expression neutral. We'd been skating for five hours already; I didn't know how much fuel I had left in the tank.

The tips of Lukas's fingers began to perform a grue-some stroking motion on the back of his hand.

'You each have sixty seconds to show me why I should keep you in the programme. I don't care what you do, but I want to see your personalities shine through. I want to see the kind of skaters you really are.'

Sixty seconds. That was nothing. Less than half the time of a typical short programme. What's more, all of us were exhausted.

He produced his prehistoric phone. 'Saskia . . . will you go first?'

She offered a creamy smile. 'It would be my pleasure.'

Lukas began jabbing at the screen. 'Kindly get into position and raise your hand once you're ready to begin. Keep going until the alarm on my stopwatch sounds.'

I was glad he hadn't asked me to go first; I needed time to work out what the hell I was going to do. As Saskia skated confidently towards the centre of the rink, my mind scrolled through my recent competition routines as I tried to pick out a sixty-second segment that played to all my strengths. But, when Saskia lifted her hand in the air, my head emptied, my focus now on my competition.

Her routine started strongly with a forward scratch spin. Then, in rapid succession, she performed an elegant twizzle, a deft cross sequence and a proficient double loop. This was followed by a preparatory half-lap of backward stroking, before a three-turn led into a decent triple Salchow. She had timed it to perfection because half a second later the alarm sounded on Lukas's phone.

'Thank you, Saskia,' Lukas said, his face giving nothing away as she skated back to the group.

I prayed my name wouldn't be the next one out of his mouth. I wasn't ready; not even close.

'Fred,' Lukas said. 'You're up.'

The Dutchman had a wonderfully fluid style and his footwork was crisp, but he over-rotated his first jump and had to put a hand down for balance as he landed. He made up for it with a nice double toe-loop, but then he fluffed the entry into his swinging camel spin and consequently didn't achieve sufficient momentum. He looked disappointed as he rejoined the group, but Melissa mouthed a reassuring 'well done' to him. I'd noticed how the two of them had grown close over the past couple of days and I was glad Fred had someone in his corner.

Next up was Gerhard. His routine contained some advanced skills, including a colourful smorgasbord of spins, an excellent split jump and a passable double Lutz. Following Saskia's lead, he too elected to show off his recently acquired triple Salchow, but he wobbled badly on the exit and only just managed to stop himself from falling over. It wasn't the best I'd seen him skate, but it was a strong performance nonetheless.

Despite her nerves, Flora also acquitted herself well with a technically demanding three-jump combination and a stylish step sequence that was full of verve and excitement. I was pleased for her. She and I were fast becoming friends and I would be genuinely disappointed if she left Schloss Eis today. I felt the same way about Nathan, but I didn't need to worry. The American moved across the ice with his usual pace and athleticism, and his triple Salchow was one click away from perfect. I would eat my leg warmers if *he* went home today.

Melissa, too, brought her A-game, delivering an inventive and near-faultless routine. She didn't waste precious seconds on a triple Salchow. She didn't need to; Lukas already knew she had it down and she chose to finish with an impressive double Axel instead. Judging by the smile on her face as she skated back over to us, she knew she was safe.

Now there were only three of us left.

'Libby,' Lukas said. 'Let's see what you've got.'

I felt a dread that was like sediment blocking the flow of my blood. I almost wished I'd gone first now. At least then I wouldn't feel so daunted, so deeply inadequate. I thought I knew what I was going to do, but, after the performances I'd just witnessed, I feared it wouldn't be enough.

As I pushed off towards the centre of the rink, my thoughts turned to liquid. For someone so young, I had a surprisingly large number of regrets: that I never knew my dad, that I didn't try harder at school, that I came to ice skating so late in life. But I was damned if this was going to be another one of them.

I wasn't stupid; I knew the odds were stacked against me, but I was still going to strain every sinew, skin cell and tendon to be the best that I could possibly be. At least then I could return to England with my head held high: no regrets, no self-pity, no if onlys.

As I turned to face Lukas, I felt a wave of calm wash over me. This could only go one of two ways and I was putting everything on red.

All the other skaters' routines had incorporated traditional figure skating movements, the ones that were on the governing body's approved list and earned you points in competition. But Lukas didn't say we had to stick to the rulebook. He said he wanted to see our personalities. And that was exactly what I intended to do. Show him a side of me he hadn't seen yet. A side that would probably come as a bit of a shock not just to him, but also to my fellow competitors.

Back home, I had forged some strong relationships at my local rink and I was friendly with several members of the ice hockey team. They had introduced me to a different, more aggressive type of skating known as freestyling. Borrowing heavily from extreme board sports, it involved jaw-dropping stunts and seemingly impossible footwork; the sort of stuff that would make the blood of most figure skaters run cold. Not mine though. In social situations, I was mousey and timid, but when I was on the ice, I had the heart of a lion. And now it was time I threw back my head and started to roar.

I made eye contact with Lukas. His phone was in his hand as he waited for me to give the signal. I took a perverse satisfaction in making him wait a few seconds longer. Taking a deep breath, I raised my hand to shoulder height.

The first element of my routine was based on a move called hydroblading, where the skater glides on a deep edge, with their body stretched in a very low position so they're almost horizontal to the ice. It was a fairly standard connecting step, frequently used in competition, but I was betting that none of the others had seen the unusual variation I was about to demonstrate.

As I lowered myself to the ground, I rotated my hips so that, instead of facing downwards in the usual way, my body was now twisted slightly to the side, my right leg extended in a straight line, with my foot a few inches above the ice. I placed my left leg over it, so my knee formed a ninety-degree angle, with the heel of my boot pressed against the opposite thigh. Next, I took my entire body weight onto my left foot, before spreading my arms out wide and placing my fingertips on the ice. All that remained was to turn on my skate's inside edge, forcing my body into a circular glide path. This is what the guys on the ice hockey team called the Spider-Man.

A few seconds later, I was pushing myself back into an upright position, ready for my next trick. The Butterfly Kick was a power move – a flying jump spin, the sort of thing you'd see in a martial arts movie, and one of my all-time favourites.

I did a basic one-eighty turn, then jumped on one leg, with the opposite leg straight out behind me. At the same time, I bent forward, rotating my upper body around my jumping leg, and used my arms to draw a U-shape in the air. This created huge momentum, propelling me upwards. For a few fractions of a second, my entire body was airborne, my torso parallel to the ice, all four of my limbs spreadeagled. It felt amazing; it always did.

As soon as my feet were back on the ice, I knocked out a fifteen-second footwork sequence, showcasing several freestyling classics – the Grapevine, the Leg Breaker, the Insanity. Not knowing how much time I had left, I started backward stroking, in readiness for my finale.

Backflips, where a skater completes a three-hundred-and-sixty-degree turn mid-air, had been banned by figure skating's regulatory body since 1976. Perform one in competition and you'd earn yourself a reprimand and a two-point deduction. But there were no judges here, and the only person whose opinion I cared about was Lukas's.

I kept skating backwards until I had achieved the required speed and then, in one clean motion, I lifted my right leg, launching myself high into the air. As my feet passed over my head, I scissored my legs open in a wide split, before completing the rotation. My landing wasn't perfect, but it was a hair's breadth away. A couple of seconds later, the alarm on Lukas's phone sounded.

I was breathing heavily as I made my way back towards the others. I had no idea what Lukas made of my routine; I just hoped it wasn't too radical for him. When I looked up into the stand, I saw that his mouth was twitching, not with a smile exactly, but somewhere in that family.

The others looked shocked as I skated over to them. I was guessing they didn't think I had it in me.

'That wasn't even proper skating,' I heard Saskia say to Gabrielle as I stopped at the fringes of the group. 'She should be disqualified.'

'Ignore her, she's just jealous,' Nathan told me. He raised his hand in a high-five. 'Way to go, Libby,' he said as our palms connected. 'I knew you were something special.'

His words lit me up from the inside and, as I watched the two remaining performances, I couldn't stop smiling to myself.

When it was all over, Lukas rose to his feet like a Roman emperor about to decide which gladiator would be put to death.

'Thank you, everyone,' he said. 'I appreciate the effort you put into your performances. You've made my decision so much easier.' He raised his chin. 'Gerhard. Thank you for your contribution to the programme, but I'm afraid this is the end of the road for you.'

I was totally blindsided; this was not the result I'd been expecting. I looked over at Gerhard. He was staring up at Lukas, his mouth twisted into an incredulous line.

'You can't be serious,' he said. 'Mine wasn't the worst performance, not by a long shot.'

Lukas seemed unmoved. 'I appreciate this is disappointing for you.'

'But I thought this programme was about learning the Grim Reaper,' Gerhard persisted, his cheeks streaked with scarlet. 'I've got my triple Salchow and there are some people here who are still struggling with it. It's not fair.'

Lukas eyed him coolly. 'Did I state at any time that mastering the triple was a prerequisite for continuation in the programme?'

'Not in so many words. I just assumed . . .' Gerhard trailed off, whatever he was about to say shrivelling under the harsh beam of Lukas's unblinking stare.

'You assumed incorrectly. Whilst learning the component parts of the Grim Reaper is an important aspect of the programme, there are other factors at play too.'

Gerhard gave an unhappy grunt. 'Such as?'

'I'm not prepared to debate this any further, Mr Völler. Kindly leave the rink and return to the library, where Annett will be waiting with instructions for your departure.'

His tone was cold and in that moment, I arrived at a dismaying realisation: Lukas Wolff was a man to whom empathy was essentially an abstract emotion.

Realising that further protestation was futile, Gerhard gave a shrug of surrender and stalked off the ice.

It was a brutal execution, but I wasn't about to shed any tears for Gerhard. Not when his departure had taken me one step further towards the glittering prize.

12

After the elimination, most of us were dismissed, free to spend the rest of the day however we liked, but Fred and Flora were told to stay behind to practise their Salchows. Lukas warned that if they hadn't mastered the triple by the time the next elimination rolled around, they would definitely be going home.

As the rest of us made our way back along the maze of corridors, the only topic of conversation was Gerhard's shock departure.

'I don't understand Lukas's thought process,' said Alexander. 'How is Fred still here? No disrespect to the guy, but Gerhard's a *much* better skater.'

'I think this competition is about more than technical ability,' said Nathan. 'Based on what went down back there, I'd say personality's just as important.'

Saskia tittered. 'I wasn't aware Fred *had* a personality – or, if he does, he keeps it very well hidden.'

'He's just shy, that's all,' said Melissa, springing to the Dutchman's defence.

'He wasn't very shy the other night when he was rolling around drunk, was he?'

'How would you know?' I asked Saskia. 'You weren't even there.'

'Gerhard told me. It sounds like Fred let himself down badly. He's lucky Annett didn't find out and snitch on him to Lukas.'

I gave Saskia my best death stare. 'Fred's got a lot going on in his life; give the guy a break, will you?'

'Oh. You mean that business with his brother; Flora told me about that,' she said. 'Like Lukas said, we've all had hurdles to overcome in our lives; I don't see why any of us should get special treatment.' She turned abruptly to Gabrielle. 'I'm going to the gym to do some conditioning work. You up for it?'

'Maybe later,' the French girl replied. 'I'm wiped out after that session. I think I'll chill for a bit; check my Insta.'

'Good luck with that,' said Nathan. 'The Wi-Fi's been in and out all day and the 5G's not much better.'

Gabrielle groaned. 'Honestly, it's like being in a third-world country.'

'I'll come to the gym with you,' Alexander told Saskia. 'Lukas says I need to work on my core strength.'

Saskia fluttered her eyelash extensions at him. 'Wonderful, I hate working out alone.'

I saw Gabrielle bristle. 'Actually, maybe I will join you,' she said, looping her arm through Alexander's. 'I can check my socials later.'

When we all came together for dinner that evening, there was another surprise in store: no Gerhard. I thought we'd get a chance to say goodbye, but when Annett arrived with the food trolley, she revealed he'd already left. His flight back to Hamburg wasn't till the morning, but apparently arrangements had been made for him to spend the night in an airport hotel. I wondered if, logistically speaking, that was strictly necessary, or, if now that Gerhard had proved surplus to requirements, Lukas simply wanted him off the premises asap. Either way, I wasn't going to dwell on it.

As Annett began serving our meals, I tried to engage her in conversation.

'Is there a TV anywhere in the castle?' I enquired.

Her face was stiff with concentration as she pulled plates out of the trolley. 'Did you want to watch something in particular?'

'Just the weather forecast,' I replied.

It had been blowing a gale for two days solid. I could hear the wind whistling around my head at night, lifting the tiles on the roof and shaking the window frames. It made for a very disturbed night's sleep.

'I'd use my phone,' I added. 'Only there's no signal.'

'*Again*,' said Saskia. 'It's very tedious because I have twenty-four thousand followers waiting for an update.'

Annett set a plate down in front of her. The food so far had been of a high standard, but tonight's offering of chicken casserole didn't look particularly appetising.

'I think a mast must be down,' she said.

'When do you think normal service might be resumed?' asked Saskia.

'I don't know.' The corners of Annett's mouth trembled as if she were fighting a smile. 'It might not be such a bad thing that you can't access your social media.'

'How do you figure that?'

'It means fewer distractions and more time to focus on your training. That *is* the reason you're here after all.'

As Annett returned to the trolley for another meal, Saskia made a one-fingered gesture behind her back.

'About that TV?' I said tentatively.

Annett looked over her shoulder at me. 'The only televisions are in the west wing, in Lukas's private quarters.'

'Ah, OK, not to worry then,' I said. 'I don't suppose *you* managed to catch the latest forecast by any chance, did you?'

Annett gave Nathan his meal. The plate caught the edge of the table mat, sending a small tsunami of gravy slopping over the side.

'No, sorry. I wouldn't be surprised if we see some snow, though; it's definitely cold enough.'

Alexander looked faintly alarmed. 'We're very isolated here. What if we get cut off?'

Annett began filling our water glasses from a jug. 'We're used to snow in Bavaria. The local authorities are well-prepared.'

Melissa shook out her napkin. 'I bet the castle looks really pretty in the snow, doesn't it?'

'I wouldn't know.'

'Oh yes, I forgot, you've only worked here a few months, haven't you?'

Annett offered no response. Her expression was tense and there were dark shadows looming beneath her eyes.

'So where do you live when you're not looking after Lukas's house guests?' asked Nathan.

'On the other side of the valley,' she replied.

I waited for her to expand on her answer, but she didn't. It was weird, this reluctance to share any personal details, even the most mundane ones. I felt a strange, creeping sense of unease, and a sudden overpowering desire to prise something more intimate from her.

'Are you married?' I asked.

The smallest shake of the head. 'Divorced.' She leaned in between me and Saskia as she put the jug down in the centre of the table. 'Enjoy your meal.'

As she stepped back, I reached out and rested my hand on her arm.

'Won't you eat with us, just this once, Annett?' I said. 'I'd love to hear more about the local area.'

She gently withdrew her arm, brushing off the sleeve of her moss green sweater as if my touch had contaminated it.

'I've already eaten. Another time, perhaps.'

After dinner, all the skaters reconvened in the library, where we sat talking for a while. Every couple of minutes, someone would check their phone, but a signal remained elusive. By nine-thirty, we had all drifted back to our rooms.

Up in the attic, my radiator was on full blast and yet

I still felt cold. I thought about having a bath to warm me up, but in the end I decided I couldn't be bothered. After changing into my pyjamas, I got into bed and started to read an Agatha Christie novel I'd pilfered from the library. As my eyes grew heavy, I checked my phone one last time (still no connectivity), put down my book and turned off the light.

Some hours later, I was woken by a loud noise. It sliced through my sleep and shook me from a dream so engrossing that for a moment I couldn't tell where the boundary between my subconscious and reality lay. Raising myself up onto my elbows, I stared around the dark room, trying to work out what had woken me, but there was only the sound of my heartbeat.

After a minute or two, I lay back down. I had barely closed my eyes when I heard it again. A loud shriek that seemed to be coming not through the dividing wall, but up through the floorboards. Now wide awake, I sat up in bed, visualising the layout on the first floor, as I tried to work out whose bedroom lay directly beneath my own.

It was Gabrielle's, I was sure of it.

I wondered what was going on down there. She could be having a nightmare. Or perhaps she'd got up to use the loo and stubbed her toe. But then I heard another noise. A series of staccato sobs; loud and agonised.

Deciding I should investigate, I got out of bed and walked towards the door, pausing only to pull on a hoodie and a pair of thick socks. As I walked along the shadowy corridor, past Alexander's room, I saw his door was open a crack. I stopped; said his name out loud. When there was no reply, I nudged the door with my foot. The bedside light was on, but Alexander himself was nowhere to be seen. He must be with Gabrielle.

I almost turned back then, thinking the two of them were probably having a lovers' tiff. It would be hugely embarrassing for all concerned if I were to burst in on them. But for some reason, I didn't turn back; I kept on going towards the stairs.

Down on the first floor, the corridor was ablaze with light, every one of the brass wall sconces burning against the encroaching darkness. Up ahead, I could hear the sound of muffled conversation.

All the doors on the left-hand side were closed, the rooms' occupants presumably asleep. On the right-hand side, two doors had been flung wide open to reveal a pair of empty beds.

The next room was Gabrielle's. The door was shut, but I could hear voices. I couldn't make out the words, but there was no mistaking the flayed undertones: fear, panic.

After a few seconds' hesitation, I rapped softly on the door with my knuckles.

Immediately, the voices fell silent.

'Who is it?' said a voice I recognised as Alexander's.

'Libby,' I replied.

A moment later, the door opened and I found myself looking not at Alexander, but Nathan. Without saying a word, he grabbed my arm and pulled me inside.

The scene that greeted me was surreal. Flora was standing by the window, clutching a first-aid kit. Alexander was sitting on the edge of the bed. He wasn't dressed in nightwear, like Flora and Nathan, but rather jogging bottoms and a sweatshirt. Lying at his feet were a pair of women's ice skates.

Gabrielle, who was also wearing activewear, was sitting in bed on top of the covers. She was white as a sheet and tears were welling in her eyes. There were several pillows propped up behind her back, while another two pillows cushioned her right foot. Her ankle was hugely swollen and I could see the bone protruding sickeningly beneath the skin.

I took a couple of steps forward, gawping at her foot in disbelief. 'What happened to you?'

'I had a fall on the ice,' Gabrielle replied, offering the valiant half-smile of someone trying to be brave. 'A bad one. Luckily, Alexander managed to get my boot off before my ankle started to swell.'

'You were practising?' I said. 'In the middle of the night?' I knew Gabrielle had a strong work ethic, but I didn't realise she was so desperate to give herself an advantage that she'd forgo sleep.

She looked faintly embarrassed. 'Alexander and I wanted to go over some of the footwork we learned in training today while it was still fresh in our minds.'

'So what happened?'

Alexander answered for her. 'One of the plugs that join the panels of synthetic ice together had worked loose and was sticking up by a couple of centimetres. Neither one of us noticed it until Gabrielle caught her boot on it and went flying.'

Flora sucked her teeth. 'This is unforgivable. Lukas should be checking the rink on a daily basis for signs of wear and tear.'

'It's a bit late for that,' Alexander said grimly. He looked at Gabrielle's foot briefly before turning away, as if the sight of it was more than he could bear. 'At first, I thought she'd just sprained her ankle, so I carried her upstairs. It wasn't until I actually saw it that I realised it was broken.'

Gabrielle gave a little shudder. 'You should've heard the noise I made when he took my boot off.'

'I think that was what woke me up,' said Nathan. 'It sounded like someone was being murdered.'

I looked at Flora. 'Did you hear it too?'

'No, but Nathan remembered I'd done some first-aid training, so he woke me up. I don't know much about broken ankles, but I've elevated the foot to help reduce the inflammation. We need to get some ice on it too. But make no mistake, this is a serious injury; Gabrielle needs medical attention asap.'

'Have you called 999, or whatever the German equivalent is?'

'We've tried, but there's no signal.' Alexander picked up the mobile phone that was lying on the nightstand, looked at the screen and sighed.

'Maybe the castle has a landline.'

'I don't know that it does,' said Flora. 'The two numbers Annett gave us to pass on to our families in case of emergency were both mobile numbers.'

'It's worth double checking though,' said Nathan. 'And if there isn't a landline, Lukas will just have to drive Gabrielle to the nearest emergency room himself. I'll go and wake him up, shall I?'

'Do you even know where his bedroom is?' I asked him.

'No, but I'll knock on every door in the west wing until I find him.'

'I'll come with you. It'll be quicker with two of us.'

Gabrielle let out a little whimper. 'Hurry, please. The pain's getting worse; I feel as if I'm about to pass out.'

Alexander put his arm around her shoulders. 'Don't worry, babe, nothing bad's going to happen to you while I'm here.'

As far as I was aware, the west wing could only be accessed via the entrance hall on the ground floor. Nathan and I took the stairs as fast as we dared, neither of us under any illusions about the potential repercussions for Gabrielle's skating career if she didn't receive prompt treatment.

Downstairs, the hall lay in darkness, but rather than waste time hunting for light switches, Nathan used the torch on his phone to light our way as we entered the west wing.

It felt strange being in Lukas's private domain, almost as if we were trespassing. We set off down a long, windowless corridor, hammering on every door we passed, but getting no response. Realising that any bedrooms were more likely to be on the upper floors, we quickly located the staircase and raced up to the first floor. The layout was different to the east wing, with not one, but two corridors, stretching in opposite directions.

'You go left, I'll go right,' said Nathan. He thrust his phone into my hand. 'Take this, I'll try to find the light switch.'

I set off at a jogging pace. All the rooms were on the right-hand side of the corridor, while the left-side wall was lined with windows.

'Lukas? Are you there?' I said in a loud voice as I thumped the first door with my clenched fist. No answer.

The door of the second room was slightly ajar. Realising it was a bathroom, I hurried on to the third door.

Before I could raise my hand, I heard a voice say, 'Who's there?'

Swinging the torch round, I saw a figure standing in an open doorway at the far end of the corridor, backlit by the soft glow from a lamp. It was Lukas, looking surprisingly boyish in striped pyjama bottoms and a white T-shirt.

'It's me, Libby,' I said, rushing towards him. 'There's been an accident.'

He rubbed his eyes with the heels of his hands. 'What sort of accident?' he said in a thick voice.

'Gabrielle was practising on the rink and she had a nasty fall; she's broken her ankle.'

Lukas stared back at me. He seemed slightly disoriented, as if I'd woken him from a very deep sleep.

'What time is it?'

'Um, I'm not sure. Two? Maybe three o'clock.' I made an impatient noise. 'Please, Lukas. Gabrielle needs to get to hospital asap, but the Wi-Fi's down and none of us can get a signal on our phones. Does the castle have a landline?'

He had to think about it for a moment or two. 'No, not any more; I had it disconnected. I didn't see the point in paying for something I never used.'

I felt like grabbing him by the shoulders and giving him a shake. Who cared about his petty cost-saving measures? Didn't he get it? A woman had been seriously injured and we needed his help.

Before I could say anything else, I saw Nathan striding down the corridor towards us. Following a few paces behind was Annett in a pair of fluffy slippers and an ankle-length dressing gown.

'There's no landline,' I told him.

He blew out a puff of air. 'Yeah, Annett said. We'll just have to take Gabrielle to hospital ourselves.'

I turned back to Lukas. 'How far is it?'

'What?'

'The hospital. How far away is it?'

He scratched his head. 'Fifteen kilometres; maybe a little more. But there's no way we can get there.'

'Why not? Surely you have a car.'

'Yes, but . . .' He gave me a long, helpless look. 'I'm guessing you haven't looked outside recently.'

'What are you talking about?' I said impatiently.

He went over to the nearest window and hoisted the Roman blind. 'Come and see for yourself.'

I did as he had asked. Outside, there was an almost-full moon and the stars in the sky were so bright they looked like sequins on an evening gown. But in spite of the ambient light, I couldn't see the shrubs, or the flower beds, or the statuary – or anything else in the garden. All of it had gone. Buried beneath a thick white quilt that stretched as far as I could see.

'It's been snowing for hours,' Lukas said. 'The roads will be treacherous; completely impassable.'

Nathan came up behind me. 'Wow, that's crazy,' he said as the two of us stared at the snow spiralling downwards. I'd never seen so much snow and it looked quite magical. At any other time, I would have loved to stand there with Nathan, our shoulders touching, as we admired the dream-like landscape. But not now. Not when Gabrielle was relying on us.

I looked at Lukas. 'We have to at least *try*,' I said. 'The roads might not be as bad as you think.'

He shook his head. 'I've got a sports car; a rear-wheel drive. It's useless in the snow; it'll skid all over the place and we'll probably end up crashing.'

Nathan gave him a withering look. 'But it must snow here all the time. How can you not have a 4x4?'

Lukas spread his arms wide. 'What can I say? If the weather's bad, I stay at home.'

I turned to Annett. 'How about you? What do *you* drive?'

She made an apologetic face. 'A ten-year-old Fiat 500.'

It was all I could do not to scream out loud.

'We've got to do something,' said Nathan. 'Gabrielle's in agony.'

Annett glanced at her boss and something indecipherable passed between them. 'Let's go and see how she is,' she said, 'And then we'll decide what to do.'

By the time we got to Gabrielle's room, her condition had worsened. She lay back on the pillows, her eyes closed, her forehead beaded with sweat.

'Thank God!' Alexander cried, jumping to his feet as we entered the room. 'You've been gone for ages.'

'How is she?' asked Annett.

'Not good,' he replied. 'She keeps falling in and out of consciousness. We need to get her to hospital immediately.'

'I'm afraid that won't be possible,' said Lukas impassively.

Flora's eyes shimmered with horror. 'Look at her ankle!' she cried. 'Can't you see this is an emergency?'

Nathan pointed to the window. 'Check out the view. I hate to say it, but Lukas is right: there's no way anyone's leaving the castle tonight.'

Frowning in confusion, Flora turned towards the window and yanked the curtains apart. 'Ho-ly shit,' she said slowly as she stared out across the grounds. 'You've got to see this, Alexander; it's a total white-out.'

As Alexander joined Flora at the window, Annett took his place at Gabrielle's bedside. Clearly not squeamish, she leaned over the young woman's body to study her foot close up. I noticed that the skin around Gabrielle's ankle had turned purple, making the deformity look even more pronounced.

Annett's brief assessment complete, she moved to the head of the bed and put the back of her hand to Gabrielle's forehead.

'She feels very hot; I think she's running a fever.' She took her hand away. 'Gabrielle, can you hear me?'

The French girl moved her head on the pillow, but her eyes remained shut. 'Mmm,' she moaned, her face contorting, as if squeezing out the syllable required enormous effort.

Alexander turned away from the window, worry etched across his face.

'There's no landline,' Nathan informed him. 'The whole time we were in the west wing, I kept checking my cellphone, just in case there was a signal, but we're in a total dead zone. Lukas and Annett only have regular cars; they'll be deathtraps in these conditions. We'd need a 4×4 to stand any chance of getting Gabrielle to a medical facility.'

Alexander released a roar of frustration. 'I'm going out there,' he said, crossing the room in three large strides. 'I'll keep on walking until I get phone coverage.'

Nathan caught him by the arm. 'Forget it, Al. All you'll be doing is putting yourself in danger. You could be walking for miles before you get a signal. Not a smart idea at night, in the middle of a blizzard.'

'And even if you did manage to call the emergency services, the nearest hospital is fifteen kilometres away,' I told him. 'No ambulance is going to risk travelling that distance in weather like this.'

Alexander wrenched his arm away. 'Doing nothing is not an option,' he snarled in Nathan's face.

I took a shallow breath. The situation suddenly felt very unstable, like a tent without pegs in a gathering storm. Somebody had to take control. By rights, it should be Lukas. This was his home and all of us were here at his behest. But he hadn't said a word since we'd stepped into the east wing. Instead of offering reassurance, he was hovering by the door, arms wrapped around his torso as if he was quite literally holding himself together. I couldn't believe what I was witnessing. Lukas was so assertive in training, so forceful – but the first sign of a crisis and he fell to pieces.

'We're not going to do nothing,' I told Alexander. 'We're going to give Gabrielle some painkillers, get some ice for her foot, make her as comfortable as we can and take turns watching over her.' Even as I spoke, I could feel the cramping inadequacy of my suggestions, but no one else had any better ideas. 'As soon as it's light the snowploughs will be out, clearing the roads – right, Annett?'

'They should be,' she said, with less conviction than I was hoping for. 'The castle's on a minor road; it might not be a priority.'

'OK, so if there's still no vehicle access in the morning, how close is the nearest doctor?'

'There's one in the next village.'

'How long will it take to hike there?'

She rolled out her lower lip. 'In these conditions? Four hours. Maybe five.'

'We can manage that. I'm sure that once we've explained how serious Gabrielle's injury is, the doctor will agree to come back to the castle with us. It won't be the same as having an orthopaedic surgeon, but it's the next best thing.'

'Sounds like a plan,' said Flora. 'You OK with that, Alexander?'

His hand was still on the door handle. I could see he wasn't convinced.

'If you go out there now and something happens to you, Gabrielle will never forgive herself,' I told him. 'You do know that, don't you?'

After a few moments, he sighed and nodded his head, grudgingly mollified.

I switched my focus back to Annett. 'Can you rustle up an ice pack and some painkillers?'

'The ice is no problem, but all I have is paracetamol.'

'I might have something a bit stronger,' said Lukas, finally spurred into action. 'I'll go and have a look.'

I was intensely worried about Gabrielle, but there was nothing more we could do. Except wait, and hope this wretched snowstorm blew over soon.

Even in my darkest days as a child, I had never felt quite so helpless. At least back home I'd always had Gran to turn to – and she had never let me down. Here, there was only Lukas: a man who, I was beginning to realise, was singularly ill-prepared to deal with the sort of medical emergency that might reasonably have been foreseen. Everyone knew there was risk involved in our sport, and it wasn't like Gabrielle was the first skater ever to suffer a broken ankle. I just hoped the delay in getting help wasn't going to impact her chances of making a full recovery.

13

It was just after 4 a.m. when I returned to my room. Nathan, Flora and I offered to take turns at Gabrielle's bedside, but Alexander had sent us away, saying he'd rather watch over her himself. I lay in bed for half an hour or so, kept awake by the distant hooting of an owl, before finally reaching for my earplugs and floating off to sleep.

When I woke up, the room seemed overly bright and shards of wintry light were leaking from the edges of the blind. I checked my alarm clock: eight forty-five; later than I thought. We were supposed to be at the rink by ten but, given the situation with Gabrielle, training would surely have been cancelled. I shifted a little under the covers. My right arm was numb, as if an invisible body had been pressing against it all night. I did a few bicep curls, the blood immediately rushing through my inert fingers and foggy brain, making them pulsate with life and allowing the memories of the previous night to surface.

I still felt cross with Lukas. His lack of action was maddening. Gabrielle was a guest in his home and he had a duty of care towards her; towards all of us. At least Annett had made herself useful, fetching a damp flannel for Gabrielle's head, a tea towel packed with ice for her ankle and a bottle of water to keep her hydrated.

I was praying we'd be able to get Gabrielle to the hospital today. She was certainly going to need surgery and the quicker she was treated, the greater the chance she would regain full function of the limb. I hoped she had good travel insurance. If not, then Lukas would just have to foot the bill – and it might not be the only financial expenditure he faced. Depending on how magnanimous Gabrielle was feeling, he could very well find himself being sued for negligence. He'd probably settle out of court; the last thing he'd want is a protracted legal case and his name plastered all over the media.

I knew I should get up and find out how the patient had fared overnight, but when I threw back the covers, it was so cold, I immediately pulled them back over me. Just five more minutes, I told myself. Even if Nathan and Flora were still in bed, Annett would have certainly apprised the others of the situation over breakfast, so it wasn't as if Gabrielle would be short of visitors.

As I lay there, staring up at the sloping ceiling, the quiet weight of the castle pressed down on me. There was a peculiar heavy silence, almost as if the building was listening with me, every fibre of wood and plaster tuned to the absence of sound.

When I did finally haul myself out of bed, I went directly to the window and raised the blind, hoping for good news. There wasn't any. It was still snowing, fat flakes coming down in a relentless torrent, obscuring the grounds in a milky haze. Even the yew trees were barely recognisable, their tops looming out of the whiteness, like ships' masts momentarily lulled before an approaching storm. In the middle distance, I could just make out the head and shoulders of a Grecian statue. It told me the snow was lying over a metre deep. I remembered what Annett had said, about the road that served the castle not being a priority for the snowploughs. I hoped for Gabrielle's sake that she was wrong.

After taking a quick shower, I put on clean underwear and yesterday's jeans and oversized sweatshirt and headed off to see Gabrielle.

As I descended the stairs to the first floor, I almost tripped over Flora and Saskia. They were sitting on the bottom stair, not saying anything, just staring into space.

'Hey, what's up?' I said as I stepped past them onto the landing.

Flora screwed up her eyes as if she was in physical pain. 'She's gone, Libby,' she said in a choked voice.

I gave her a curious look. 'What are you talking about?'

'Gabrielle's dead,' Saskia said bluntly.

I suddenly felt very light-headed, as though the air in the corridor was too tightly squeezed around us, making it difficult to breathe.

'She can't be.'

Flora stood up. 'It's true.' Her mouth did a sideways twist as if she was trying not to cry. 'Alexander fell asleep in the chair and when he woke up a couple of hours later, she wasn't breathing. He didn't know what to do, so he woke me and Nathan up. We moved Gabrielle onto the floor and I started doing CPR. I told Alexander to run and get Saskia because she knows CPR too.'

Saskia looked up at me. 'The two of us took it in turns. I don't know how long we were going for, but it must've been nearly half an hour.' Her lips trembled. 'It was too late though; we couldn't get her back.'

I pressed my hands to my temples. It felt as if I'd stuck my fingers into an electrical socket and the current was pulsing through me over and over again. 'But how? How can this have happened? People don't die from a broken ankle.'

Flora shrugged. 'I know; we don't understand it either.'

'I'm surprised you didn't hear all the commotion,' said Saskia. 'Your room's directly above Gabrielle's, isn't it?'

'I had my earplugs in.' Guilt rinsed through me. I hadn't been trained in CPR, but maybe I could've done something to help. 'Does Lukas know?'

'Yeah, Nathan woke him and Annett up. They both came to Gabrielle's room straight away, but they could see she was dead. I wanted to wake you too, but Nathan said I may as well let you get some sleep because there was nothing you could do.'

I could feel myself coming apart inside, growing ragged, bits of me flailing around. 'Have you told Melissa and Fred?'

Flora nodded. 'I think they're both in a state of shock.'

I remembered the last thing I said to Gabrielle. I told her not to worry, that everything was going to be all right. Despite the enormous pain she was in, she'd smiled as I left the room and said she'd see me in the morning.

I tipped back my head to stop the tears sliding down my face. 'Where's Lukas now?'

'He's gone for a walk, to see if he can find a mobile signal. He wants to call a doctor so Gabrielle's death can be certified – and, of course, he'll have to notify her poor parents. I'm not holding my breath though. It's been snowing all night; I doubt he'll be able to get very far on foot.'

My mind returned to Lukas's odd demeanour in the night; how distant he'd seemed; how removed from everything that was going on around him. Just before I left Gabrielle's room, he did something strange. He reached out and laid a hand on my shoulder, the weight of it doing nothing to reassure me, a dump of fuel on the bonfire of my internal panic.

'How did he react when he found out Gabrielle had died?' I asked them.

Saskia's face puckered. 'How would *you* react if one of your guests suddenly dropped dead? He was utterly horrified.'

I chewed this over in my mind. Of course Lukas was horrified. His strange, slightly befuddled reaction last night must've been because he was still half-asleep. 'And where's Annett?'

'Preparing breakfast – not that any of us feel like eating right now,' said Flora. 'Fred and Melissa are helping her.'

'How's Alexander doing?'

'He's completely distraught,' said Flora. 'He wanted to stay in the room with Gabrielle, but the rest of us didn't think that was such a good idea. He took a bit of persuasion, but eventually he agreed to go to the library with Nathan.' She produced a crumpled tissue from her sleeve and dabbed her nose with it. 'The poor guy thinks it's *his* fault she died.'

'It kind of is, in a way,' said Saskia. 'He did fall asleep after all.'

There was a long silence that we all seemed reluctant to fill. Saskia might have had a point, but it seemed rather cruel to bring it up. It wasn't like Alexander *meant* to fall asleep.

Flora sniffed loudly. 'Sas and I offered to stay here and clean Gabrielle up. We were just bracing ourselves for the task when you appeared.'

'Clean her up?' I said, not understanding.

'She'd been sick,' said Saskia. 'It didn't seem right to leave her like that.'

Something swayed and lurched in my gut. 'Do you think she might have choked on her vomit?'

'I don't think so,' said Flora. 'I checked her airway before I started CPR and it was clear.'

She covered her face with her hand and I could see how traumatised she was.

'I can do it if you like – clean her face, I mean.'

Saskia looked surprised at the offer. 'Really?'

'Absolutely.' It was only fair. My way of making up

for the fact that I'd been sleeping like a baby, while the others battled to save Gabrielle's life. 'You two have just been through an awful experience; you don't need this on top of it.'

'Thanks, Libby, that's kind of you,' said Flora. 'I must admit I don't think I could face going back in there just now.' She pointed to a door halfway along the corridor. 'That's the bathroom; there's a cupboard in there with clean towels.'

'OK.'

She seemed to hesitate. 'Are you sure you can do this? None of us will think any less of you if you can't.'

I gave her a buckled smile. 'It's fine, honestly. Go and have some breakfast – and save me some coffee; I think I'm going to need it.'

As I opened the door to Gabrielle's room, I felt an unpleasant vibration in my centre. The heaviness I sensed in the air when I'd woken up no longer seemed atmospheric. Now it was inside my head – a nauseating pressure pushing outward against my skull.

Gabrielle was lying on her back on the pale carpet. Her skin had a yellowish tinge and her eyes were open in a glassy stare, her lips slightly parted. In life, her irises were a bright, sparkling blue, but now they had a kind of dullness to them, like smeared glass.

I knelt down and placed the towel and the damp washcloth I was holding on the floor. As I gently closed Gabrielle's eyelids with my fingertips, her skin still felt warm; she clearly hadn't been dead for very long. Vomit was smeared at the corners of her mouth. A small amount had stained the front of her pink top – a top I had complimented her on the first time she wore it. Suddenly, a flood of emotion threatened to overwhelm me and I had to bite the inside of my cheek to stop myself crying.

My gaze travelled downwards. The flesh on Gabrielle's lower leg was a mottled bluish purple, the broken ankle bone protruding so sharply I was surprised it hadn't pierced the skin. It reminded me of one of those grisly fake prosthetics people took to Halloween parties.

Taking a deep breath, I reached for the washcloth. As I gently wiped Gabrielle's mouth, I thought about her parents and about how devastated they'd be when they realised the daughter they had waved off to Bavaria little more than a week ago would be returning home in a coffin. I tried to remember if Gabrielle had any siblings. I was sure she'd mentioned a younger sister; only fourteen or fifteen years old. Another heart soon to be broken. I wondered how her parents would break the news that Gabrielle had died; if the teenager would ever be able to get over the loss of her big sister.

Once Gabrielle's face was clean and dried, I took a pillow off the bed and eased it gently under her head. It didn't seem enough, so I closed my eyes and said the Our Father in my head. It was the only prayer I knew.

I stood up and looked around the room, trying to remember what had changed since I was last here, a few short hours ago. The armchair that had been in the corner was now beside the bed, and a rumpled blanket lay on the floor beside it.

Something else caught my eye: a small amber pill bottle, sitting on the nightstand, next to an empty glass and a half-drunk bottle of Evian. It must be the pain medication that Lukas had offered to get for Gabrielle. I picked up the pill bottle and saw that it was empty. The label on the front had been torn off and only a sticky residue remained. I put it back down and then, with a last, lingering look around the room, I headed off to join the living.

14

When I arrived in the dining room, the others were already there. The breakfast buffet was laid out on the sideboard, but hardly anybody was eating. It was as if an invisible atomic bomb had gone off, billowing out poisonous gases to everyone in the fallout radius.

Most of the skaters were sitting at the table, but Alexander was standing up, leaning against the wall. His face was drained of its usual animation and the pain in his eyes was raw. I went over and gave him a hug because I didn't know what else to do. It felt desperately awkward.

As we drew apart, I could see his eyelashes working wildly to hold back his tears.

'Flora said you've been taking care of Gabrielle. I appreciate it, Libby; I know it can't have been easy.'

'No problem, I was happy to do it.' I looked around the room, noting the absence of Annett and our host. 'Is Lukas still out searching for a phone signal?'

'Yes,' Melissa confirmed. 'He's been gone for over an hour. I don't know about anyone else, but I'm starting to get worried. The conditions out there are brutal.'

I glanced at the window. The snow was still coming down, but now it was being driven sideways, indicating the strength of the wind.

'Personally, I don't think he should've risked it, at least not on his own,' said Nathan. 'Alexander and I offered to go with him, but he wouldn't let us; I don't know why not.'

Fred pulled the crust off a piece of bread and rolled it between his forefinger and thumb. 'Because battling your way through a blizzard is probably easier than facing the music.'

Nathan raised an eyebrow. 'Meaning?'

'Meaning it's his fault Gabrielle died. If the rink had been properly maintained, none of this would've happened.' He let the crust fall onto the tablecloth. 'Fate can be very cruel; it's terrifying how everything can change in the blink of an eye. All it takes is one bad decision; one wrong turn; one trip on the ice.'

His words were like cold fingers caressing the back of my neck.

'I'm going to get some coffee,' I said. 'Does anyone need a top-up?'

'No, thanks, but I wouldn't mind a bran muffin,' said Saskia.

I poured a cup of black coffee from the flask and carried it to the table, along with Saskia's muffin and one for myself. I sat down, deliberately avoiding the spot where Gabrielle usually sat, and peeled the paper case from my muffin. I was feeling quite hungry, but the first bite nearly choked me, so I put the muffin back down on my plate. I felt on the verge of tears, every emotion of the past twelve hours crystallising into a hard ball inside my stomach.

As I sipped my coffee in silence, I discreetly observed the other skaters, watching to see how they were dealing with the tragedy. Flora sat almost motionless, staring into space, as if the rest of us weren't even there. Fred, by contrast, seemed twitchy. He gulped his coffee and made a couple of inane remarks that made me wonder if he'd been at the Jäger again. Melissa and Nathan made stilted conversation but seemed to have no appetite, their breakfasts lying untouched in front of them. As for Alexander – he looked bewildered; punch-drunk; like a man who'd lost everything. Only Saskia seemed anything like her usual self. She tucked into her muffin with gusto and every couple of minutes she picked her phone up off the table, tapping at the screen as if the persistent action could somehow summon a signal out of thin air.

After a little while, the dining-room door opened. I was hoping to see Lukas, but it was only Annett. She looked tired and she kept her eyes downcast.

'I've just been listening to the local news on the radio,' she said without preamble. 'I thought you'd like an update on the weather.'

'Ooh, yes,' said Flora. 'What's the latest?'

'The region received forty centimetres of snowfall overnight. They said it was some sort of record.'

'Jeez, that's a shitload of snow,' said Nathan. 'Is the worst of the weather over now?'

Annett shook her head. 'More heavy snowfall is expected over the next seventy-two hours, accompanied by strengthening winds. The government is advising every-one to stay indoors.'

Melissa groaned. 'Three days? That's terrible; we need to get Gabrielle's body back to her family sooner than that.'

'And that's the best-case scenario,' Annett went on. 'The German Weather Service has advised that the current conditions could persist for even longer. Apparently it's down to the slow movement of a low-pressure front over western Europe.' She pulled the sleeves of her jumper down over her hands as if she were feeling the cold. 'All flights at Munich airport have been grounded until fur-ther notice, bus and tram services have been suspended and most of the local roads are completely impassable, even for 4×4s.' She pointed to the phone that seemed to be glued to Saskia's hand. 'I was right about the mast, by the way. There's no internet or mobile signal for a ten-kilometre radius and no indication of when it's going to be up and running again.'

'So, what are we supposed to do in the meantime?' Saskia enquired petulantly.

'What *can* we do?' said Melissa. 'We're trapped; we'll have to sit here and wait it out. There's no way I'm going back on that ice rink after what's just happened.'

A couple of the others murmured their agreement.

'What about food?' asked Fred. 'I assume the catering company won't be delivering anytime soon.'

'We have a well-stocked freezer,' said Annett. 'No one's going to go hungry.'

Somewhere in the distance, I heard a door slam. Less than a minute later, Lukas appeared in the doorway. He was wearing a knee-length parka and a fur-lined trapper hat. There was defeat in his posture and something else I couldn't quite put my finger on.

In a flash, Alexander was on his feet.

'Did you find a signal?'

Lukas shook his head and a shower of snowflakes fell from his hat. 'It's awful out there; it's snowing so hard, there's practically zero visibility.'

'How far did you get?' Nathan asked him.

'Less than a kilometre.'

Alexander slammed his palm against the botanical wallpaper. 'Is that all?' he said angrily. 'I knew I should've gone myself.'

Lukas's eyes darkened. Something in his expression made me think of a simmering pan of milk about to boil over.

'I'm sure Lukas did his best,' I said in an effort to calm the situation. Things were bad enough already; the last thing we needed was people blowing up at each other, especially when none of us could leave. 'Annett just heard on the radio that there's no mobile reception for a ten K radius. That's much too far for anyone to walk in these conditions.'

Lukas flicked his eyes towards his assistant, who was standing at the breakfast buffet pouring coffee into a mug. 'Is that right?'

Annett nodded. 'Even the snowploughs haven't been

able to make it out of the depot; it's just too dangerous.' She carried the hot drink over to him. 'Did you see
anyone else while you were out there?'

'Not a living soul,' he said, taking the mug from her
and cupping it in both hands. 'I might as well have been
on the moon.'

Fred sat stiffly upright. 'The snowstorm's got another
three days to run, possibly more. What are we going to
do about Gabrielle in the meantime? We can't leave her
where she is – not when our bedrooms are in such close
proximity.'

'He's right,' said Flora. 'My room's right next door. I
really wouldn't feel comfortable sleeping there.'

'Perhaps we could all relocate to the west wing,'
Melissa suggested.

'There aren't enough rooms for you all,' said Lukas. He
pulled off his hat and stuffed it into his pocket. Beneath it,
his strawberry blond hair was damp and tousled. 'I do
have an alternative suggestion, however. We could utilise
the walk-in freezer. It would help preserve Gabrielle's
body and ensure that she can be returned to her family in
a reasonable condition.'

Alexander flinched, but raised no objection.

'You have a walk-in freezer?' Flora said in surprise.

'Yes, it was here when I bought the property. I assumed
it was a hangover from the days when Schloss Eis operated
as a hotel.'

Saskia gave an appalled shudder. 'Annett says we're
going to be relying on the freezer for our meals until the

catering service resumes. I don't mean to sound crass, but there's no way I'm eating food that's been stored next to a dead body.'

'How about the basement?' asked Nathan. 'Does the castle have one?'

'It does, but it's damp and humidity will only speed up the rate of decomposition,' said Lukas.

His careless tone made me blench.

'What about outbuildings?' said Nathan.

'There's the garage and the summer house, but neither of them are rodent-proof.'

Alexander placed a hand on each cheek. 'Are we really having this conversation?'

'Sorry, Al,' Flora said gently. 'We're just trying to do what's best for her.'

'Why don't we take the food out of the freezer and put it in the fridge?' Melissa proposed.

Annett looked doubtful. 'The fridge is already half full and there are so many of us. We'd probably only be able to get enough food in there to last us a day or two.'

Suddenly, the solution hit me like a slap around the face. 'Why don't we use nature's freezer?'

Saskia sighed. 'What are you on about, Libby?'

'It must be well below freezing outside. We can dig a hole in the snow and bury the food. It'll be fine, so long as it's well wrapped up.'

Nathan broke into a smile. 'Libby, you're a genius.'

Lukas was nodding too. 'Yes, I think that would work.'

'Good, then that's what we'll do,' said Melissa. 'Who's

going to move Gabrielle? It's a horrible job, but someone's got to do it.'

'I will,' said Lukas.

I gave him a grateful smile. It was good to see him taking charge at last. He was more like his usual self today; more like the Lukas I'd seen in training.

'I'll help you,' said Nathan.

'Thank you,' said Lukas, bowing his head slightly. 'Are those arrangements all right with you, Alexander?'

'I suppose they'll have to be,' came the short reply.

Lukas took a quick drink of coffee and put his mug down on the dining table.

'I want you all to know how incredibly sorry I am about Gabrielle. Her death is a terrible loss to the skating community.' He drew the back of his hand across his mouth as if there was a nasty taste on his lips. 'Right now, none of us knows the precise cause of her death and I would respectfully ask you to refrain from speculating, as it serves no useful purpose. All we can be sure of at this stage is that she sustained a broken ankle following a fall and that some sort of obstruction on the ice may have been a contributing factor.'

Alexander peeled back his lips, baring his incisors. 'There's no *may* about it. I was there, I know what happened. And it wasn't an obstruction; it was a defect in the ice panels, due to *your* inadequate maintenance.'

'I'm not suggesting you fabricated your account,' said Lukas in a measured tone. 'However, I carried out an inspection of the rink earlier. I examined every square centimetre of ice and nothing was misaligned. The entire surface was perfectly level.'

Alexander's face clouded with confusion. 'But that can't be right. One of the plugs was sticking up, I saw it with my own eyes.'

'I don't suppose you took a photograph, did you?'

'No, I did not.' There was a steely strain in Alexander's voice, like a guitar string twisted too tight. 'My girlfriend was lying on the ice, screaming in agony. My immediate concern was getting help for her.'

I looked from one to the other. Without any physical evidence, it was one man's word against the others. And in that moment, I wasn't sure who to believe.

'Perhaps the plug settled back into position by itself,' Fred suggested.

'Yes, you could be right,' said Lukas.

'I don't wish to debate the issue any further,' Alexander said tightly. 'But I shall be giving Gabrielle's parents my version of events. It's up to them what they choose to do with the information, but if I were in their position, I would certainly be taking legal advice.'

Despite the clear threat in his words, Lukas seemed unruffled. 'I also intend to reach out to Gabrielle's family to offer whatever information or support they require,' he said. 'And now you must excuse me, I need to get out of these wet clothes.' He checked his watch. 'Nathan, meet me in the entrance hall in half an hour.' He looked at his assistant. 'Will that give you enough time to clear the freezer?'

Annett pulled on her chapped top lip. 'I think so.'

'I can lend a hand,' I told her.

'Me too,' said Melissa. 'Anything to take my mind off this nightmare.'

Lukas gave a watery smile. 'Thank you, ladies. I suggest you wear an extra layer of clothing; it's very cold in there.'

As he walked towards the door, he seemed to be concentrating very hard on each step, as if any break in rhythm would shatter his self-control.

It was the first time Melissa and I had seen the castle's kitchen. The flagstone floor looked original, but everything else was achingly modern, from the stark forensic lighting and hand-painted cabinetry to the vast, granite-topped island with its upholstered bar stools. There wasn't much time to look around because Annett took us directly to the walk-in freezer – a white metal box, roughly two metres square, discreetly positioned in an alcove.

Annett opened the door, treating us all to a blast of chilly air. 'If you two want to start taking things down from the shelves, I'll go and get some plastic crates to put it all in.'

As she went to a cupboard on the other side of the room, Melissa and I stepped into the freezer. Its walls were lined with metal shelves, most of them laden with food. It all looked pretty healthy. I saw chicken breasts and fish fillets and vegetarian sausages, but not a pizza or a French fry in sight. I wondered if this was what Lukas lived off when he was on his own.

We set to work, knowing we only had half an hour to empty the freezer, ready for its precious consignment. I was hoping the task would be a distraction, but as I pulled bags of vegetables off the shelves, all I could see was Gabrielle's face, cold and white as marble, her eyes staring sightlessly ahead. I was desperate to talk to Melissa about what had happened. Although she hadn't seen Gabrielle in the aftermath of her accident, I was interested to hear her thoughts and find out if she had any theories about what might have caused her death. But, mindful of Lukas's request that we avoid speculating, I opted to stay silent. With Annett never far away, I was sure that anything we did say would be reported straight back to her boss.

I had never been very good in confined spaces and it wasn't long before the freezer started to feel claustrophobic. As I stood on tiptoe to reach a whole salmon on the top shelf, the air blurred around me and I suddenly felt very faint. Letting the fish fall from my hand, I pushed past Melissa and stumbled, half-blind, into the kitchen. I managed to make it to the sink, where I clung to the draining board as a cold sweat bloomed over my body. The next minute, Melissa was behind me.

'You poor thing,' she said, rubbing my back as I dry heaved into the sink. 'I'm not surprised you're feeling ill. You were so brave, going back into Gabrielle's room after she died; there was no way *I* could have done it.'

I stopped retching and raised my head. 'I'll be all right in a minute. I think I just need to sit down.'

She gently escorted me to the island, while Annett went to get me a glass of water. My scalp was prickling with embarrassment as I manoeuvred myself onto one of the bar stools. Poor Alexander had woken up to find his girlfriend dead and was still managing to hold it together, while here I was falling apart, like a Victorian heroine with a fit of the vapours. I couldn't help feeling disappointed in myself; I really thought I was made of stronger stuff.

Annett appeared with my water and put it down in front of me. She hovered at my elbow and asked if there was anything else she could do. I had the same feeling I always did when I was around her: that she was simply going through the motions. I wondered if she resented us being here. I wouldn't blame her if she did; we must have created a lot of extra work that probably wasn't in her job description. And now she was having to deal with the most horrific event imaginable.

'Honestly, I'm feeling better already,' I lied. 'You two go and finish off in the freezer; the others will be here soon.'

Less than ten minutes later, Lukas appeared in the kitchen. His wet hair was slicked back and he was wearing a thick sweater with a jolly Nordic pattern that seemed inappropriate for the occasion.

'Is the freezer ready?' he said. 'Nathan and I are just about to go and get her.'

Annett emerged from the freezer, a tub of frozen yoghurt in her hand. 'Perfect timing, we've just finished.' She gestured to the half-dozen crates of food sitting on the worktop. 'All we need now is a volunteer to bury that lot outside.'

'I'm sure Fred will oblige,' I said, slipping off the stool. I didn't want to be there when they brought Gabrielle's body down. 'Come on, Melissa, let's go and find him.'

We went to the dining room first but found it empty, the breakfast things still sitting, uncovered, on the sideboard. It occurred to me that we should probably save the leftovers for tomorrow, but there was no time to worry about that now. Our immediate priority was to get the contents of the freezer into the ground before they started to defrost.

Our next port of call was the library. Alexander and Saskia were there, sitting next to each other on the sofa, so close their heads were almost touching. Saskia glared at us, as if we were interrupting something.

'Have they moved Gabrielle yet?' Alexander asked.

'Lukas and Nathan went to get her a few minutes ago,' Melissa told him.

He scrubbed a hand over his face. 'This all seems unreal. It's like I'm having the worst nightmare and any minute now I'm going to wake up and realise she's still alive.'

Saskia made a clucking sound and reached out with one of her manicured hands, letting it rest on Alexander's thigh. 'I know you're going through hell right now, but

I'm going to help you get through it,' she said, as if Melissa and I weren't in the room.

His chin dropped onto his chest. 'She was super close to her father; he was the one who taught her to skate. I don't know how I'm going to tell him he's never going to see his daughter again.'

'I'd leave that to Lukas if I were you,' said Saskia. 'It's the very least he can do.'

'No,' he said fiercely. 'I want them to hear it from me.'

I felt deeply for Alexander, but right now, we had a more pressing concern. 'I don't suppose either of you know where Fred is, do you?'

Saskia removed her hand from Alexander's leg. 'We saw him about fifteen minutes ago. He said he was going to the hydrotherapy pool.'

'Oh, great,' I muttered. I turned to Melissa. 'We haven't got time to wait for him to put his clothes back on. Maybe you and I could dig the hole between us. We can ask Nathan to give us a hand.'

'Is this for the food?' asked Alexander, getting up from the sofa. 'I'll do it. I could use some fresh air.'

Saskia sprung to her feet. 'I'll help you.'

'No, it's fine, I'd quite like some time on my own, to be honest.'

Her face fell. 'Oh, OK then, no problem.' She hooked her long hair back behind her ears. 'Be careful out there, won't you?'

I too had a sudden, strong urge to be by myself. I needed a break from everyone; my nerve endings felt exposed, my sense of security shattered. I gave Alexander directions to the kitchen and then, after telling Melissa I was going for a lie-down, I headed up to my room, where I lay on top of the covers in a foetal position, hugging a pillow to my chest and wishing I was back home.

Not being able to communicate with Mum and Gran felt horrible. I missed them so much, it was painful – a low-level burning, like acid in my blood. I hoped they weren't too worried by my lack of contact. With any luck, they'd heard about the snowstorm and realised it was the reason for my silence.

I comforted myself with the thought that it wouldn't be long before we were reunited. Once the roads were cleared of snow and the airport had reopened, Annett would surely set about arranging return flights for all of us. There was no way the programme could continue now. Lukas was probably ruing the day he dreamed up the crazy idea to teach the Grim Reaper to a bunch of amateurs.

I couldn't help feeling a twinge of sympathy for him. Once Gabrielle's death became public knowledge, he would be facing a lot of difficult questions. I wouldn't be at all surprised if he brought his retirement date forward and withdrew from the public eye permanently.

Tossing the pillow aside, I checked my phone for the millionth time – still no signal – and then, unable to think of anything else to do, I picked up the Agatha Christie from my nightstand and started to read.

Despite the tumultuous real-life events in the castle, I was soon immersed in a fictional world. I had completely lost track of the time when I heard a knock at my bed-room door. I told whoever it was to come in and was pleased when I saw that it was Nathan.

'Hey,' I said, putting down my book. 'What's up?'

'Have you seen Alexander?' he said tersely.

'Not since he offered to go and bury the food from the freezer. Why?'

'He's gone missing.'

15

'What do you mean – *missing*?'

'I can't find him,' Nathan said. 'I've looked everywhere.'

My mind went back to Alexander and Saskia; how intimate they'd looked, sitting together on the sofa. 'He might be with Saskia; I know the two of them are close.'

He shook his head. 'I just spoke with her; she hasn't seen him for a few hours.'

I got up off the bed. 'Do you know if anyone saw him go outside?'

'Annett did. There's a boot room off the kitchen with an external door; Annett said she unlocked it for him.' A stitch of concern appeared between his eyebrows. 'She watched him carry the first crate through the door, then she left him to it. That was nearly three hours ago.'

'So nobody saw him come back in?'

'Nope, but all the crates have gone from the kitchen. I opened the door from the boot room and hollered his name a few times, but there was no answer. I can't see him through any of the windows either.'

'Does Lukas know he's missing?'

'Not yet. I didn't want to bother him until I'd checked with everyone.'

I couldn't help feeling annoyed. I understood that

Alexander was hurting, but it was thoughtless of him to go AWOL. We already had enough to worry about, without him adding to our stress levels. I remembered what he'd said in the library, about wanting to be by himself.

'What about the summer house, over by the tennis court? He could have gone there after he buried the food to get some alone time.'

'In sub-zero temperatures?'

'There might be an electric heater in there, or blankets. It's got to be worth a look.'

He nodded. 'Yeah, OK. I'll grab my coat and head out there now.'

I went to the wardrobe and pulled a coat off the rail, before picking up my Doc Marten boots from the shelf below. 'Not on your own you won't.'

Nathan and I went downstairs to the kitchen and he led the way to the boot room. No bigger than a walk-in wardrobe, it was crammed with assorted outerwear that hung from hooks on the walls. A pile of sports equipment was piled up in one corner, testament to Lukas's various hobbies: tennis rackets, golf clubs, a long padded case that looked as if it might contain a fishing rod. Nathan grabbed a couple of thick scarves and handed one to me.

'We're going to need gloves too,' I said, spotting a wicker basket filled with them. After finding a couple of pairs that more or less fitted us, Nathan turned the key in the external door and pulled it open.

The scene that greeted us when we stepped outside was almost apocalyptic. The view was the same in every direction – a bleak, monochrome canvas, with precious few points of reference. It was still snowing heavily, sharp flakes that tumbled from rents in the sagging grey sky. A vicious wind drove them into our eyes and noses, forcing us to pull our scarves up over our faces. It was bitterly cold, a sharp-edged chill that seared my lungs every time I took a breath.

Nathan pulled down his scarf to speak. 'Are you sure you're OK with this? It's pretty gnarly out here.' The wind snatched the words out of his mouth almost before he'd spoken them.

Reluctant to remove my own scarf, even momentarily, I gave him a nod.

'I'll go in front,' he said. 'That way, you can walk in my tracks.'

The summer house was less than fifty metres away, but our progress was painfully slow. With each step he took, Nathan sank into the snow almost up to his knee. Even just using the holes he'd created was hard work since it required lifting my legs much higher than usual. The snow clung to the soles of my boots, creating heavy weights that seemed determined to anchor me in place. Every now and then, I lifted my head to scan the castle grounds, eyes straining to make out any distinguishing features in the landscape. But there weren't any.

By the time we finally reached the summer house, my hands and feet were numb and my leg muscles were screaming. I knew I'd be feeling ten times worse if I wasn't so fit from skating.

Every contour of the wooden building was covered with snow. Icicles hung like crystal daggers from its eaves and its windows were veiled by a frosty mosaic. A thick layer of pristine snow covered the veranda, suggesting that nobody had been here in the last few hours. When I tried the French windows, they were locked, but just to be certain, Nathan and I peered through the glass, hands cupped around our eyes. Alexander wasn't there and everything inside was shrouded in dust sheets.

I lifted my scarf from my mouth. 'Do you think he might've ventured further afield?'

'Left the castle grounds, you mean? Why would he do that?'

'To find a phone signal. He told me earlier he wanted to be the one to tell Gabrielle's parents she'd died.'

'Well, if he has, we're not going out there to look for him; it's just too dangerous.' He swiped away a drop of moisture from the end of his nose. 'We'd better get back. I just realised we didn't tell anyone where we were going. If the others see that we're missing too, they'll freak out.'

'Hang on a minute. Didn't Lukas say something about a garage?'

'Yeah, it's on the other side of the castle; I've seen it on my morning runs.'

'Shouldn't we check it out? At least then we'll be able to tell Lukas we've looked everywhere.'

'All right then, but let's be quick; I'm freezing my ass off out here.'

We headed back the way we'd come. We followed

our original tracks for a while, which were already filling with fresh snow, but then Nathan veered in the opposite direction so that now we were walking parallel to the front of the castle. It became increasingly difficult to keep up with him and I found myself lagging further and further behind. Each step felt like a battle and several times I stumbled on an unseen obstacle, hidden under the surface. The visibility was atrocious and by the time Nathan reached the westernmost corner of the castle, I could barely make him out. It was mid-afternoon, but the air was so thick with swirling snow, it might as well have been dusk. It distorted my vision, creating an ethereal scene that seemed to shift and dance in front of my eyes.

Not wanting to lose sight of Nathan entirely, I picked up my pace. Speed came at the cost of caution, however, and, as I lifted my back foot out of the hole it was encased in, the toe of my boot caught on the compacted snow. The next second, I was falling forwards, arms cartwheeling in the air. I tried to regain my balance, but it was too late and I landed on my stomach, winding myself badly.

Hearing my cry of shock, Nathan's voice came towards me on the wind. 'Libby! I can't see you. Are you OK?'

Pulling down my scarf, I waved a hand in the air. 'Here!' My chest felt so tight, I could hardly get the word out.

He began retracing his footsteps, peering through the curtain of snow until he spotted me sprawled on the ground. By the time he reached me, I'd managed to haul myself up onto all fours.

He leaned down and pulled his scarf away. 'What happened? Have you hurt yourself?'

The tender note in his voice gave me a tiny squeeze of pleasure.

Opening my mouth wide like a stranded fish, I gulped down a lungful of freezing air. 'I was going too fast.' Another shallow breath. 'I'm just winded.'

'Sorry, it's totally my fault. I should've checked to see you were still behind me.' He rested his hand on the small of my back. 'Don't try to get up yet. Just concentrate on taking slow, deep breaths in through your nose and out through your mouth. Come on, I'll do it with you. Inhale . . .' He took a deep breath, held it for a couple of seconds, then blew the air back out. '. . . And exhale.'

I couldn't help smiling to myself. This was what I loved about Nathan. His kindness, his unflappability, his quiet reserve of strength. Even though we'd only met a week ago, I knew instinctively that he was the sort of person who could be relied on in a crisis, someone who would never let you down. It was just bloody bad luck that we lived on different continents.

'Feeling better?' he said after a minute or two.

'Much,' I replied, sitting back on my haunches.

'Good, let's keep moving then.'

He stood up and reached out his hand. As our gloved fingers connected, he lifted me to my feet so powerfully that I rebounded into his chest. Grabbing my upper arms, he leaned in to steady himself. As our eyes locked together, every fantasy that I'd tried to box away seemed to bloom in the space beneath my ribs, so that there was an exquisite kind of pleasure-pain pushing against my internal organs. All at once, I forgot that we were caught in the middle of a raging blizzard. In that moment, it was just me and him and our two beating hearts.

The next moment, I came crashing back down to earth. Because just over Nathan's shoulder I could see something lying on the ground, off to the left. A flash of neon standing out against the sea of white.

'What's that?' I said, pointing to it.

Nathan looked behind him. 'What are you looking at?'

'There's something bright orange sticking out of the snow over there.'

'Yeah, I see it,' he said after a couple of seconds. 'Could be the stuff Alexander buried.'

I didn't recall seeing any orange packaging when we'd emptied the freezer. But at the same time, there was something familiar about the colour.

I started moving towards the object. My feet felt like lead weights as I dragged them through the snow, but a mounting sense of dread drove me on. As I got closer, I felt something ugly crawl across my skin, put its fingers tightly around my throat.

'Hey, wait for me,' I heard Nathan say.

Ignoring him, I kept on going. When I reached the scrap of colour, I fell to my knees and began digging frantically in the snow. Within seconds, the sleeve of an orange ski jacket had been revealed. My heart cracked.

'Hurry,' I shouted to Nathan. 'I think I've found him.'

A few seconds later, Nathan was beside me. Our numb hands clawed at the snow, working upwards from the sleeve. My worst fears were realised when a face appeared: Alexander's face. His skin was pale and his eyes were closed. The hood of his jacket was pulled half-way up over his head and there was blood leaking from one of his ears.

'Fuck, no!' Nathan cried, tearing off one of his gloves.

As he put his fingers to Alexander's neck, the hood of the jacket fell back, revealing a gaping wound in the side of the Polish man's head. It was encrusted with blood and brain matter – confirmation, as if we needed it, that any resuscitation attempt would be pointless.

Nausea rose up from my stomach and into my throat, making me gag. I looked at Nathan. He stared back at me in such pure, feral panic that I wanted to grab him and hold him tight. I didn't though. My mind had seized up. I could barely think, let alone move.

As I struggled to make sense of what I was seeing, a line ran through my mind like a news crawler at the bottom of a TV screen: *This can't be happening. Not again.* Two deaths in less than twenty-four hours. I wouldn't believe it if I hadn't seen both lifeless bodies with my own eyes.

It felt as if I had fallen through the cracks into an alternate universe. A universe where nothing was as I'd believed it to be, leaving me flailing round, trying to catch hold of something solid.

Nathan rubbed his eyes as if he couldn't believe it either. 'What do you think happened here?'

'I don't know,' I said in a voice that seemed to be coming from a very long way off. 'But judging by the amount of snow on top of him, he's been dead for a couple of hours at least.'

Nathan stood up abruptly. 'We need to get back to the castle – *now*.'

'Hang on a sec.'

I knew that if the snow continued to fall at the current rate, it wouldn't be long before Alexander's body was covered up again. This might be the only chance we had before the snow thawed to find some clue about how he had sustained his head injury.

I began carefully excavating the snow around his head.

'What are you doing?' Nathan asked.

'He didn't get that injury just by falling over in the snow. Something made contact with his head; a rock or something. I want to know what it was.'

'Does it matter?' Nathan said impatiently. 'I think it's more important we tell the others Alexander's dead, don't you?'

I was slightly taken aback; I'd never heard him speak so gruffly. I looked up at him. His cheeks were flushed and a vein on his forehead was standing out like a cord.

'You go back if you want,' I said obstinately. 'But I'm staying here.'

Sighing, he put his glove back on and knelt down beside me. We dug for several minutes, but found nothing.

'This is a waste of time,' Nathan said. 'We can't help him now. Come on, Libby, let's go.'

I knew he was right, but still I hesitated. Rising to my feet, I scanned our surroundings, looking for anything that seemed out of place. Something a couple of metres away stood out. A subtle disturbance in the otherwise pristine blanket of snow; a patch of ground, slightly raised and uneven. I began walking towards it.

'Where are you going?' Nathan said.

When I arrived at the uneven area, I began to circle it, digging my heel into the snow at intervals. The third time I did it, my foot made contact with something hard and unyielding. I squatted down and began to dig with my hands.

'There's something here!' I shouted as I spotted what looked like a piece of wood poking out through the snow.

'What is it?'

'I don't know, but I'm going to try to get it out.'

Together, we began scraping away the snow from around the object. It was bigger than I'd thought – a long, smooth shaft of pale-coloured wood. At one end was a T-shaped hand grip; a walking stick perhaps. We worked our way carefully down the shaft until, suddenly, I saw the dark edge of something metallic glinting through the snow.

Nathan reached across me for the hand grip and yanked it hard. All at once, the object emerged from its icy cocoon.

It was a spade.

And clinging to one corner of its curved blade was the missing piece of flesh from Alexander's scalp.

I reared back, hands pressed to my mouth. As we both stared dumbly at the spade, fear rose inside me, filling my brain like a swell of music I couldn't contain.

I turned to Nathan. 'I don't understand what's going on,' I said slowly.

'I don't either.' He laid the spade carefully back down, the piece of bloody tissue still attached to it. 'We need to get back; it's not safe out here.'

I didn't know if he was referring to the weather, or something else, but I felt a bead of sweat slide down my spine and settle in the small of my back.

'What about Alexander? We can't just leave him here.'

'We don't have a choice. The guy must weigh a hundred and sixty pounds; there's no way we can get him back to the castle.'

My head was starting to throb, a dull beat at the base of my skull. 'We ought to at least mark his location.'

'What with? There's nothing out here.'

I looked around, but all I saw were a few small twigs, lying on the surface of the snow.

Nathan nudged the spade with his foot. 'We could always use this.'

I thought about it for a moment. It wasn't ideal, but if we didn't mark the spot somehow, we might not be able to find Alexander's body again until the snow thawed, which could be days – if not weeks.

'Fine, use the spade.' I fumbled in the pocket of my jacket for my phone, grateful that I'd had the presence of mind to bring it with me. 'I'm going to take some photos.'

Raising my phone, I fired off a series of shots, all the while trying to ignore the heave in my stomach, the taste of fear that lapped against my teeth like some bitter herb. Recording the grisly scene was the last thing I wanted to be doing, but if foul play was involved, then I needed to gather what evidence I could, before it was lost to the elements.

'Stand next to his body,' I instructed Nathan. 'I want to take a picture of you with the castle in the background, as a reference point.'

Reluctantly, he got into position, the lines around his mouth drawn tight. When I was done, he picked up the spade and plunged it into the ground. 'Can we go now?'

I looked at Alexander. Snow was already covering his chest, his lips, his hair. There was no time to pray; every second we stayed out here felt like a second too long.

As we set off towards the castle, I was in a state of hyperarousal, every one of my senses on high alert. But there was only a featureless white abyss and the muffled crunch of our footsteps.

16

The air in the library was charged with a suffocating mix of shock and disbelief. Six people were staring at Nathan and me, all of them looking as if they'd just been hit by an avalanche.

We'd rounded everyone up as soon as we got back; we figured it was only fair to tell them all at once. Nathan was the one who broke it to them. He just came straight out with it. There was no build-up, no forewarning, no time for anyone to brace or cover their eyes.

Saskia was the first to speak. 'Is this some kind of sick joke?'

'No,' I told her. 'It's real.'

She gave a low moan and buried her face in her hands.

Flora stared down at the floor, shaking her head in bewilderment. 'I can't believe it,' she said softly. 'First Gabrielle, and now Alexander. How is this even possible?'

'And you think he died from this head wound?' said Fred.

'It looks that way.'

Lukas was rocking back and forward on his heels. His pupils were dilated, giving his gaze an almost unblinking quality. His loss of composure unsettled me. Now, more than ever, we needed a strong leader.

'Do you have any idea how Alexander might have sustained this apparently fatal injury?' he asked.

'Um, yes, actually, we do.' My shoulders slumped under the weight of what I was about to reveal. 'There was a spade lying next to his body.' I hesitated, wondering how best to phrase it. 'It was obvious its blade had made contact with Alexander's head.'

There were several audible expressions of horror.

Lukas stopped rocking. 'When you say *obvious* . . .'

I pushed a strand of hair out of my eyes. I didn't think I could bear to describe what I saw on that spade – and judging by Nathan's silence, neither could he.

My hand closed around the phone in my pocket. 'I took some photos if you want to see them – but I have to warn you, they're pretty graphic.'

Melissa's lip curled in distaste. 'You took *pictures* of Alexander?'

'Yes, but not for sharing on social media or anything like that,' I said hurriedly. 'It just seemed like a sensible precaution . . . you know . . . to have a record of what we saw, especially as it might be some time until his body can be recovered.'

Saskia gave a little whimper. 'I don't want to see; I'd rather remember Alexander as he was.'

'Of course, nobody's going to make you look at them.'

'*I'd* like to see them,' said Fred.

There was a brief pause before Lukas stepped forward. 'So would I.'

They all gathered round as I started looking for the

pictures on my phone. Only Saskia hung back, clutching the two sides of her cardigan tightly around her throat. I knew that she and Alexander had been close, but still, there was something staged about her behaviour. It was almost as if, no matter the circumstances, she had to be the centre of attention.

I pulled up the first image. It showed Alexander's upper body, his head injury clearly visible. Melissa gasped; Flora stifled a sob; someone else uttered an expletive.

Drawing the phone back to my chest, I swiped past a close-up of the wound. I would spare them that one; it was something they would never be able to unsee.

'This is the spade,' I said, turning the screen around.

Melissa looked as if she was about to be sick.

'OK, so we know what caused Alexander's injury,' said Fred. 'The question now is *how* did it happen?'

Flora looked deep in thought. 'Based on what you saw, is it possible that this was some kind of accident? I'm guessing it would be pretty easy for someone to fall over out there – and if the spade had been lying in the snow, blade up . . .'

Nathan scratched his head. 'I'm no CSI – but, yeah, I'd say it could've happened that way.'

'But it's not the only possibility,' I said.

'The other one being that someone hit him with the spade,' said Fred, vocalising what I had been reluctant to.

'You're suggesting Alexander might have been murdered?' said Melissa, her voice swerving up, high and panicky.

'We can't rule it out,' Nathan replied.

'But what sort of person would do that?' Saskia's voice came shrilly from the back of the room.

Her question hung in the air unanswered.

'Do we know where the spade came from?' asked Melissa. 'That might give us a clue.'

Annett coughed lightly. Up until then she'd been silent; I'd almost forgotten she was there.

'It was in the boot room,' she said. 'We keep a few tools there for the gardener. I gave it to Alexander when he went outside to bury the food.'

'Do we know for sure that he *did* bury the food?' said Flora.

It was a very good question.

'I think he must have done,' I told her. 'It had all been taken from the kitchen and there was no sign of it anywhere outside.'

'Unless the person who attacked him stole the food,' said Annett.

'Forget the damn food!' Fred's voice echoed around the room like a gunshot. 'I'm more concerned that a killer might be stalking the grounds. What if they're still out there? What if they try to break into the castle and hurt someone else?'

Melissa's face froze in a rictus of fear. 'You two did lock the boot-room door when you came back in, didn't you?'

Nathan assured her that we had.

'What about the front door?' said Saskia. 'Is that secure too?'

'Yes,' said Annett. 'Locked and bolted.'

Flora crossed her arms over her chest. 'So is anyone going to address the elephant in the room?'

'Elephant?' said Fred, clearly not understanding the English idiom.

Flora's lower lip wobbled. 'I'm talking about the fact that two people have died in unexplained circumstances. I know there's no obvious connection between their deaths, but can it really be coincidence?'

Nathan frowned. 'But Gabrielle's death was clearly accidental.'

'We don't know that for sure,' said Melissa. 'For all we know, she was asphyxiated.' She started pacing up and down. 'Let's think about this for a second, shall we? Who was the only person who witnessed Gabrielle's fall on the ice?'

'Alexander,' said Nathan.

'Correct.'

'And who was the only person present when she died?'

Saskia eyed Melissa with suspicion. 'So what are you suggesting – that Alexander killed her?'

'I'm just thinking out loud, that's all. Don't you think it's odd that Alexander insisted Gabrielle tripped on a faulty section of synthetic ice – and yet Lukas didn't spot anything amiss when he inspected the rink just a few hours later? What if her fall wasn't caused by a misaligned panel; what if it was caused by something else?'

Flora frowned. 'Like what?'

'Alexander could easily have placed some sort of obstacle on the ice without Gabrielle noticing,' said Melissa. 'A small object that was difficult to see; something that could be removed after the event and slipped into a pocket.'

'It seems like a very strange way to try to murder someone,' said Fred. 'The vast majority of falls on the ice aren't fatal.'

'Not kill her, *disable* her,' said Melissa. 'Make her vulnerable, so it would be easier to kill her later on, without it looking too suspicious.'

'But Alexander was crazy about her,' said Flora. 'At least, that's the impression I got. Why would he want to kill her?'

Melissa shrugged. 'Why does anyone kill their partner? Jealousy? Revenge? A desire to control?'

Saskia was shaking her head. 'No, I don't buy it. Alexander wasn't a murderer.'

'How can you say that when you hardly even knew the guy?' said Fred. He gave a knowing smirk. 'Although I noticed you didn't waste any time moving in on him after Gabrielle died.'

'How dare you?' she hit back angrily.

'Oh, don't play the innocent. Even when Gabrielle was alive, it was obvious you were crushing on him. All those flirty sideways glances and little arm touches; laughing at things he said, even when they weren't even funny.'

'Fuck you, Fred,' she spat. 'You know nothing about me.'

Fred gave a small, hard smile. 'On the contrary, I know more than you think.'

'Enough, guys,' Nathan intervened, making a slicing motion under his chin. 'I know emotions are running high, but this isn't the time to be bitching at each other.'

'Nathan's right,' said Flora, laying a calming hand on Saskia's shoulder. 'We need to stick together; it's the only way we're going to get through this.'

Saskia stuck her chin in the air. 'Fine, but Alexander and I were friends. Nothing more.'

'We'll take your word for it,' I said shortly. 'Just for the sake of argument, let's say Alexander did kill Gabrielle. How would that tie in to his own death?'

'Maybe he felt bad about what he'd done and decided to commit suicide,' said Melissa.

Fred snorted. 'You think Alexander hit himself over the head with a spade? I don't think so. There are plenty of easier ways to get the job done.'

'Personally, I think Fred's theory about a psycho stalking the grounds makes more sense,' said Flora. 'Isn't it possible that the same person broke into the castle, sabotaged the ice rink and then, when they knew Gabrielle was vulnerable, they finished her off?'

'How would they be able to do that with Alexander in the room?' I said. 'Even if he was asleep.'

'Maybe he lied about falling asleep. Maybe he felt embarrassed because he left Gabrielle on her own for whatever reason, and it was while he was gone that the killer struck.'

Annett made a face. 'I don't see how this person could have got into the castle. If there were any signs of a break-in, I'd have noticed.'

'Maybe they didn't have to break in,' said Saskia. 'Maybe it was someone who used to work here; someone with a set of keys.'

'Unlikely,' said Lukas, finally finding his voice. 'I take my personal security very seriously. The only employee who's ever had a set of keys to the property is Annett.'

'Did you change all the locks when you moved in?' Saskia asked him.

His confident look wavered. 'Only the front door.'

'There you are then,' she said triumphantly. 'For all you know, the previous owners were handing out back door keys to all and sundry.'

It was a plausible notion, but the seed of something even more terrible was growing in my mind. *What if the person responsible didn't need a set of keys?* The seed pushed forth sick tendrils. *What if they were in the room right now?*

I forced the thought back down and listened as the others continued to trade theories.

As the discussion went on, I found myself becoming increasingly frustrated. Idle speculation was pointless. What we needed was a plan; a way to dig ourselves out of this crisis. Thankfully, Nathan was thinking the same.

'All this talk is getting us nowhere,' he said in a loud voice. 'Two of our friends are dead, and until we know how they died, the rest of us are in a very precarious position. We need to stop wasting time and find a way of raising the alarm.'

I waited for Lukas to suggest a way we might achieve this, but he was staring straight ahead with an unsettling vacancy. It was the same way he'd looked when I found him in his office half an hour ago, half-sitting, half-lying in a leather recliner. I'd thought he might be asleep at first since he didn't react when I'd tapped on the door. But then, when I'd entered the room, I'd realised his eyes were open. He'd jumped up when he saw me and looked almost guilty as I'd explained that his presence was required in the library.

'What do *you* think we should do, Lukas?' I asked him now.

He raked a hand through his shock of hair. 'The way I see it, we don't have many options. There's no point in taking unnecessary risks; the last thing we want is more deaths on our hands. I think the best plan of action is to stay here and wait out the storm.'

'I disagree,' said Melissa. 'Who knows how long this blizzard's going to last? We need to find a way of making contact with the outside world before then. Maybe some of us should try to hike to the nearest village. How far away is it anyway?'

'Nine kilometres by road,' said Annett. 'Seven if you go through the forest.'

Melissa looked crestfallen. 'I didn't realise it was that far, but if we set off at daybreak, we might be able to—'

'It's a physical impossibility,' said Nathan, interrupting her mid-flow. 'You haven't been out there. It took me and Libby half an hour just to walk to the summer house. There are only eight hours of daylight, so even if you set off at dawn, you'll probably only have travelled four Ks by sunset, and that's if you don't die of hypothermia along the way. If you had skis, you might stand half a chance, but in regular footwear – no way.'

Suddenly, Annett's face brightened. 'But we *do* have skis.'

Lukas looked nonplussed. 'Do we?'

'Yes, they're in the attic. I saw them there in the summer when I was laying the mousetraps.'

'How many pairs?' asked Flora eagerly.

'Three or four; I'm not sure. There are ski poles too.'

'Well, they're not mine,' said Lukas. 'I don't ski. The castle's previous owners must have left them behind when they moved out.'

Flora turned to Saskia, her eyes glistening. 'What do you reckon, Sas? We can do this, can't we?'

'Course we can,' replied Saskia. 'Both of us are decent cross-country skiers. This will be a walk in the park.'

'I really don't think it's a good idea,' said Lukas. 'You aren't at all familiar with the area; it would be very easy for you to get lost.'

'You have maps though, don't you?' said Saskia. 'I've seen them in the library.'

He stroked his chin. 'Yes, but—'

'I want to come with you,' said Fred. 'I've never tried cross-country, but I'm a competent downhill skier.'

'That's fine, we can give you a quick lesson,' said Flora. She looked around the group. 'Anyone else?'

Fred reached out to Melissa and gave her forearm a little squeeze. 'You ski, Melissa, don't you?'

She smiled uncertainly. 'I'm probably not as good as the rest of you, but I can manage a red run.'

'Libby?' said Flora expectantly.

'No,' I said. 'I've never been skiing.' Sadly, I didn't come from the sort of family who trotted off to Val d'Isère for a week every Christmas.

'Me neither,' said Nathan. He gave me a wink, so quick I almost missed it. 'I've always thought skiing was overrated, to be honest.'

Lukas let out a noisy breath. 'I understand your desire to help, but please believe me when I tell you this is a foolish fantasy that's doomed to failure.' There was a complex edge to his voice, dismay or disappointment, and something harder, like anger. 'Your families have entrusted you into my care and I take my responsibilities very seriously. Therefore, I must insist you remain in the castle until the weather improves.'

Saskia gave a mocking laugh. 'Given that two of us are dead, you haven't done a very good job of looking after us so far, have you? We're not children, we're grown adults and we're perfectly capable of deciding what's in our own best interests, thank you very much.'

Lukas didn't reply but his face took on a strange expression – exasperation, tinged with another, darker emotion; one I couldn't read.

Flora went over to Annett. 'How do we get to the attic?'

'It's in the west wing.'

'Will you take us there?'

Annett looked over at Lukas, as if seeking his approval. There was an unmistakeable note of warning in his eyes, but either she didn't see it, or she chose to ignore it. 'The others are right,' she told him. 'We have to try *something*.'

I expected Lukas to let rip, but he just tossed his head imperiously. I sensed the tension in him, banked and ready to explode, the threat of it hanging like a cloud of noxious fumes above our heads.

'Do what you like,' he said, 'but I want it on record that I advised you against this course of action. Anything that happens to you from now on is entirely of your own making.'

'Whatever,' said Saskia flippantly. She smiled at Annett. 'Lead the way.'

17

I stared up at the ceiling. It was several minutes since Annett had disappeared through the hatch that led to the attic. I wasn't the only one waiting in anticipation. Everyone was there; everyone except Lukas.

Fred climbed the first rung of the retractable ladder. 'How are you doing up there? Do you need any help?'

'I'm fine, thank you,' a distant voice replied.

I heard the sound of something being dragged across the floorboards above our heads, and then Annett appeared at the top of the ladder. There was a greyish smear of dirt on one of her cheeks.

'Here's the first pair, I'll pass them down to you.'

Fred climbed another couple of rungs as Annett manoeuvred first one ski and then the other through the small aperture.

'Wow,' he said as he took hold of them. 'These look ancient.'

He gave them to Flora, who was waiting at the foot of the ladder.

'Who cares?' she said as she leaned them up against the wall. 'So long as they do the job.'

The next thing to emerge through the hatch was a pair of ski poles.

'Those are for downhill, not cross-country,' grumbled Saskia.

'What's the difference?' I asked her.

'Cross-country poles are longer. They give you more propulsion when you're gliding across flat surfaces.'

'Can you manage with these ones?'

She shrugged. 'What choice do we have?'

Annett produced two more pairs of skis, both of them well-used, judging by the amount of scratches on them. They were followed by another set of poles, thick with dust and draped in cobwebs. As Fred handed them to Flora, I saw that one had a forty-five-degree bend in its lower quadrant, which was going to make life difficult for whoever drew the short straw.

'That's all of them,' said Annett as she passed Fred the final pair of skis, these ones noticeably shorter than the others.

'These look like they're for kids,' he said with a scowl.

Melissa went over to the ladder and took them out of his hands. 'I'm not very tall; I think I can work with these.' She looked up at Annett. 'I don't suppose there are any helmets, are there?'

'No, sorry. I've found a couple of pairs of snowshoes though. Shall I bring them down?'

'Don't bother,' said Saskia. 'We'll be able to travel much quicker on skis.'

As Annett began descending the ladder, the rest of us scrutinised the kit.

'These haven't been waxed in a while,' said Fred, as he ran a finger along one of the skis. 'Look how corroded the edges are.'

'I'm more concerned about that damaged pole,' said Melissa. 'Do you think we'll be able to straighten it out?'

Nathan picked it up. 'Depends what it's made of.'

'Must be aluminium,' said Fred. 'Carbon fibre wouldn't have bent like that.'

'What if we heat it up with a hairdryer?' asked Nathan.

Fred shook his head. 'It's not worth the risk. We won't be able to straighten it without fatiguing the metal, and if it breaks, it'll be useless.'

Flora went over to Annett, who was hovering on the periphery of the group, and gave her a quick hug. The assistant looked faintly startled, but not altogether displeased, by this spontaneous display of affection.

'Thanks for this, Annett,' said Flora. 'Remembering those skis were up there was a stroke of bloody genius.'

The older woman smiled at her. 'It's like you said before, we're all in this together.'

'I hope we haven't got you into trouble with Lukas. He seemed pretty angry with us.'

'Don't worry about him; he's just a little highly strung,' said Annett. 'I'm sure that once he's had a chance to think about it, he'll realise this is our only option.'

'Is he?' I said. 'Highly strung, I mean? Only that's not the impression I get.'

'Lukas is good at putting on a front. He doesn't like people seeing the real him.'

Fred gave a hard little smile. 'I can believe that.'

'So when are we setting off?' asked Melissa.

'Tomorrow, at dawn,' Flora said. 'Hopefully the snow will have eased up by then.'

'I'll be sure to listen to the weather forecast,' said Annett. 'I'll fetch a map for you too. I can show you the two different routes to the village.'

'Do *you* ski, Annett?' I asked her. 'I don't think you said.'

'Yes, but I'm out of practice.'

'Why don't you come with us?' Saskia suggested. 'I'm sure one of the others wouldn't mind giving up their place for you.'

'That's a really good idea,' I said. 'That way you won't need the map; Annett can lead the way.'

'No, honestly,' Annett protested, 'I'm not very good; I'd only hold you up.'

'Don't worry, we'll manage,' Flora told her. 'We're perfectly capable of reading a map.'

I caught a flicker of relief in Annett's eyes. I rubbed my hand along my brow. Whilst it was clear that action was needed, I still had a few misgivings. 'Why do four of you need to go? Wouldn't it better if just a couple of you went – the two best skiers, say?'

'No,' Saskia hit back. 'Safety in numbers and all that.'

'Fine,' I said, not wanting to start an argument. 'But I'd stick to the roads if I were you; there's less chance of getting lost. You might even run into someone in a vehicle; someone who can help us.'

'Yeah, that's a good call,' said Nathan. He clapped Fred on the shoulder. 'I wish I was going with you, but I know you guys have got this.'

'We won't let you down, I promise,' said Flora. 'We're going to get to that village if it kills us.'

18

'How far do you think they've got?'

Nathan, who was lying prone on the sofa, raised his arm in the air and checked his watch. 'They should be at least halfway there by now.'

I gave a little shiver. My arms were covered in goose-bumps, even though the heating was on full blast. The library felt different today. It was as if my body was reacting to something in the room, something living, breathing, something woven into the DNA of the build-ing, as much a part of it as its walls and floors.

'They won't be able to get there *and* back before it gets dark though, will they?' I said, turning away from the window.

'No. If they've got any sense, they'll take shelter in the village overnight. I'm sure there'll be some place they can stay – a church, or an inn.'

He yawned loudly. Both of us had got up early to see the others off; so had Annett. She had helpfully filled an old rucksack of Lukas's with bottles of water and snacks, as well as a map, on which she'd marked the two routes to the village with a highlighter pen. Lukas, meanwhile, was conspicuous by his absence; none of us had seen him since yesterday's awkward stand-off in the library.

It was still snowing when they left but, thankfully, the

wind had died down. After wishing them luck, the three of us had watched through the boot-room door as Saskia gave Fred and Melissa a crash course in cross-country skiing. Ten minutes later, the four of them were off, skimming over the surface of the snow, their graceful movements a stark contrast to my own clumsy trek to the summer house the previous day.

Reassured by Nathan's prediction, I abandoned my post and took a seat in a leather armchair. I had been waiting for the right moment to broach something with him and now seemed as good a time as any.

'There's been a lot of speculation about Gabrielle and Alexander's deaths,' I said, leaning sideways on the chair and curling my legs up beneath me. 'I just wondered what you were thinking; you haven't really said.'

He stared at the chandelier that hung above his head. 'I'd like to think that both their deaths were accidental,' he said carefully.

I wasn't going to let him off the hook that easily. 'Liking an idea and actually believing it are two different things.'

He drew his thumbnail back and forth across his forehead. 'Truthfully, Libby, I don't know what to think. I really can't see Alexander killing Gabrielle, especially not in the cold-blooded way Melissa was suggesting.'

I felt the same. It was just about plausible that the two of them had had a blazing row and Alexander had lashed out in the heat of the moment. But stage-managing Gabrielle's fall on the ice, getting us all to bear witness to her injury and then shooing us out of the room so he could finish the job? So improbable it didn't warrant serious consideration in my book. Nor did the idea that, mere hours later, he had a sudden crisis of conscience and whacked himself over the head with a spade.

'What about Fred's theory – that there's a psycho out there, watching us?' It was a deeply unsettling thought and one that had kept me awake as I tossed and turned in bed last night.

'Maybe. Although Annett did say there was no sign of a break-in.'

'It could be someone with keys to the castle, like Saskia said.'

'It's possible, I guess.'

I was quiet for a few moments, my thoughts churning as I tried to piece together fact and conjecture, but I felt agitated; twitchy. My brain wasn't working like it should.

'Or it could be someone closer to home.'

Nathan's eyes met mine. 'Yeah, the thought had occurred to me.'

A ripple of relief; the two of us were on the same page. 'Lukas's behaviour has been very erratic since Gabrielle had her accident,' I ventured. 'One minute he's completely disconnected, the next he's throwing his weight around.'

'He definitely wasn't happy about having his authority challenged yesterday. For a minute there in the dining room, I thought he was going to lose his shit. We're supposed to be a team, but sometimes I get the feeling he's working against us.'

My hand went to the back of my neck. My skin was crawling as if a swarm of ants were making their way from my collar up into my hair. 'Do you think we can trust him?'

Nathan adjusted the cushion beneath his head. 'I don't think we should rush to judge him. Some people just aren't very good in a crisis; maybe Lukas is one of them. It's only a matter of time before his adoring public finds out about what's gone on here. He must be crapping himself, wondering how all this is going to affect his future earning potential.'

I thought back to my first impressions of Lukas; how in awe of him I was when I'd arrived at Schloss Eis. His reputation, his charisma, his skill on the ice, his sheer physical presence. But now, after the events of the past thirty-six hours, he seemed strangely diminished in my mind. With every hour that passed, he seemed to be retreating further and further from the rest of us. And, more than that, I had a disconcerting sense of déjà vu. His moods that seemed to swing like a pendulum, from moments of intense focus to sudden outbursts of anger, or withdrawal. It reminded me of the turbulent waters I'd navigated as a child, when every interaction with Mum felt like walking on fragile ground, never quite sure what would happen next. I wasn't saying that Lukas was an alcoholic, but he was fighting some sort of demons; that much was obvious. But if the rest of us were going to get through this nightmare, we needed him on side. We had to find a way to repair our relationship with him, to paper over the cracks before they widened into irreparable fractures.

Nathan yawned again. 'I'm falling asleep here,' he said. 'I think I'll head up to my room and take a nap.'

'Good idea,' I said, trying to mask my disappointment. It was rare I got to spend time with Nathan without one of the others being present, and there was still so much I wanted to say to him.

He got up from the sofa. 'Will you be OK on your own?'

'Of course,' I said, before I had a chance to really think about it.

After he'd gone, I rested my head against the back of the chair and began twirling a strand of hair around my finger. It was an old self-soothing gesture from childhood; something I hadn't done in ages.

I wasn't sure how I was going to fill the rest of the day. I would have liked to hit the rink, but in the light of recent events, it didn't seem right somehow. I thought about going to look for Annett, who I hadn't seen for several hours. It was well past lunchtime and, with Nathan and I the only skaters left, I wasn't sure if we were expected to help ourselves from the fridge. Perhaps I'd wait until Nathan resurfaced and then the two of us could eat together.

I stood up and went over to the book shelves. The Agatha Christie was lying, unfinished, on my nightstand, but I couldn't be bothered to walk up two flights of stairs to get it. I ran my fingertips across the spines, looking for a fantasy novel I could lose myself in. Lukas's tastes didn't run to science fiction, but I spotted an English language version of *Brave New World*. I'd started reading it when I was sixteen or seventeen, but never got past the first few chapters. I pulled it off the shelf and took it back to my chair.

I only managed a few pages before my eyelids grew heavy. Laying the book on the floor, I leaned back and closed my eyes.

The next thing I knew, someone was screaming my name.

I jumped to my feet in a panic, heart beating out of my chest. 'I'm in the library!' I shouted back.

Before I could reach the door, it flew open and Flora burst into the room. She was wearing her coat and her face was red raw from the cold.

Disoriented as I was, I could see it was still light outside. I didn't understand what she was doing back so soon. They'd only been gone a few hours; not nearly enough time to get to the village and back.

'Something awful's happened,' she said, her breath hitching in her throat. She gripped my forearms, her eyes huge and frightened.

'What is it?' I said. 'Where are the others?'

She started to answer, but then her face folded and she pressed a hand to her mouth as if she didn't trust herself to speak.

'We need to organise a search party.'

Hearing another voice, I turned around. Fred was standing in the open doorway. Like Flora, he was clad in his outdoor gear.

'Will someone please tell me what's going on?' I demanded.

'Melissa's missing,' he said. 'We lost her in the forest.' His voice was weary and flat.

I felt like I hadn't woken up and I was having one of those twisted dreams that only happen when you fall asleep at the wrong time. 'What do you mean, you lost her?'

'The group got split up,' said Flora.

'So why have you come back?' I said, not understanding.

Fred began unzipping his jacket. 'We had no choice. We spent a couple of hours looking for her, but the forest's huge; she could be anywhere. We need more manpower, so we came back to get you guys.'

There was a horrible chewing sensation in my gut. Melissa was alone. In the forest. In freezing temperatures. She must be scared out of her mind.

'What were you even doing in the forest? I thought you were going to stick to the roads.'

'The skiing was more challenging than we anticipated,' said Flora. 'If we'd taken the longer route, we wouldn't have reached the village before it got dark.'

Fred nodded. 'Annett had shown us the way on the map; it looked straightforward enough. We didn't feel we were taking any unnecessary risks.'

Something skittered across my heart – a portent of

fear I wasn't ready to face just yet. 'How did you manage to get split up?'

'It's my fault,' said Flora. 'Saskia and I were skiing too fast. We should've made allowances for Fred and Melissa's lack of experience, but we were so focused on making up for lost time, we didn't notice they'd fallen behind.'

'Skiing through that forest was really tough,' said Fred. 'There were all kinds of hazards hidden under the snow – rocks and tree roots and God knows what else. Melissa kept falling over, and every time she did, I had to stop and wait for her to get back up. I could see how tired she was getting, so when I saw a spotted a fallen tree, I told her to sit down and rest up, while I skied on ahead to find the others and tell them to wait for us.' His mouth tightened. 'They'd gone much further than I thought. I didn't even know if I was headed in the right direction because the others had the map. I thought I could follow their tracks, but the snow had already started to cover them up. It was a miracle I managed to find them.'

'As soon as Fred caught up with us, we went straight back to get Melissa,' said Flora, breathlessly. 'But when we got to the fallen tree, she wasn't there.'

'Are you sure you were in the right place?'

'Totally,' said Fred. 'The tree was there – but Melissa had gone.'

Flora brushed a tear away from her cheek. 'We split up and started looking for her. I shouted her name until my throat was sore, but it was like she'd vanished into thin air. We were only a couple of Ks from the castle, so it made sense to come back here, rather than continue on to the village and try to get help there.'

'So where's Saskia?' I asked her.

'She's gone to find Lukas; we need Nathan too. Do you know where he is?'

'He went to his room for a nap. You two wait here for Lukas; I'll go and get him.'

I took the stairs two at a time. There weren't many hours of daylight left and the thought of Melissa spending a night out in the open was unbearable.

When I got to Nathan's room, I knocked loudly once, then walked straight in. I expected him to be asleep, but he was sitting up in bed, staring at his iPad, the screen lending his face a sickly glow. When I told him what had happened, he tossed the iPad down and bolted from the room.

By the time we got to the library, Lukas, Annett and Saskia were there. The three women seemed relieved to see us, but Lukas and Fred barely looked up, locked as they were in a heated conversation.

'Are you out of your mind?' Lukas was saying. 'What you're proposing isn't a rescue attempt, it's a suicide mission.'

Fred stared daggers at him. 'We have to at least try. What if she's injured? What if she's suffering from hypothermia?'

'And we *will* try – but not tonight.' Lukas gestured to the window and the rapidly darkening landscape beyond it. 'It'll be pitch-black out there in an hour's time.'

Saskia was nodding. 'I hate to say it, but Lukas is right. Even with head torches, it's still too dangerous. One of us could easily fall and break a leg. How would we get back to the castle then?'

'We should never have left her,' Flora said in a strangulated voice.

Annett patted her forearm comfortingly. It was the first time I'd seen her initiate physical contact with any of us. 'No, I think you made the right decision coming back here when you did.'

Fred started walking towards the door. 'I don't care what the rest of you think. I'm going out there anyway.'

'I can't let you do that,' said Nathan, as he stepped in front of him, blocking his way.

Fred's jaw flexed. 'Get out of my way, Nathan.'

'Please don't go, Fred,' Flora pleaded with him. 'None of us wants to see you come to any harm. Haven't we lost enough friends already?'

'You never know, Melissa might even find her own way back,' offered Annett.

'No, she won't,' said Fred. 'Don't you remember her joking that she had a terrible sense of direction when you were showing us the way on the map?'

Nathan laid his hands on Fred's shoulders. 'We'll go first thing in the morning, I promise,' he said. 'Melissa's tough; resourceful. Wherever she is, she'll find a way to survive the night.' His voice was strong and steady, but his eyes didn't seem to carry the same conviction.

Fred looked as if he was about to cry. 'I'm so stupid. I was carrying all our supplies in the rucksack. If only I'd left it with her before I skied off to find the others, at least she'd have food and water.'

'Don't blame yourself. How were you to know she'd wander off?'

Fred hung his head so his chin almost touched his chest. I could see that the fight had gone out of him. I wondered what he was thinking. If he knew, as I did, that the odds were not in Melissa's favour.

19

The search party set out at first light: Flora, Saskia and Fred on skis; Nathan and Lukas wearing the snowshoes that Annett found in the attic. I wanted to go with them, but there were only two pairs of snowshoes and I knew I wouldn't get far in my DMs.

'Be careful out there, won't you?' I said to Nathan as I stood in the boot room, watching him strap on the unfamiliar footwear.

He gave me a lopsided smile. 'Don't worry, we'll be back with Melissa before you know it.'

Despite his reassuring words, I had an uneasy feeling as I waved them off – not a premonition exactly, more a sense that events were spiralling out of our control. On a slightly more positive note, Annett had heard on the radio that engineers would be carrying out emergency repairs to the damaged mast today. All being well, communications would be restored within the next forty-eight hours. But, until then, Schloss Eis remained completely cut off from the outside world.

Needing some sort of distraction, I offered to help Annett with some chores; anything to stave off the lethal undertow of my thoughts. She set me to work in the kitchen, while she headed off to take care of some unspecified administrative task in Lukas's office. It struck me as odd – that she would think of doing admin at a time like this – but maybe she just wanted something to take her mind off the dreadful situation we were in.

After tidying away the breakfast things, I tried to find solace in the mundane rhythm of mopping, but I hadn't slept properly for the last two nights and my exhausted, overworked mind kept imagining things. I jumped at the sound of creaking pipework. Shrieked out loud when a bony hand clawed at the window, before realising it was only a strand of ivy trembling in the wind.

I couldn't shake the feeling that I was being watched. I kept glancing over my shoulder, half-expecting to catch a glimpse of some phantom lingering in the shadows. Of course, it didn't help knowing that there was a dead body, lying just feet away in the freezer. Or that Gabrielle's parents still didn't know what had happened to her. The thought of them going about their daily lives in ignorance back in France was like a blade lodged in my stomach.

I kept checking the clock on the wall, watching the minutes leak slowly away. The waiting, the not knowing what was happening, felt like torture. What if someone else went missing out there? What if that someone was Nathan?

At midday, Annett reappeared and we had lunch together, sitting at the kitchen island, random odds and ends from the fridge: leftover grilled chicken, gherkins straight from the jar, half a wheel of over-ripe camembert. I wasn't very hungry, but I ate it anyway. Next time, it might be *me* having to trek for miles in the snow. I needed to keep up my strength; just in case.

As we ate, Annett studiously avoided all mention of the others. Instead, she told me about the summer holiday she was planning to Greece, and the box set she'd been enjoying before the Wi-Fi went down. I knew she was only trying to keep our spirits up, but her mundane chat grated on me and I found myself wishing I was alone again.

After lunch, we washed our plates and wiped the worktop free of crumbs. Then Annett made tea and we drank it in silence as morning bled into afternoon.

It was just before two o'clock when Annett, rinsing our mugs in the sink, spotted a group of people trudging in single file across the lawn.

'They're back!' she cried, reaching for a towel to dry her hands.

Springing off my stool, I rushed to the kitchen window, hoping to see Melissa. But, as the group veered right and began heading towards the boot-room door, a thin seam of cold opened up inside me. *Five*. There were still only five of them.

'They didn't find her,' I said.

Annett sighed, mournful notes in her breath. 'I'll go and put the kettle on.'

I went to the boot room and unlocked the door, watching through its glass panel as the group approached. Nathan was at the head of the crocodile, his legs pumping in a solid rhythm. His head was down against the driving snow, but I recognised his green waterproof.

When he was almost at the door, I wrenched it open. An icy chill rushed in, making me gasp out loud. Nathan lifted his head. His eyebrows were encrusted with snow and his cheeks were ruddy. He gave the tiniest shake of his head, then let his chin fall back onto his chest as if he couldn't bear to look me in the eye. Behind him, the others broke ranks. Flora's eyes were puffy, as if she had been crying. Fred was white as a sheet. Saskia's bottom lip seemed to be in permanent spasm. As for Lukas . . . Lukas looked hollow; it was the only word I could think of to describe him.

Nathan stepped into the boot room, moving clumsily in his snowshoes.

'Melissa's dead,' he said. His voice was like a scalpel: so sharp it took whole seconds before I felt the pain.

'*Nein!*' I heard Annett cry from the kitchen.

Hot tears welled in my eyes, blurring everything around me. I staggered back against the wall. It felt like there was something solid in my chest, an obstruction stopping me from breathing.

Annett sidestepped me and beckoned to the others. 'Quickly, get those skis off and come inside,' she said. 'I'll make you all a hot cup of tea.'

Nathan unzipped his snow-covered jacket. As he tossed it over the nearest hook, I saw that his hands were shaking. 'I don't suppose you have anything stronger, do you?'

'There's a bottle of schnapps in the pantry,' said Lukas as he stepped out of his snowshoes and followed Nathan over the threshold. 'I think we could all use a glass.'

He fixed me with eyes that looked even bluer than usual; the cold blue of Venetian glass.

'You too, Libby. You're going to need it when you hear what we found in the forest.'

20

We stood around the kitchen island, a shot glass of schnapps in front of each of us.

'Lukas was the one who found her,' Nathan began, his words scattering like beads from a broken necklace.

'Her body was almost completely covered with snow,' said Lukas. 'If one of her skis hadn't been sticking up in the air, I wouldn't have known she was there.'

'That poor girl,' Annett murmured. 'They said on the radio that temperatures fell to minus eleven overnight. It wouldn't have taken very long for hypothermia to set in.'

Nathan and Lukas looked at each other across the island and I saw something ponderous and painful pass between them.

'She didn't die of the cold,' said Lukas.

I frowned. 'No?'

Nathan took a long breath, as if galvanising himself. 'She had a deep laceration to her neck. It looks like she bled out.'

A series of violent shudders radiated out from somewhere deep inside me, one after the other, like tiny depth charges.

'How?' I said hoarsely. 'How could she possibly have got an injury like that?'

Nathan reached for his phone. Pulled up a photo.

Slid the phone across the island towards me. The image showed a narrow trail, thickly carpeted with snow. In the foreground were two slender trees, one on each side of the trail. More trees extended behind them, forming an attractive avenue.

'Is this where you found her?'

'Yes, she's just out of shot.'

Annett leaned over my shoulder. Together, we stared at the photo for a few seconds. The others were silent, waiting for our reaction. At first, I couldn't spot anything out of the ordinary. It was only when I pincered my fingers on the screen to enlarge the image that I saw it.

A thin length of wire. Strung between the first set of trees. At approximately neck height.

My mind tipped sideways.

Annett saw it too. I heard her say something in German; it sounded like a swear word.

'You think Melissa skied into this,' she said.

'There was blood on the wire,' said Flora. She squeezed her eyes shut as if the words caused her physical pain. 'I took it down, to stop the same thing happening to someone else.'

As nausea bubbled up inside me, I pressed the back of my hand to my mouth.

'You can't see it very well in the photo, but the trail slopes downwards quite sharply,' Nathan explained. 'The wire would've been practically invisible to someone on skis, travelling at speed.' He swallowed hard. 'Melissa was lying at the side of the trail, underneath a big fir tree. It looks like she managed to stagger a short distance before she collapsed.'

Fred downed his schnapps in one and slammed the shot glass down on the island. His face was crumpled and white, like something botched and screwed into a ball. 'I hope for her sake it was quick.'

My mind was reeling, my thoughts turned upside down. Trying to put the pieces together was like trying to assemble a shattered mirror – the shards jagged and scattered.

'Whoever set this trap must've known it could be deadly,' I said, voicing the uncomfortable truth.

'For sure,' Saskia agreed. 'But what sort of person would do something so awful?' I could see the effort of holding back tears in the tiny convulsions of her lips.

Nathan braced himself on the worktop with both hands. 'A sick son of a bitch, that's who.'

'Did you leave Melissa in the forest?' I asked them.

'We had to,' said Lukas, his face a rigid mask. 'We would have needed a sled to bring her back to the castle.'

Nathan pulled a map from his trouser pocket and tossed it down in the centre of the island. 'I've marked the location on here. I just hope the local wildlife doesn't get to her before we can recover her body.'

I closed my eyes. It felt as if I was standing on the edge of a crevasse and it was going to take everything I had to hold myself back from the brink.

'How far was she from the place where Fred last saw her?'

'Quite a way,' said Flora. 'She was in an area we hadn't searched yesterday. We didn't think she could've travelled so far in such a short amount of time.'

Annett pulled the map towards her. 'When do you think she died?'

'Based on the half a metre of snow she was buried under, I'd say it was more likely to be yesterday than this morning,' said Lukas.

Annett pointed to the biro cross that Nathan had marked on the map. 'She was skiing in completely the wrong direction.'

'Where does that trail lead?' I asked her.

'Nowhere. It just goes deeper into the forest and ends when it hits the railroad tracks.'

'So what was she doing there?' I wondered out loud.

'My guess is she got tired of waiting for Fred and decided to try to catch up with us,' said Saskia. 'Only she took a wrong turn and lost her bearings. The poor thing must've been completely disoriented.'

An idea came to me. It became strong, thick fingers tightening around my windpipe. I cleared my clotted throat. 'What if Melissa knew she was headed in the wrong direction?'

Nathan frowned. 'Why would she decide to go off and explore some random trail on her own?'

'Something might have caught her attention,' I said, choosing my words carefully.

'What sort of something?' asked Fred.

'I don't know . . . she might've seen another person in the distance, or heard a voice calling for help.'

Flora looked shocked. 'Are you suggesting someone deliberately lured her down that trail?'

'I think they could've done.'

'Jesus,' said Saskia. 'I never even thought of that.'

Nathan picked up his shot glass. There was something hard and metallic behind his eyes. 'However it happened, it's still murder and the police need to find the person responsible before they pull the same sick stunt again.'

'Unfortunately, we have no means of contacting them at the present time,' Lukas pointed out.

'There are engineers working on the mast as we speak,' said Annett. 'I heard it on the radio. Our phones should be operational in the next day or two.'

'But, in the meantime, we're all trapped here like sitting ducks,' said Flora. She put her face into her palms and breathed inwards, then shakily out again, trying to steady herself. 'There's someone evil out there and they won't stop until we're all dead.'

The starkness of her words turned my blood to ice.

Lukas seemed less concerned. 'I know you're upset about losing your friends,' he said. 'But let's try to think rationally about this.'

'Upset!' Flora shrieked. 'Upset doesn't even come close.'

He held up a calming hand. 'I'm sorry, I didn't mean to be insensitive. I'm devastated about what happened to

Gabrielle, Alexander and Melissa and I intend to support their families in any way I can.'

Fred looked unimpressed. 'A pay-off, you mean? To stop them going to the press?'

'I was referring to *emotional* support,' Lukas replied tightly. 'And perhaps a bursary for aspiring skaters, set up in their child's name.'

'Oh *pur-lease*,' said Saskia. She drew quote marks in the air. '*Your kids didn't live long enough to realise their full potential, but hey – here's a few grand to help someone else's crotchfruit achieve sporting greatness.*'

Lukas didn't respond, but his face closed, became hostile and aloof.

I took a small sip of schnapps. It felt good, so I took another one. 'For what it's worth, I think Flora's on the right track. It does look as if we're being deliberately targeted. Someone doesn't want us here and they're willing to do whatever it takes to get rid of us.'

'But why would they be gunning for a bunch of amateur skaters with no connection to the local area?' said Fred.

'Maybe it's not *us* they want to hurt,' suggested Saskia. 'Maybe it's Lukas. Let's face it, when the media gets wind that three young people he was supposed to be looking after have died, it's not going to do much for his reputation.'

A silence stretched out, thinning until it became awkward. It was Lukas who finally broke it.

'I don't have any enemies and I can't think of a single person who'd want to hurt me.'

'Oh, don't be so naive,' Saskia retaliated. 'You're a public figure; you have been for more than two decades, and we all know there are some very sick puppies out there who get their kicks from stalking celebs.' She jabbed a finger at him. 'If I were you, Lukas, I'd watch my back.'

Lukas gripped his schnapps glass so tightly I was surprised it didn't break. 'Do you seriously think a deranged fan is holed up in the grounds of Schloss Eis, in the middle of a blizzard, just waiting for an opportunity to murder my guests?' he said through clenched teeth. 'And then what? They kill me and wait for the authorities to arrive, thereby guaranteeing their place in the history books? If you believe that, then you're more deranged than they are.'

Saskia leaned towards him across the island, showing she wasn't intimidated. 'Let's just say I don't think we should rule anything out.'

Lukas stood up abruptly and the stool he was sitting on crashed to the tiled floor. A dark energy emanated from him, something bottled and ferocious.

'I'm not enjoying the direction this conversation is going, so I think it's best I remove myself from it.' He gave an awkward little bow. 'Once again, I'm very sorry for your loss.'

'That's right, run away,' Saskia taunted him as he walked towards the door. 'That's your answer to everything, isn't it?'

The tension in the room was like a long, lithe ribbon, winding around us, pulling us tight. I wanted to leave myself. I needed some time to gather my thoughts and grieve in private for Melissa.

'There's something about that man I don't trust,' Fred said ominously. 'Does anyone else think it's strange – the way he managed to find Melissa's body so quickly? It's almost like he knew where to look.'

'He saw her ski sticking up out of the snow, didn't he?' said Nathan.

'So he said,' Fred retorted. 'None of us saw it for ourselves.' He eyed Annett suspiciously. 'I expect you're going to report back to him later, aren't you? Tell him everything we've said.'

'Not at all,' she replied. 'Lukas might be my employer, but I do have a mind of my own, and, believe it or not, I'm on *your* side. However . . .' She rose from her stool. 'I have no wish to make you feel uncomfortable, so I shall give you some privacy.'

'You don't have to go,' said Flora.

'It's no problem. I'll be back in a little while to start on dinner.'

Flora managed a feeble smile. 'Up to you. I can give you a hand with the food if you like.'

'That would be appreciated, thank you.'

As Annett closed the kitchen door behind her, Flora sank onto a high stool. She looked washed out; exhausted.

'Melissa was such a lovely person,' she remarked, her

face working with the effort of speaking. 'I can't believe we're never going to see her again.'

'It's her family I feel sorry for,' said Nathan.

'Me too,' I said quietly.

Fred picked up the bottle of schnapps and poured himself a generous measure. 'Anyone else for another drink?'

I placed a hand over the top of my glass. 'Not for me, thanks; I want to keep a clear head.'

'Yeah, take it easy, bud,' said Nathan.

Fred glowered at him. 'Who are you – my father?'

Nathan held his gaze. 'I just don't think any of us should be getting drunk right now. It's only going to make us more vulnerable than we already are.'

'Thanks for the advice, but it's *my* body; I'll abuse it any way I choose.' Fred raised his glass to Nathan. 'To your very good health,' he said, downing the schnapps in one.

Flora let out a huff of breath. 'Why are you being like this, Fred?'

'Like what?'

'Weird.'

'I don't know what you mean.'

Saskia gave him a sly, sideways look. 'You don't seem very cut up about Melissa. I thought the two of you were close.'

He set his empty glass back down. 'People show their feelings in different ways.'

'Yeah, I get that – but when you saw her, lying in the

snow with that appalling gash across her throat, you barely even flinched. Flora and I both had to turn away; I actually thought I was going to be sick.'

'Perhaps I just have a stronger stomach than you.'

'How can you be so matter-of-fact?' said Flora, anger flaring in her voice. 'Even if you couldn't care less about Melissa, aren't you feeling scared right now? I know I am.'

Nathan gave a short, mirthless laugh. 'Maybe the reason Fred's so calm is because he knows nothing's going to happen to him.'

The Dutchman's body stiffened, like an animal scenting danger. 'What are you insinuating?'

'Nothing – at the moment,' said Nathan. 'But how about we review the facts . . . see where they take us?'

I felt a queasy inner slide. I had a horrible sense of where this conversation was headed.

'Fact number one: you were the last one to see Melissa alive.'

Fred picked up the schnapps bottle and filled his glass again. 'That's not proof of anything.'

'Fact number two. We only have your word that you left her sitting on that fallen tree.'

'So, what . . . you think I took her down that other trail instead?'

'Fact number three,' Nathan steamrollered on. 'It was your idea to take the shortcut through the forest.'

'Who told you that?' said Fred.

'Libby.'

Fred glared at me. 'I never said that.'

I could've sworn he did, but I wasn't about to risk a confrontation; the situation was tense enough already. 'Sorry, Fred, I must've misunderstood. I thought that's what you told me in the library, right after you got back yesterday.'

'It was a joint decision,' said Fred. 'We all agreed it was the right call.'

'You were the first one to suggest it though,' remarked Flora.

Fred frowned. 'Was I? I don't remember.' He looked around the group. 'You can't really think I had anything to do with what happened to Melissa. She was my friend. Why would I want to kill her?'

'Psychopaths don't need a motive,' said Saskia. 'They kill because they enjoy it.'

Fred's chin buckled. 'I suppose you think I killed Alexander and Gabrielle as well.'

'Did you?'

'Of course I didn't.' Fred's expression was defiant. 'I don't know why you're all ganging up on me. I've got nothing to hide, I promise you. Everything I've told you is one hundred per cent true.' He passed his tongue back and forth across his front teeth. 'But there *is* someone here who's keeping a secret.'

21

'Oh, here we go,' said Saskia in a bored tone. 'Fred's so desperate to deflect attention away from himself, he's going to try to paint someone else as the bad guy.'

'Don't be like that, Sas,' said Flora. 'We need to hear Fred out; it's only fair.'

I agreed with her. Secrets could be dangerous and if someone here was holding back, I needed to know. 'Who are you referring to?' I asked Fred.

'It's Lukas,' he said. 'He's a drug addict.'

The words were so startling, I actually took a step backwards.

'Whoa,' Nathan said, putting both hands up in a defensive gesture. 'That's a very serious accusation.'

'It's true; I've seen the evidence with my own eyes.'

'So what are we talking about?' said Flora. 'Weed? Coke?'

Fred shook his head. 'Hydrocodone.'

'Hydro-*what*?'

'It's a prescription analgesic, almost as powerful as morphine. It blocks pain receptors in the brain, but it also triggers a rush of dopamine, producing a temporary high.'

Saskia gave him a withering look. 'So, what – you're a medical expert now?'

'No. I googled it. Right after I found Lukas's stash.'

Nathan made a disbelieving noise in the back of his throat. 'You expect us to believe Lukas left a pile of pills lying around in plain sight? He'd never be that careless.'

'They weren't in plain sight. On the contrary, they were very imaginatively concealed.'

Nathan's eyes narrowed. 'So how did you find them?'

'I searched Lukas's quarters while he was away on business.'

Flora's mouth dropped open. 'But that was the day we arrived.'

Fred nodded. 'I said I was going to bed, but I didn't go to my room; I went to the west wing instead.'

'But Annett expressly told us the west wing was out of bounds,' said Flora. 'Weren't you worried she'd find you there?'

He shrugged. 'If she had, I would've pretended to be looking for the bathroom.'

'So what *were* you looking for?' I asked him.

He looked at me as if the answer was obvious. 'Lukas's drugs, of course.'

'But how did you know they were there?'

'I was acting on a tip-off.' Fred took a leisurely drink of schnapps. 'Let's just leave it at that.'

'So where exactly were these meds?' asked Saskia. 'In Lukas's bedroom?'

'No, I looked there first and found nothing. I went to his office next, but the desk drawers and the filing cabinet were both locked. I was about to give up when I noticed a display case mounted on the wall; it was full of trophies and medals.'

He released the words slowly, grudgingly, before reaching for his glass again.

'One trophy in particular caught my eye – a golden ice skate, mounted on a wooden base. I opened the door of the display case and picked it up for a closer look. As I turned it over in my hands, it made a rattling sound. That's when I realised the skate was hollow. I put my hand inside it and pulled out a bottle of prescription tablets. The printed label on the front said Vicodin; I found out later it's a brand name for hydrocodone. There was a patient's name on the label too; someone I'd never heard of. I put the skate back and picked up another trophy, a silver cup. There was more hydrocodone inside it, three bottles this time. The prescriptions had been filled in three different names, none of them Lukas's.'

All of us were staring at Fred, utterly incredulous.

'I checked every single trophy. Two more contained similar bottles, a different name on every label. There must have been nearly a hundred tablets in total. Far more than one person would reasonably require for occasional pain relief.'

Flora's eyes were out on stalks. 'How did he manage to get hold of so many?'

'You can get anything on the dark web,' said Saskia.

'Or he knows a rogue doctor who's willing to bend the rules for the right price,' said Nathan.

I put my fingers to my temples. It felt like I was

standing in the eye of a tornado and everything around me was moving too fast and too chaotically for me to keep up. 'Just so we're clear, Fred, are you saying you knew about Lukas's addiction before you even came here?'

'I had a suspicion; nothing more.'

'I haven't heard any rumours,' I said, thinking back to the Wolff Man fan forum I'd trawled through as part of my research. I was sure there hadn't been any mention of drugs.

'Nor have I,' said Flora. 'In fact, I don't think Lukas has ever had any negative publicity, has he? He's always been held in such high regard; *idolised* almost, especially here in Germany.'

'I guess it just goes to show how clever he's been in covering his tracks.'

'So who tipped you off?' Nathan demanded to know.

'I don't think I should say.'

'If you want us to take you seriously, you have to tell us everything.'

Fred rolled his eyes. 'OK, it was Fabian, my coach. He knows Lukas from way back; the two of them came up the ranks together. They used to be very close, although Fab hasn't heard from Lukas in years.'

Fred reached for the schnapps bottle again, but Nathan was quicker. He swiped it off the worktop and hugged it to his chest.

'You can have another drink when you've told us everything,' he said. 'And I mean *everything* – right from the very beginning.'

Fred shook his head, as if Nathan was something to be dislodged. For a moment, I thought he was going to storm off, but then he steepled his fingers together under his chin and resumed his tale.

'In that case, we need to go back to 2018. Lukas wasn't competing any more; he was working as a coach, but he'd been offered a lot of money to do a showcase at a competition in the US. He was attempting a triple Axel, but he miscalculated his take-off. He fell really awkwardly, injuring his hip, and had to be helped off the ice.'

'I read about that,' I said, remembering one of the interviews I'd come across online. 'He had to have surgery for a labral tear, didn't he?'

'That's right, and afterwards he was prescribed powerful analgesics to help with his recovery. That much is in the public domain. Fabian didn't hear much from Lukas during that period, but in the spring of 2021 they ran into each other by chance. Lukas was the after-dinner speaker at a corporate event in The Hague that Fabian had been invited to. Fab told me that when he watched Lukas deliver his speech, he was shocked by what he saw.

'For one thing, Lukas seemed very nervous. His hands were trembling and he lost the thread of what he was saying several times. It jarred with Fab, because Lukas had never really suffered from nerves and by that point in his career he was an experienced public speaker, known for his polished performances. There was something else too: Fab noticed that even though the air con in the room was on full blast, Lukas was sweating profusely, so much so that he had to take his jacket off. And then, the second his speech was over, he left the podium before the event host had finished thanking him and practically ran out of the room. Fab was so concerned, he followed him.

'He found Lukas in the bathroom, slumped in a cubicle, pouring with sweat and shaking all over. Fab wanted to call an ambulance, but Lukas wouldn't let him, so Fab called a cab instead and took him back to his hotel room. It was then that Lukas revealed the real reason for his strange behaviour: a secret addiction to prescription pain-killers that dated back to his 2018 surgery.'

Fred paused. I got the impression he was enjoying holding court; seeing the enthralled looks on our faces.

'Lukas told Fabian he was trying to kick the habit. He'd chosen the trip to the Netherlands to go cold turkey, not realising how severe the side effects would be. Fab offered to get a doctor, but Lukas refused. He was too worried the story would be leaked to the press.'

'So what did Fab do?' asked Flora.

'Dosed his old friend up with paracetamol and spent the night sitting in a chair, watching over him as he writhed in bed. By the time a car came to take Lukas to the airport the next morning, he seemed a lot better. Before they parted ways, Lukas swore Fab to secrecy and promised that as soon as he got back to Germany he'd seek professional help.'

'And did he?' asked Saskia.

Fred shrugged. 'Your guess is as good as mine. Fabian said he never heard from Lukas again, despite reaching out to him via email and text several times. He assumed Lukas was embarrassed and that his lack of communication was a way of distancing himself from the whole episode. By the end of the following year, Lukas had stopped working as a coach and all but disappeared from public view.

'Fabian gave up trying to contact him, but he kept his word and never told anyone about that night in the hotel room. Like a lot of people, he assumed Lukas had turned his back on skating for good – until, that is, I told him about my invitation to Bavaria.'

Nathan nodded thoughtfully. 'And that's when he broke his promise to Lukas.'

'Yeah. Fab didn't think Schloss Eis was a safe environment for a young skater, especially as we both believed I'd be the only skater here. He thought if Lukas was still addicted, he might be volatile. Dangerous, even. He tried to talk me out of coming here. I couldn't understand why he was so against it, and at first he wouldn't say. But, eventually, when he found out I'd accepted Lukas's invitation, he told me everything. He thought it would be enough to make me back out, but it wasn't. I didn't really care what Lukas got up to in his private time. My only concern was that eight weeks wouldn't be long to learn everything I needed to know from him.'

'So if you weren't worried, why did you go looking for evidence that he was still hooked?' I asked him.

Fred gave a crooked grin. 'I didn't come here with the intention of spying on Lukas. But when I got here, I was forced to rethink my plans.'

'What made you change your mind?'

'You did – or should I say, *all* of you.' He leaned forward, resting his forearms on the island. 'I was horrified when I arrived at Schloss Eis and realised I wasn't the only student Lukas had offered to coach. No doubt you all felt the same way, except everyone was too polite to admit it.

'I've competed against some of you in the past, others I knew by reputation, and I don't mind admitting that I felt completely out of my depth. Of course, at that stage I had no idea Lukas planned to teach us the Grim Reaper – or that one of us would be going home every week – but what I did know was that we'd all be competing for his attention. I was scared that I'd be overlooked; pushed into the background. I realised I had to get ahead of the game somehow. That's when I had the idea to try to find out if Lukas was still using. At that stage, I wasn't sure what I was going to do with any evidence I uncovered; it would just be collateral. But then, when I found out about the weekly trials on the first day of training, I knew exactly what I had to do.'

He hesitated, and in that moment, the dirt-encrusted penny dropped. 'You blackmailed Lukas,' I said baldly.

He peeled back his lips, showing his teeth. 'I hate that word.'

'It's true though, isn't it?'

He didn't give me the satisfaction of a straight answer.

'On day three of training, I approached Lukas at the end of our session and asked if I could have a word in private. He tried to brush me off at first, but I persuaded him to give me five minutes. We sat down together and I told him I knew what was hidden inside the trophies. I also admitted I'd taken photographs of the medication in situ.'

Nathan scrubbed a hand across his face. 'Jeez, Fred; you've got a big pair of balls.'

'I'll take that as a compliment.'

'How did Lukas react?' I asked Fred.

'He was obviously shocked, but he didn't confirm or deny anything. When he asked me what I wanted, I told him he had to keep me in the competition until the end. Otherwise, I'd post the photos on my socials and tell the whole world about his addiction. He said the photos weren't proof of anything and that nobody would believe me. But then I revealed Fabian had told me about that night in The Hague and was prepared to back up my claims – even though Fab had said no such thing.' He shaped his face into a ghastly sort of smile. 'Until that moment, Lukas had no idea Fab was my coach. I suppose it's not that surprising; we've only been working together for a couple of months, although we've moved in the same circles for years. If he had known, I think he would've thought twice about inviting me here.'

Nathan's face had contorted as if he'd bitten into something rotten. 'Did Lukas agree to your demand?'

'He said he'd have to think about it. We haven't discussed the matter since, but, based on the outcome of the first trial, I think I managed to persuade him.'

'So *that's* why Gerhard went home instead of you,' said Saskia, her cheeks flaming. 'You really are a piece of shit, Fred. We've all given up so much to be here: sacrificed our time, put our careers on hold, abandoned our families. But we did it willingly because we thought we were competing on a level playing field. Meanwhile, you were busy manipulating Lukas for your own selfish ends and throwing the rest of us under the bus. Honestly, I don't know how you sleep at night.'

Fred looked embarrassed, but unrepentant. 'Look, I'm not proud of what I did, but I didn't do it for myself; I did it for my brother.'

'Ah yes . . . Pieter,' Saskia said. 'I'm genuinely sorry about what happened to him and I know you need money for his treatment, but that still doesn't justify what you did.' Her mouth set in a mutinous line. 'You know what, I wouldn't be surprised if you *were* involved in all these mysterious deaths, since you're obviously willing to do anything to claw your way to the top.'

'But don't you see?' said Fred. 'This proves I had nothing to do with what happened to the others.'

'How do you figure that?' asked Nathan.

'If I was going to learn the Grim Reaper in its entirety, I had to let the competition run its course. Why would I risk killing off the opposition and derailing the entire programme, when all I had to do was sit back and watch as Lukas sent you home, one by one?'

Fred's argument was a convincing one. His actions were reprehensible – not least because he'd failed to warn us we were cohabiting with a potentially unpredictable drug addict – but it didn't make sense that he was the killer.

'I swear on my brother's life I had nothing to do with Melissa's death, or anybody else's,' Fred said. His long fingers went *tap, tap, tap* on the worktop; a morse code of warning. 'So stop looking at me and focus your attention elsewhere. Otherwise, I have a very bad feeling that Melissa won't be the last skater going home in a body bag.'

22

A dark mood had spread throughout the castle, tender as a bruise. It was several hours since the search party had returned and I was still trying to digest the latest horrifying developments; chewing on their sinuous fibres and choking on their bitter juices. I had survived some hellish experiences as a child, but I had never been as scared and confused as I was right then.

At dinner, there was more concerning news when Annett provided an update on our provisions. 'We've got jam, tea, coffee, crackers, and a few tins of soup. That's it,' she said as she served a sausage cassoulet she and Flora had cobbled together from the last remaining items in the fridge.

'What about all the stuff from the freezer?' asked Saskia. 'There should've been enough there to last us for days.'

'There's just one small problem,' Nathan told her, his face pale and stoical. 'We don't know where Alexander buried it.'

'Won't it be close to where you found his body?'

'Probably,' he replied. 'But are *you* willing to go outside and spend a couple of hours digging? Personally, I'd rather go hungry than end up sharing a grave with him.'

After that, there was no more discussion about trying to find the food.

Meanwhile, there was no let-up in the foul weather and our phones still had no connectivity. The latest local news report revealed that the mast wouldn't be fixed for several more days, as engineers awaited the arrival of a vital component. It had also been reported that freezing rain had caused the overhead power lines to become sheathed in ice, making them so heavy that in some instances they had broken, cutting off electricity supplies. Whichever way you looked at it, the situation was dire.

At dinner, the mood was muted, all of us lost in the toxic swill of our thoughts. Unusually, Annett had chosen to eat with us. Her presence proved slightly inhibiting and nobody brought up Lukas's alleged drug habit. Melissa's name wasn't mentioned either – not because she wasn't uppermost in all of our thoughts, but because the subject was simply too painful.

When I enquired after Lukas, Annett said he was holed up in his office. She had taken him a plate of cassoulet, but when she'd knocked on the door, there was no answer, so she'd left the tray on the floor outside.

After dinner, Flora, Saskia and Fred excused themselves and went upstairs. Flora mentioned she was probably going to spend the night in Saskia's room. She was clearly feeling vulnerable; we all were. Annett disappeared too, saying she was going to do the washing-up.

I offered to give her a hand, but she insisted she could manage by herself. That just left Nathan and me.

I wasn't looking forward to spending the evening alone in my room, so when Nathan suggested heading to the library, I jumped at the chance. The room felt cold, even though the radiators were blazing. Feeling uneasy, I went round the room checking to see if a window was open, but they were all securely shut. There was a wicker basket of logs on the hearth and Nathan and I debated whether or not to light a fire. After realising that both of us lacked the requisite skills, we wrapped ourselves in a couple of sofa throws instead.

'Do you think Annett knows about Lukas's habit?' said Nathan, as we sat in twin armchairs, staring at the uncooperative fireplace.

'Even if she's signed a non-disclosure agreement, I doubt Lukas has told her,' I said, drawing the scratchy throw more tightly around me. 'I suppose she might have guessed though. It's hard to see how she could spend so much time with him and not notice how unstable he is.'

'Would you still have come to Bavaria if you'd known the truth about him?'

'Probably not. I had to think twice about coming as it was.'

'Really?' he said, looking at me in surprise.

'Yeah, I'd decided to quit skating and focus on a new career in the thrilling world of local government.'

'But that's crazy; you're one of the most naturally gifted skaters I've ever met.'

I felt a wave of heat move through me. 'It's nice of you to say that, but I know I'm not in the same league as the rest of you.'

'It's true that you're not as polished as Saskia or Flora, but you have the potential to be better than both of them. Your work ethic is amazing and you pick things up really quickly.'

Now my cheeks were on fire. 'Thanks; that means a lot coming from you.'

His soft brown eyes bored into mine. 'So what convinced you to take up Lukas's offer?'

'My grandmother. She said I'd regret it for the rest of my life if I didn't come to Bavaria.' As I spoke, tears pricked the back of my eyeballs. I blinked them back, not wanting to break down in front of Nathan.

'I guess you and your grandmother are close, huh?'

'Super close; she's always been there for me.'

'What about your parents?'

'I never knew my dad; he died before I was born.'

'Oh. Sorry about that. What about your mom?'

'She tried her best, but . . .' I looked away. 'It's complicated.'

'Yeah, families usually are.' His head lolled against one of the chair's wings. 'The stuff Fred said about Lukas – it changes things. I think we need to be very careful around him.'

'I agree,' I said. 'If Lukas really is an addict, he'll struggle to make rational choices.'

'Do you think he knows what happened to the others?' He looked down at his lap. 'Do you think he could be involved somehow?'

'I don't know; I hope not. What I do know is that substance abuse can damage the frontal lobes of the brain; it's the part that controls morality and judgement. It's the reason some addicts exhibit the kind of behaviour that most normal people find abhorrent.'

'Like killing someone, you mean?'

It was a horrifying thought. 'That's an extreme example – but yes.'

'How do you know all that stuff about the brain?' he asked.

'I have first-hand experience of addiction. Not me – a family member; someone very close to me.'

I saw sympathy percolate in his eyes. 'That must've been tough.'

'It was, but it's all in the past now.' I plucked at the fringed end of the throw, reluctant to share any more. Nathan might think differently about me if he knew the truth. I had to redirect the conversation away from myself. 'What about Fred? Do you still think he might have had something to do with Melissa's death?'

'No, I probably shouldn't have accused him; I was just pissed at the guy.' His eyes slipped sideways. 'When you think about it, there's more circumstantial evidence pointing at Lukas.'

My mind went back to the scene in Gabrielle's room. To the little amber bottle on her nightstand. 'Do you remember how Lukas went to get those painkillers for Gabrielle, the night of her accident?'

He nodded.

'When I went to her room, after she died, there was an empty bottle of tablets on her nightstand. The label had been torn off, so I have no idea what she took, or how many, but I'm wondering now if Lukas gave her Vicodin.'

Nathan's face clouded over. 'And encouraged her to take so many she OD-ed?'

'I think he might have done.' The words were thick in the back of my throat. I didn't want to believe it, but I couldn't ignore the possibility any longer. 'He could easily have sabotaged the rink too. He knows exactly how those synthetic ice panels fit together; he probably watched the whole thing being installed. And then the next day, he fixed up the rink and claimed there was nothing wrong with it. That way, we'd think there was some other reason Gabrielle fell – one that had nothing to do with him.'

A muscle ticked in Nathan's jaw. 'He obviously knows that most falls on the ice aren't fatal but, if his plan all along was to kill one of us with an overdose of Vicodin, then that person would need to have a reason to take them.'

I covered my face with my hands. It was all sounding scarily plausible.

'And if we're right about Lukas, then Alexander was the obvious choice for his next victim,' Nathan said.

I spread my fingers and peeked between them. 'Why do you say that?'

'He was the only other person in the room when Lukas brought Gabrielle the meds; the rest of us had already left by that point. Alexander must've heard him advising her about the dosage.'

My hands fell away from my face. 'You're saying Lukas murdered Alexander before he could work out how Gabrielle died?'

'Correct,' said Nathan. 'It's easy to see how it might have played out. Lukas followed Alexander outside; maybe he even offered to show him a good place to bury the food. Then, as soon as Alexander's back was turned, he grabbed the spade and whacked him over the head. The poor guy didn't stand a chance.'

The thought of Alexander's vulnerability, his helplessness against the man he thought was his mentor, caused a small tearing sensation inside me.

'What about Melissa? If Lukas killed her too, he would've had to set that trap before the group got to the forest.'

'He could've strung that wire up any time, even before we arrived at Schloss Eis,' said Nathan, growing more animated. 'Maybe he was planning to deploy it during another one of his team-building exercises. You wouldn't have to be on skis; a mountain biker would be just as vulnerable. But then the blizzard hit and he had to make another plan.'

I scrambled back through my memory. 'But don't you remember? Lukas didn't want anyone to ski to the village. He told us in no uncertain terms it was a bad idea.'

'That's because he wanted to keep us all trapped in the castle, where we'd be totally at his mercy. And then, when he couldn't talk the others out of it, he decided to turn the situation to his advantage.'

'But how could he possibly have known they'd take the shortcut through the forest?'

'An educated guess? He knew how challenging the conditions were out there. It isn't too much of a stretch to think they'd want to get to the village by the quickest and most direct route possible.'

'But that means he must've followed them.'

'Exactly. And when he saw that Melissa was alone, he lured her down that trail to her death. I didn't see Lukas anywhere in the castle the whole time they were gone, did you?'

'No,' I admitted. 'But how could he have got to the forest so quickly when he can't even ski?'

'Correction: Lukas *told us* he can't ski. For all we know, the guy's a semi-pro.'

The gnawing agitation inside me grew. 'But wasn't it Lukas who found Melissa's body? Why would he lead the rest of you directly to her if he was responsible for her death?'

'To throw us off the scent,' he said. 'The sick bastard probably got a thrill out of seeing our shocked reaction when we realised what had happened to her.'

It was feasible, but I still wasn't quite there yet. I'd seen Lukas in a state of controlled passive-aggression plenty of times. Making cruel comments. Tracking our tender points like a sniper. But he'd never shown physical aggression, or the kind of sadistic predisposition I imagined a cold-blooded killer to have. Another thing occurred to me; something else that didn't quite add up. 'So why is Fred still here? Given that he was blackmailing Lukas, you'd think he'd be top of his hit list.'

'Lack of opportunity would be my best guess.'

'But why?' I persisted. 'Why would someone like Lukas, a man who's held in such high regard, a man with so much to lose, invite a bunch of people he's never even met before to his home, spend a week convincing them they were enrolled on a unique training programme, and then start bumping them off? And even if he is the murderer, wouldn't it be easier to take us all out at once?'

'I know, I'm struggling to see a motive too. I wish we had all the answers; maybe then we'd be able to predict his next move.' Nathan's hands went to his head, his fingers pushing into the roots of his hair. 'What was it Saskia said earlier? *Psychopaths don't need a reason. They kill because they enjoy it.* For all we know this is just another form of sport for Lukas.' He gave a bitter laugh. 'When he promised to introduce us to the Grim Reaper, maybe he wasn't just referring to his signature skating move.'

I felt sharp fingers throttling my natural reserves of courage. The theory we'd hammered out between us sounded like a plot from a movie, but could we be right? Had I unwittingly been playing a twisted game of 'survival of the fittest'? Was I so blinded by ambition that I had willingly delivered myself into the hands of a monster?

As we lapsed into discomfited silence, my thoughts turned to Mum and Gran, and the idea that I might never see them again. It stirred something in me. Something desperate and raw. It was time to draw on the survival skills I'd learned as a child; to do everything in my power to ensure that I, and all the remaining skaters, left Schloss Eis unharmed.

I looked at Nathan, my resolve hardening. First thing in the morning, I'm taking a pair of snowshoes and I'm hiking to the village. I don't care how hard it snows, or how exhausted I feel, I'm not going to stop walking until I've got help for us all.'

Nathan regarded me for a long moment. 'You're serious, aren't you?'

'You bet I am.'

'You know I can't let you do that, don't you?'

A sudden blaze of fury ripped through me. 'Don't even think about trying to stop me, Nathan.'

He laughed. 'Chill, Libby. What I meant was, I can't let you do it on your own. There are *two* pairs of snowshoes, remember?'

Our eyes met and I imagined a delicate filament reaching from my heart to his, tautening and relaxing with both our breaths. I wished I could tell him how I felt, but it was too complex to tease apart, even in my own head.

'Great!' I said emphatically. 'In that case, we'd better get an early night. We're going to need all our strength for tomorrow.'

'You're right.' He checked his watch. 'Although I'm not sure I'll be able to sleep. I'll be too worried I'll wake up to find Lukas standing over me.'

I glossed my lips with the tip of my tongue. I wasn't relishing the thought of spending the night alone, the only skater on the second floor. 'The two of us could always spend the night here, in the library,' I said. 'We could take it in turns to sleep; that way, the other person can keep watch.'

He smiled. 'You know what, that's actually not a bad idea. We can bring some pillows and blankets down from our rooms.'

He flung back the throw that was covering him and stood up.

'What are you doing?' I asked as he began pacing around the room.

'Looking for a weapon.'

'A weapon?' I repeated dumbly.

'For protection.'

'Ah,' I said, shucking off my own throw. 'I think I might be able to help with that.'

I went over to the fireplace, where a medieval-looking collection of forged iron tools hung on a rack beside the log basket. Selecting a heavy pewter poker and a log grabber with a pair of sharply pointed ends, I held them up for inspection.

'Will these do?'

He grinned. 'Those'll do just fine.'

23

I woke with a start, not sure where I was for a moment. As I turned my head on the pillow, books slid into view, row upon row of them.

Then I remembered: Nathan and I had spent the night in the library. He had slept first, curled up on the sofa under a heap of blankets, hands tucked neatly under his chin. I'd sat in the armchair and watched him for a while, mesmerised by his dark eyelashes and the soft rise and fall of his chest.

At two-thirty, I'd woken him up and we'd swapped places. I was exhausted, and despite my racing mind, I fell asleep quickly and deeply. I had no idea what time it was now, but the armchair was empty and the slivers of brittle light bleeding around the edges of the curtains told me dawn was breaking. Nathan and I had agreed that we would hike out as soon as it got light and I was surprised he hadn't woken me.

I sat up and reached for a nearby table lamp, eyes still heavy as I fumbled for the switch on its base. But when I depressed it, nothing happened.

Pushing back the blankets, I swung my feet to the floor. I'd slept fully clothed, which was probably just as well because it felt even colder than it did last night. Shivering, I went over to the window and opened the curtains. In the distance, the first blush of morning was painting the sky in shades of pink and gold. Amazingly, it had stopped snowing, but there was no sign of an imminent thaw.

As I turned away from the window, my thighs brushed against the radiator. It was stone cold. I squinted at the clock on the mantelpiece; the central heating was usually on by now. I checked the radiator on the other side of the room. It, too, was cold.

There was a sick feeling in my stomach as I flicked a light switch on the wall, and then two more. All of them were dead.

'Shit,' I said under my breath. The electricity was down. It must be that issue with ice on the power lines that Annett had heard about on the radio. One more reason I needed to get the hell out of this place, as if I didn't have enough of them already.

Returning to the sofa, I picked up a blanket and wrapped it around my shoulders like a pashmina. I needed to find Nathan. He was probably in the kitchen, drinking coffee or preparing the kit for our hike.

As I passed through the entrance hall and entered the west wing, I had a sudden sensation that I wasn't alone; the instinct urgent and strong. I half expected a fist to slam into me at any moment, but there was nobody there, just a sense of foreboding sticking to me like a second skin.

As I hurried down the shadow-filled corridor, my mind replayed the last conversation I'd had with Nathan. He seemed to have made up his mind that Lukas was the killer, but I was going to need more proof. Pointing the finger at the wrong person could be dangerous and only make the situation even more volatile than it already was.

When I entered the kitchen, the first thing I saw was Nathan's broad back. He was standing at the island, not doing anything, just staring into space.

'Good morning,' I said, wishing I'd thought to check my appearance in the mirror before I came looking for him.

He turned around. His face looked drawn and weary. 'I'd return the greeting, but everything that's happened so far this morning has been spectacularly *bad*.'

'Yeah, I know, the electricity's down,' I said, lifting up the blanket so it didn't trail on the floor. 'It's just as well we're getting out of here today.'

'Actually, I don't think we are.'

Panic rattled around my chest like a loose marble. 'What?'

Nathan indicated to the boot room. 'Everything's gone: the snowshoes, the skis, the poles – the whole lot.'

The marble became a golf ball. 'Please tell me you're kidding.'

'I wish I was. Go and see for yourself.'

I crossed the kitchen and stepped into the boot room. Yesterday afternoon, there were three sets of skis propped up against the wall and two pairs of snowshoes on the mat by the door. But now they were nowhere to be seen.

I went to the row of hooks and started wrenching coats down, just in case the skis were buried amongst them, even though, deep down, I knew they weren't.

'Honestly, Libby, they're not here,' said Nathan, coming up behind me. 'I've checked every square inch of this room.'

'Then where the hell are they?' I said angrily.

'Someone's taken them.'

I frowned. 'It must've been Annett.'

'It wasn't; I've already asked her,' Nathan told me. 'She came by about ten minutes ago to check the circuit breakers.' He pointed to a metal cabinet mounted high on the boot-room wall. Its door hung open, revealing two long rows of switches. 'She wasn't sure if there was a power cut or if the switches had just tripped.'

Disappointment punched me in the stomach. Without the snowshoes, there was no way of getting to the village. Who had moved them? Could it be someone who didn't want us to leave?

'Where's Annett now?' I asked Nathan as we stepped back into the kitchen.

'She thinks there might be a couple of gas heaters somewhere that'll tide us over until the power comes back on; she's gone to look for them. I asked her to keep an eye out for the snowshoes at the same time.'

'Did you tell her we were planning to hike to the village?'

He shook his head. 'I didn't want it getting back to Lukas.'

I sat down on one of the stools. 'Those snowshoes

can't have vanished into thin air; someone must know where they—' I broke off as Annett entered the room. She looked bulkier than usual, as if she was wearing several layers of clothing. 'Did you find the snowshoes?' I asked in lieu of a greeting.

'No, sorry, I can't think where they might be.' She went to the kettle, picked it up, then put it back down again. 'I was forgetting we have no electricity. I'll have to boil some water on the stove.' She opened a cupboard door. 'Do you two want coffee? It'll have to be black because we're out of milk.'

'Yes, please,' said Nathan. 'I take mine black anyway.'

'Libby?'

'Er, yeah, coffee would be great. Thanks, Annett.'

She took out a saucepan, carried it over to the sink and began filling it with water. 'What did you want the snowshoes for anyway?'

'We thought we'd try to find where Alexander buried the food,' said Nathan.

She gave him a penetrating look. 'Really? I thought you said yesterday you weren't willing to risk it.'

'We had second thoughts,' I ad-libbed. 'We need to eat, after all.'

'It's your decision,' she replied. She placed the saucepan on the gas hob.

'I wonder how long this power cut's going to last,' said Nathan.

'It might be a few days. They can't fix the overhead lines while the roads are impassable.'

I buried my cold hands in the folds of the blanket. 'Did you find the gas heaters?'

'No, I think they must be in the basement.'

'Do you want me to have a look?' Nathan offered.

'No, don't worry. Lukas keeps the basement locked and I don't know where the key is.'

'Where *is* Lukas?' I asked her.

'Still in bed, I assume.'

'Perhaps you could take him some coffee,' suggested Nathan. 'You can ask him where the key is at the same time.'

'Ask him if he knows where the snowshoes are, while you're at it,' I added. '*Someone* must know where they are.'

A shadow passed over Annett's face, like a fine cloud on a spring day. I wondered what she was thinking. A second later, it was gone.

'I'll give him another half an hour and then I'll go.'

'I'm sure he'd like to know about the power outage sooner rather than later,' I remarked. 'It is his house after all.'

She opened a drawer, removed a box of matches and lit the ring under the saucepan.

'When I took him his dinner last night, he told me I wasn't to disturb him before 9 a.m. – under any circumstances.'

I watched as she spooned instant coffee into three mugs. 'I thought he didn't answer when you knocked.'

'What?' she said off-handedly.

'You told us yesterday that when you took Lukas's dinner to him, he didn't respond when you knocked on his office door. You said you left the tray on the floor outside.'

'Oh,' she said, looking flustered. 'It must've been later on then; when I went to collect the tray.' She turned her attention back to the hob, staring fixedly at the saucepan as if she could speed up the boiling process by sheer willpower. 'Yes, that's right, I remember now. Lukas must've heard me picking up the tray because he called out through the closed door and told me he wanted to sleep in this morning.'

Behind her back, Nathan and I exchanged a quick look. Annett's delivery seemed unnatural to me; almost as if she was eyeing up the puzzle pieces and moving them around to make them fit. But why would she do that?

Suddenly, she spun around to face us. 'I've just remembered – we have some creamer!' she exclaimed with more enthusiasm than the announcement warranted.

She went to the pantry and flung back the double doors. When she said we were running low on food, she hadn't been exaggerating. Even with an influx of hungry house guests and an unforeseen snowstorm, I was surprised the shelves were quite so bare. Mum and I weren't the most organised of shoppers, but even we had a stock of baked beans, cup-a-soups and instant noodles in our food cupboard at home. But perhaps Lukas didn't care for convenience food – and, to be fair, the freezer *had* been very well stocked. All at once, Gabrielle's face bobbed up to the surface of my mind, like a body that had been pushed deep underwater and suddenly released.

Annett was standing on tiptoes now, blindly moving her hand back and forth across the top shelf. Her fingers closed around something and she lifted it down. It was a cardboard tray containing a dozen or so tiny pots of UHT milk, the type you got in hotel rooms. 'Will you have some of this, Libby?'

'Uh, OK then, thanks.' I looked at Nathan. 'I've just had a horrible thought.'

'What's that?'

'We've got no electricity. Won't Gabrielle's body be . . .' I could hardly bring myself to say it. 'Defrosting.' My eyes went to the alcove where the freezer was housed. 'Do you think we should check on her? If the air's too warm in the freezer, we might have to think about moving her outside.'

'There's no need,' said Annett as she peeled the lid from a pot of milk. She muttered something in German as half its contents splashed onto the worktop. 'The freezer's well insulated; it'll stay cold for at least twenty-four hours.' She gave me a warning look. 'And I'm sure you'd rather not see your friend in her current state.'

I got up from the stool. 'I won't look. I'll just open the door a crack and stick my hand inside, just to gauge the temperature.'

Annett took a step towards me. 'I really wouldn't; you'll only let the warm air in.'

'What warm air?' I said. 'It's freezing in here.'

Nathan pointed to the saucepan. 'I think that water's boiling.'

'Oh.' Annett turned back to the hob and began fiddling with one of the knobs.

I went over to the freezer. Without the overhead light, it was dark in the alcove, but I could see that a small pool of liquid had collected on the floor. 'I think it's defrosting already,' I said. 'Do you have something I can clean that water up with, Annett?'

Nathan picked up a dish towel that was lying on the worktop. 'Use this,' he said, tossing it over the island to me.

I dropped the towel onto the floor, moving it into position with my foot. As it made contact with the liquid, a dark stain began to spread across the white fabric. Frowning, I picked the towel up and carried it into the main body of the kitchen, where there was more light.

My stomach constricted. 'This isn't water,' I said, holding up the crimson-stained fabric. 'I think it's blood.'

Annett glanced up. She seemed tense all of a sudden; the tendons in her throat were standing out. 'It must be Gabrielle's.'

I shook my head. 'Gabrielle didn't have any open wounds. And, anyway, dead bodies don't bleed.' I dropped the towel on the island and started walking back towards the alcove. 'I'm opening the door.'

'I don't think that's a good idea,' Annett said.

Ignoring her, I grasped the handle of the freezer door and yanked it open. There seemed to be something lying directly behind the door, a heavy weight, because the door opened with such force that it sent me flying backwards. I fell onto the floor, jarring my coccyx painfully.

I caught sight of a claw-like hand reaching for me, before it brushed against my foot, making me shriek.

'What the fuck?' said Nathan as he came rushing over.

I gaped in horror at the sight in front of me. Lying on the floor, half in and half out of the freezer, was a person. But it wasn't Gabrielle.

It was Lukas. But he was almost unrecognisable.

His skin was an unearthly shade of blue, almost translucent. Frost crystals clung to his eyebrows and the ends of his hair. His eyes were wide open, staring blankly into the void, and covered with a thin layer of ice. His lips were parted slightly, revealing teeth that must have been chattering violently. His fingers were curled inward, locked in a final despairing grasp, the nails tinted indigo. The fabric of his loose shirt was stiff, its frozen folds cloaking him like a shroud. He looked less like a man and more like a macabre statue.

For several long seconds, we both stared at him, as my ears filled with the ghastly arrhythmic drum of my pounding heart. Then Nathan bent down and put his fingers to Lukas's neck.

'Anything?' I asked him, even though I already knew the answer.

He shook his head, his face twisted by some harsh emotion.

'Look,' I said, extending a trembling hand towards the alcove.

The back of the freezer door was streaked with blood, and so were the tiles beneath it. I glanced at Annett. She was staring straight ahead, her pale lips pinched with unsaid words. With some considerable effort, I turned my attention back to Lukas. I noticed that his hands were swollen and covered in blood; the knuckles beaten almost to a pulp. He must have been banging on the door for hours, trying to alert one of us to his plight. But nobody came.

I felt a stinging in my eyes and something wet fell onto my arm. I lifted the edge of the blanket that was still wrapped around my shoulders and drew it roughly across my eyes.

'Does anyone know why the heating hasn't come on?'

I turned around to see Fred standing at the door to the kitchen. The island lay in between him and us, blocking his view of Lukas. He was wearing a thick sweater and there was a scarf looped around his neck.

'The electricity's out.' Nathan looked at him gravely. 'And I'm very sorry to tell you that Lukas is dead.'

Fred's legs seemed to go from under him. He grabbed the doorframe for support. 'I don't believe it.'

Nathan heaved his shoulders up and down. 'We've literally just found him.'

Steadying himself, Fred walked around the island, stopping abruptly when he saw Lukas's body. 'What happened to him?' he gasped.

'He got locked in the freezer overnight,' I told him.

Fred blanched. 'He died of hypothermia?'

'Or lack of oxygen,' said Nathan. 'With the door closed, there's probably only a few hours' air supply in there.'

Fred collapsed onto the nearest stool. 'Don't walk-in freezers have emergency release mechanisms?'

'Not this one,' said Annett, who had apparently recovered her powers of speech. 'It must be at least twenty years old; the regulations were different back then. I did raise it as a health and safety concern in my first week of employment. Lukas said he'd think about upgrading it, but for whatever reason, it never happened.'

Her admission seemed to trigger something in me. An unpleasant pressure inside my skull. It felt like air was being pumped in until my head was as hard as a bicycle tyre, but still more air pushed in.

'Is there any way Lukas could have shut himself in the freezer on purpose?' Fred asked.

Annett shook her head. 'Someone has to manually depress the door handle from the outside, or the locking mechanism won't engage.'

'Which can only mean one of two things: either someone shut the door without realising Lukas was inside, or . . .' I took a breath, trying to slow my racing pulse. 'They deliberately locked him in there.'

I looked at Annett. She stared right through me, her pupils spreading like ink blots.

'You came here after we had dinner, didn't you – to do the washing-up?'

'Yes,' she replied calmly. 'I was here till eight-thirty or thereabouts.'

I saw Nathan measuring her with his eyes. 'And if Lukas had been locked in the freezer at that point, presumably you would have heard him banging on the door.'

'Naturally.' Her lips twitched almost imperceptibly. 'Which narrows down the timeframe.'

'It does rather, doesn't it?' Nathan replied stonily.

Unease crept up my spine like the point of a knife. I could feel each cut; a sharp, inescapable force that was pushing me towards a total meltdown.

'Is Gabrielle still in there?' I could hear the tremor in my voice.

Nathan went to look inside. 'Yeah,' he said. 'She's here.' He turned to Fred. 'We'd better get him back in the freezer for now. Can you give me a hand?'

I looked away as the two men begin manhandling Lukas's rigid corpse.

'I'll go and wake Flora and Saskia,' I said, suddenly desperate to get out of there. 'They need to know what's happened.'

Nathan said something in reply I didn't quite catch.

I felt curiously light-headed as I made my way back to the east wing. The atmosphere in this place was toxic. It felt like a virus had invaded the castle, capable of destroying everything in its path.

Lukas's death had proved that none of us were immune – and if he wasn't the killer, then who was?

24

The remaining skaters had gathered in the library. The mood was sombre. What had once been a luxurious haven now felt like a frigid mausoleum, devoid of any warmth or hope. The situation was beyond desperate and, with still no sign of the missing skis and snowshoes, we were fast running out of options.

Fred was slumped in an armchair. He looked dazed; shellshocked. Flora was curled on the sofa, wrapped in a throw, her eyes puffy and red. She'd been crying on and off ever since she found out about Lukas. Nathan and Saskia were crouched beside the hearth, trying to get a fire going. Meanwhile, Annett was still hunting for the elusive gas heaters.

I sat slightly apart from the group, at an antique writing desk in the corner of the room. A map was spread out in front of me. It was the map Annett had given to the original ski party, the same one Nathan had used to mark the location of Melissa's body. I couldn't find it at first; it seemed to have vanished into thin air. Eventually, I spotted it tucked out of sight, behind the knife block in the kitchen. It was almost as if it had been hidden deliberately.

As I pored over it, trying to make sense of the unfamiliar terrain, snatches of conversation drifted over to me.

'How's that fire coming along?' asked Flora.

'I think these logs are too big,' Nathan replied. 'We need more kindling.'

Fred gave a sour laugh. 'I think I can help you with that.'

Glancing up, I watched as he went over to the bookshelves and helped himself to half a dozen paperbacks, before carrying them over to the fireplace.

'There you go,' he said, tossing one into the grate. The small flame that Nathan and Saskia had been nurturing for the past fifteen minutes suddenly flared into life.

Flora tutted. 'How do you know that isn't a first edition?'

'So what if it is?' said Saskia. 'It's no use to Lukas now.' The two of us made eye contact. 'I don't know what you're up to over there, Libby,' she said, 'but any time you want to do something useful, like help us get this wretched fire going, just let me know.'

She was already annoyed with me because I'd mentioned that Nathan and I had been planning to hike to the village. 'It's every person for themselves now, is it?' she'd said nastily. 'And here I was, thinking we were a team.'

I didn't rise to the bait; I had more important things to worry about.

'I can't feel my toes any more,' said Flora, as I turned back to the map. 'I wonder if Annett's managed to find those heaters yet.'

Nathan asked Fred to pass him another book. 'That's if they even exist.'

'Why would she say she was looking for them if she knew there weren't any?' Flora asked.

I heard Nathan tearing some pages from the book. 'I don't trust Annett. I think she knows more about recent events than she's letting on.'

So it wasn't just me then.

'Yeah, she gives off a weird vibe,' said Saskia. 'I've always thought there was something off about her.'

'Have you?' said Flora. 'You never told me.'

'I'm telling you now, aren't I?'

'I mean, what do we really know about her?' Nathan carried on.

'Nothing,' said Flora. 'Whenever you ask her a personal question, she always changes the subject.'

'She tried to convince Libby not to open the freezer,' said Nathan. 'And when Lukas's body fell out, she didn't seem that surprised. It was like she already knew he was in there. Plus she was the only one who knew the emergency release mechanism was broken.'

Somebody wailed softly. It sounded like Flora.

'What about the others?' asked Saskia. 'Do you really think Annett was involved in their deaths?'

Nathan began to outline the theory I had advanced the previous evening – that Gabrielle might have overdosed on Vicodin. Except now he was suggesting Annett was the one who had administered the fatal dose.

'Oh my God, yes!' cried Saskia.

'But it wasn't Annett's medication, it was Lukas's,'

said Fred. 'How would she have known how many pills to give Gabrielle?'

'If she already knew about Lukas's habit, she could've researched the meds online,' said Nathan.

Fred seemed unconvinced. 'But Gabrielle wasn't stupid. Would she really have swallowed down a handful of pills without question?'

'You didn't see her,' said Flora. 'She was in so much pain, she probably wasn't thinking straight. In any case, she trusted Annett. She had no reason to think she might be trying to harm her.'

The group spent several more minutes discussing the likelihood of this, before turning their attention to Alexander. Having reminded the others that Annett was the last person to see the Polish man alive, Nathan pointed out that she had also handed him the murder weapon.

Yet again, Fred was the one picking holes in the theory.

'But if Annett did kill him, why would she admit to giving him the spade?'

'Because she knew it would look weird if she didn't,' said Saskia. 'How else would Alexander have known where to find one?'

Melissa's death was the next under scrutiny. This time, Saskia took the lead. It was Annett, she reminded the group, who had first mentioned the shortcut through the forest.

'But, for all she knew, we could've decided to stick to the highway,' said Fred.

'Yes, but she did spend an awfully long time going through that shortcut with us on the map,' said Flora. 'I wonder now if she was trying to cement the idea in our minds.'

'But why?' Fred persisted. 'Why would Annett kill the person who pays her wages?'

'Perhaps that's the whole reason she took the job,' said Saskia. 'Because she had some sort of grudge against Lukas and she wanted to take him out.'

'But if Lukas was the intended target, why did the other three have to die?'

'Because Annett was worried they were on to her,' Saskia replied.

'I still think it's more likely to be someone on the outside,' said Fred. 'Someone who's been watching us from the day we arrived.'

'Maybe you're both right,' said Nathan. 'Annett could be working with a third party; feeding them information; tipping them off about our movements; letting them know when we're easy targets.'

'But the phones are down, so how are they communicating with each other?' asked Fred.

'Two-way radio?' advanced Flora. She sighed. 'I don't really see Annett as a serial killer, if I'm honest.'

'She could be acting under duress,' suggested Saskia. 'The perpetrator could be holding her family hostage and threatening to hurt them unless she cooperates.'

As more hypotheses were tossed back and forth, their

voices got louder, more strident. Even Nathan, who was usually so calm, was beginning to sound quite agitated.

'The truth is, none of us have a fucking clue what's going on here,' declared Flora when finally they had exhausted all the possibilities. 'The only thing I'm sure of right now is that I don't want to be next.' Her voice sounded choked; the words hard, angry clots. 'All I want to do is get away from this place and go home to my family.'

'That's what all of us want,' said Nathan. 'But unless those skis and snowshoes miraculously appear, there's no way out of here. All we can do is sit tight until the snow thaws and pray that no one else gets hurt in the meantime.'

I looked up from the map. 'There is a way.'

Everyone turned to look at me.

'What?' said Flora.

'There is a way out of here.'

'Don't tell me, let me guess,' said Saskia archly. 'You're thinking we can pull up the floorboards and fashion our own skis.' She gave an unpleasant scrape of a laugh. 'No? Let me try again. You want us to set fire to the summer house and send up a smoke signal.'

I sucked in my lips, letting her sarcasm wash over me.

'Wrong again? OK, let me have one last go.'

'For Christ's sake, Sas,' Flora snapped. She gave me a weak smile. 'Sorry, Libby, you were saying . . .'

I took a deep breath. 'We skate out.'

There was a brief, stunned silence.

Saskia was staring at me as if I'd gone quite mad. 'Skate? On *snow*? What planet are you on, Libby?'

I got up from the chair. 'The river, the one from the team-building challenge; it'll be frozen solid right now. It feeds into the Danube; we'll be able to travel for miles on it – and at a decent speed too.'

A spark of interest burned in Saskia's eyes. 'But the river's miles away; it's too far to hike.'

'There's another tributary three quarters of a kilometre from here; I've seen it on the map. It should be doable, even in regular footwear.'

'Show us,' said Nathan, abandoning the fire and crossing the room in three large strides. The others were right behind him.

'This is the source of the tributary, right here.' I pointed to a thin line of blue on the map, tracing its length with my finger. 'It travels for approximately three kilometres before it joins the Danube.' My finger followed the line as it dog-legged right before attaching itself to a more substantial sliver of blue. 'Unfortunately, it doesn't pass through any settlements for quite some distance – or at least none within hiking distance.' I moved my finger to another part of the map. 'But look here . . . after approximately twenty kilometres, it passes right through the centre of a town.' I showed them the word *Polizei* on the map. 'It looks like it has a police station; we'll be able to get help there.'

Nathan looked pensive. 'Twenty Ks, huh? We should be able to cover that in a couple of hours, maybe less.'

Fred seemed less certain. 'I think you're being optimistic. This is a frozen river, remember, not a freshly resurfaced rink. There'll be all sorts of stuff on the ice: lying snow, twigs, plant debris . . . things we might not see until it's too late. It wouldn't take much for one of us to fall and sustain a serious injury.'

I gave him a look of understanding. 'I'm not saying it won't be dangerous, Fred, but it's better than staying here and doing nothing. And twenty Ks really isn't that far; if we set off now, we'll get to the town well before nightfall.'

His eyes bulged. 'You want to go *today*?'

'Our lives are at stake; I don't think we can afford to wait.' I flung my arms wide in a gesture of hopelessness. 'Look, I'm just as confused as the rest of you. I have absolutely no idea what's going on here. Every time I think I might have a handle on it, something else happens to change my mind. But Schloss Eis isn't safe any more; that much I do know.'

'What about when we're hiking to the tributary?' said Saskia. 'We'll be out in the open; easy to spot. What if someone tries to attack us? How are we going to fight back?'

'We'll take weapons,' said Nathan. 'And we'll make sure we stick together. Alexander and Melissa were both alone when they were killed; they were a soft target. *We* won't make the same mistake.'

I smiled at him, pleased that he seemed to be on board. 'And once we're on the ice, we'll be able to relax,'

I told them. 'Yes, there'll be challenges to contend with, but thankfully none of them will be human.'

'What's to stop someone following us onto the ice?' said Flora.

'Nothing,' I admitted. I looked around the group, making eye contact with each of them in turn. Trying to instil confidence in them, even while my own was wavering by the second. 'But we're all highly proficient skaters. The only person who could have outpaced us on the ice is sadly no longer alive.' I started folding up the map. 'I'm not going to try to persuade you; there's no time. If you'd rather stay here, I completely understand. I'll send help as soon as I get to the town, I promise.'

I tucked the map under my arm and started walking towards the door.

'I'm going upstairs to change. I'll be in the entrance hall in twenty minutes; anyone who wants to come should meet me there.'

Up in my room, I wasted no time assembling what I needed. Warm clothing was clearly crucial, but it was a little more complicated than that. I had to protect myself from wind chill and moisture, but anything too bulky would restrict my range of motion on the ice and create more air resistance, making it harder to maintain speed and momentum.

I opted for several thin layers: two pairs of tights, topped with thermal leggings, and on my upper half, a merino base layer, funnel-neck fleece and a lightly padded waterproof jacket. I stuffed a woollen beanie and a pair of gloves in my jacket pockets. A scarf was a definite no-no; if it came loose while I was skating, it would be a trip hazard.

Once dressed, I took a small backpack and filled it with the bare essentials: skates, spare socks, map, water bottle, passport, debit card, phone and charger. Some snacks would've been nice, but I would have to do without. If I went to the kitchen and started poking round in the fridge, I might run into Annett – and the less she knew about my intentions, the better. I had a very strong feeling she was involved in all of this; I just didn't know to what extent.

I was deliberately running five minutes late as I left my room and walked down the corridor, heading for the stairs. I didn't want to be on pins in the entrance hall, waiting to see which, if any, of the skaters were coming with me. At least this way I'd know as soon as I got there. Nathan had seemed pretty enthusiastic, but even he might have got cold feet once he'd had a chance to think about it.

As I reached the first-floor landing, my heart spiralled up into my throat. If I leaned over the rail, I'd be able to see who was waiting there. Perversely, I delayed the moment of truth by turning my head away and continuing on towards the last flight. As I rounded the staircase's graceful curve, the entrance hall appeared beneath me.

When I saw Nathan standing in the centre of the room, the relief was instant. And he wasn't alone. To my surprise, all the skaters were there.

'Here she is,' said Flora, as I jogged down the last few stairs. 'Our expedition leader.'

Nathan picked his backpack up off the floor and slung it over one shoulder. 'We were worried you'd gone without us,' he said in a teasing tone.

'Not a chance.' I noticed Fred was wearing the same loose-fitting sweats I'd seen him in earlier. 'Are you going to be warm enough like that?' I asked him.

'I'm staying at the castle,' he said. 'I just came to say goodbye.'

I felt a surge of frustration. It didn't feel right, leaving one skater behind. Even if Annett had nothing to do with the deaths, Fred would still be vulnerable to whatever dark force was at work here. 'Please come with us,' I begged him.

He shook his head. 'I'm not at the same level as the rest of you; I wouldn't be able to keep up.'

'We can go at your pace, Fred. Honestly, it's not a problem.'

'No, really. The truth is, I'm too scared to skate on the river; I'd rather take my chances here.'

I wanted to discuss it with him some more, but if we were going to get to the town before dusk, we had to leave now.

'All right,' I said reluctantly. 'But as soon as we've gone, I want you to barricade yourself in your room and don't come out till either we – or the police – come back for you. Will you do that?'

He nodded and reached towards me, hooking an arm around my neck and pulling me towards him. 'Good luck,' he whispered in my ear. 'I'll be with you in spirit every step of the way and I know four other skaters who will be too.'

A lump rose in my throat. 'We'll send help as soon as we get to the police station,' I said as we drew apart. 'All you have to do is stay alive for one more day.'

'I'll do my best.' He smiled, but I could see it was an effort. 'What shall I tell Annett when she asks where you are?'

'Just say we're trying to hike to the nearest village on foot.'

'Whatever you do, don't mention the river,' Flora warned him. 'We don't want Annett, or anyone she might be working with, coming after us.'

'Understood.'

Nathan went over to the console table. Sitting on top of it were several familiar items from the library. The poker and log grabber from the fireplace, a brass candlestick, and the silver paper knife that had been sitting on the antique desk.

'For our personal protection,' he said. He handed me the log grabber and gave the candlestick and letter opener to the other two. 'Let's hope we don't need to use them.'

25

The cold was ferocious; like a thousand needles pricking at my skin. Shivering, I pulled my beanie further down over my ears, thankful that at least it wasn't snowing.

I did a quick scan of the grounds, but there was no movement, no footsteps in the snow; nothing to indicate any imminent threat or danger.

'We all need to be hyper-vigilant,' Nathan said as he closed the front door behind us – gently, so as not to alert Annett to our departure. 'If you see anything out of the ordinary, anything that feels even slightly off, you must let the rest of us know right away.' He clamped the poker between his knees while he adjusted the straps on his backpack. 'Stay close together. If anybody falls behind, we all stop and wait for them, OK?'

Flora raised her left hand in a salute; her right was tightly gripped around the candlestick.

We set off down the drive in single file with Nathan leading the way. The snow was even deeper than the last time I'd ventured outside and every step felt like an effort. We were halfway down the drive when something made me stop and look over my shoulder. Behind me, Schloss Eis looked almost otherworldly, its pale stucco walls framed against the slate grey sky. As I took in its grandeur, its soaring turrets dusted with icing sugar, I wondered if I would ever see it again.

Frankly, I hoped I never did.

As I turned away, I thought I saw something: a figure standing at one of the second-floor windows. But when I looked again, there was nobody there.

After twenty exhausting minutes, we finally arrived at the security gates, only to discover we'd overlooked an important detail.

The gates were locked and none of us had the code for the keypad. Flora grabbed hold of one of them and tried to pull it open with brute force, but it wouldn't budge. She kicked it in frustration. 'We'll have to go back and ask Annett for the pin.'

'No way,' said Saskia. 'We need to get as far away from here as possible before she finds out we're gone. And anyway, the electricity's out, remember? The keypad won't work.'

Nathan began looking around. 'There must be a manual release somewhere.'

He went over to a small metal cube that was attached low down on the left-hand gate's supporting pillar.

'I bet it's in there.' He began brushing away the snow from the cube, trying to find a way in. A rubber stopper appeared and when Nathan flipped it up, there was a keyhole underneath.

'Oh, crap,' Saskia groaned. 'What are we going to do now?' She looked up at the row of metal spikes on top of the gates and then at the towering perimeter fence that encircled the castle grounds. 'We can't get over this without a ladder.'

Nathan seemed unfazed. He held out his hand to me. 'Give me that log grabber, Libby.'

I handed it over, watching as he spread the implement's two arms apart, and pushed one of the pointed ends into the narrow aperture at the side of the cube. He began working the makeshift jemmy backwards and forwards in the gap, while the rest of us looked on.

We all cheered when, after only a few seconds, the front of the box sprang open. Inside was a small lever. Nathan gripped it between his fingers and rotated it to the right.

'Try the gate now.'

Flora pulled it towards her and this time it was more obliging.

The snow on the road lay deep and undisturbed. It came as a blow; I'd been hoping to see tyre tracks: an indication that help was closer than we thought; that we might not have to skate the river after all.

We headed north, following the same route the 4×4s had taken on the first day. We'd already discovered that trying to walk and talk at the same time made us out of breath, so we kept conversation to a minimum.

It was eerily quiet. There was no birdsong, no rustling of small mammals in the underbrush, or wind blowing through the trees, but the scenery was rather beautiful.

I wished I could take time to admire the icicles hanging from the telegraph poles, the birds of prey soaring majestically overhead, the rugged peaks of the Alps shimmering in the distance. But it was a luxury I couldn't afford. I had to be on my guard; watching for anyone who might be hiding among the trees that lined one side of the road.

After half a kilometre or so, we arrived at the first waypoint: a derelict barn set back from the road. According to the map, this was where we left the highway and followed a footpath in a diagonal trajectory across an open field.

I checked the time on my phone. We'd been walking for almost an hour, but it felt much longer than that. 'See those trees over there?' I said, pointing to a patch of woodland on the other side of the field. 'That's where the tributary is.'

'That's not too far,' said Flora. 'Is it OK if we stop and rest for a couple of minutes?'

Nathan surveyed the landscape as if he were a KGB agent in enemy territory. 'No, we're too exposed here; we need to get to the woods.'

We started trekking across the field. It was harder than walking on the road; the surface of the snow was more uneven. Our progress was agonisingly slow and at times it almost felt as if we were moving in slow motion. Nathan's words were ringing in my ears. He was right: we *were* exposed. Nowhere to run. Nowhere to hide. If someone was holed up in that barn, lying in wait for us, we wouldn't stand a chance. The logical part of my brain knew this was unlikely. Only the four of us – and Fred, of course – knew where we were headed. But the intuitive part believed that, given what had already come to pass, anything was possible.

I tried to shove the thought of a shotgun-wielding assassin aside and replace it with a more pleasant image, but I couldn't. Fear had taken over and my brain was a sick centrifuge operating at full tilt.

It seemed to take forever to reach the woods, but finally we made it. With snow covering whatever path there might have been, the way ahead wasn't immediately obvious. While the others took a quick breather, I got the map out of my backpack and tried to get my bearings.

'Do you need some help?' Nathan asked when I was still staring at it a minute or two later.

'No, it's fine,' I said, folding up the map and stuffing it in my jacket pocket. 'Follow me.'

We started to pick our way through the tall conifers, mindful of any obstacles that might be hiding beneath the snow.

'Are you sure you know where you're going, Libby?' Saskia asked as I stopped and consulted the map once again.

'Don't worry,' I replied, sounding more confident than I felt. 'It's not much further now.'

After fifteen minutes or so, we emerged into a large clearing. It was surrounded by tall trees and studded with snow-capped boulders that rose from the ground like ancient sentinels.

I walked to the centre of the clearing; stopped and looked around.

Behind me, Saskia released an exasperated breath. 'Please don't tell me we're lost.'

I pulled the map out of my pocket. 'No, I'm sure this is the right spot; I just don't see the tributary, that's all.'

Nathan came up to me. 'Let me see that map.'

I offered it up to him, pointing to where I thought we were.

He studied it for a few seconds, then looked up, comparing it to the surrounding landscape. 'Yup, this is definitely it,' he said, handing the map back to me. 'There must be water here somewhere.'

Flora kicked a patch of brambles. 'The map could be out of date. Maybe the tributary's dried up.'

Her words made me feel sick. It was a possibility I hadn't even considered. What if I'd led the others on a mission that was doomed to failure? What if we'd come all this way for nothing? If we couldn't find the tributary, we'd have to go back to Schloss Eis. The prospect was unbearable.

'It has to be here somewhere,' I said. 'It might be buried underneath the snow.'

'In that case, we'll probably never find it,' said Saskia unhelpfully.

I noticed that the ground dropped sharply away on the

other side of the clearing. When I walked over to it and looked down, my heart vaulted with relief.

It was a ditch.

A ditch filled with a shimmering ribbon of ice.

'Guys,' I said, breaking into a smile, 'I think I've found it.'

The others hurried over, but when Saskia saw the ditch, a mulish expression settled on her face.

'You've got to be joking,' she said. 'There's no way we can skate on this; it's not even two metres wide.'

I was forced to concur. In order to skate successfully, the ice had to be wide enough to accommodate the width of our stride, whilst also providing enough space to manoeuvre around any hazards. In practical terms, that meant several metres at least.

Nathan came up behind her. 'Don't get your panties in a bunch, Sas,' he told her. 'This is only the source of the tributary. It'll get wider downstream.'

She frowned at him. 'You're sure of that, are you?'

He didn't answer. He was already walking away. 'Are you coming?' he called over his shoulder.

Sighing, Saskia stomped off after him.

'Ignore her,' Flora said to me quietly. 'You're doing amazing, Libby, I can't believe you've managed to get us this far.'

I smiled at her, grateful for the morale boost. But I knew this was just the beginning.

Fortunately, Nathan's prediction proved to be correct. As we walked alongside the ditch, following the tributary's course, the ribbon of ice steadily expanded. By the

time it left the woods, it was roughly four metres across
– wide enough to accommodate even Nathan's generous
stride. After identifying a suitable entry point, we wasted
no time unpacking our skates.

'What shall I do with this?' said Flora, holding the
candlestick aloft. 'It won't fit in my backpack and if I
skate with it in my hand, my centre of balance will be off.'

'Dump it,' said Nathan. 'We're safe now.' He tossed
the poker down on the snow. 'And get rid of anything else
that's going to slow you down.'

I threw away the log grabber and sat down on a tree
stump to change my footwear. As I laced up my skates, I
took even more care than usual. Today was going to be
the most important skate of my life and I couldn't afford
to be slapdash. The laces had to be tight enough to support my feet. That way, all my energy would be directed
towards the blade and not lost within the boot. At the
same time, they mustn't be so tight that they restricted
my circulation and gave me foot cramps.

Saskia had already finished putting her skates on and
was now hefting her backpack onto her shoulders. She
tottered towards the bank, dropping the paper knife on
the ground en route. Then, after some hesitation, she
added what appeared to be a hardback book, wrapped
in a polythene bag.

I looked at her in surprise. 'You brought a *book* with
you?'

'It's not a book, it's my journal,' she replied. 'I didn't
want to leave it behind in case Annett found it.' She gave

it a final, longing long. 'When all this is over, I'm going to come back for it.'

'Good luck with that,' I said as I stuffed my trainers and damp socks into my backpack. I, for one, had no desire to ever set foot in this place again.

Once we all had our skates on, Nathan volunteered to do a test run. After removing his blade guards and tucking them into the side pocket of his backpack, he lowered himself gingerly onto the ice. The three of us watched anxiously from the bank as he pushed off with his back foot. As he propelled himself forwards, the rest of us were silent, ears straining for any telltale sound of cracking or groaning.

After travelling a short distance, he turned around and carefully retraced his steps, his face drawn in concentration.

'How does it feel?' I asked him.

'The texture's a little rough, but it seems pretty solid,' he replied. 'If it's like this all the way, we should be fine.'

Reaching out his hand, he helped us onto the ice, one by one. It had been several days since I'd last skated and, despite the unusual surroundings, it felt good to be back in my natural environment.

We set off in single file, with Nathan at the front, acting as lookout. I thought back to the last time we were on the river, albeit a different part of it. It seemed like a lifetime ago. I recalled Lukas's words of caution; his warning that the ice could be an unforgiving mistress, and the importance he had placed on balancing risk and reward.

As we proceeded downstream, one question was caught in a loop in my mind, a marker on the way to the point of no return.

Had we made a sensible risk assessment – or, just like the time before, were we utter idiots for thinking we could tame this powerful beast?

26

We proceeded warily as the tributary carved a serpentine path through the countryside, not knowing what dangers might be around the next bend.

The first stretch traversed open farmland. We passed one snow-covered field after another, the monotony of the landscape only broken by the occasional stable or cowshed. We kept our eyes peeled for any signs of life, but we saw nothing; not even a solitary sheep.

After a kilometre or so, the fields gave way to a dense pine forest. Although the tributary was slightly wider here, the skating was more challenging. With every twist and turn, there was a new obstacle to contend with: a part-submerged rock, a mound of leaf litter, the skeletal remains of a deer.

I was grateful when we finally emerged from the forest into a small valley. In the distance, I spotted a village nestling in the shadows of the Alps, its colourful rooftops peeking out from beneath the snow. In better weather, we'd be able to hike there in a couple of hours, but in these conditions, it might as well have been in another galaxy. Turning our heads away, we pressed on, our blades slicing through the ice in a soothing hum. Push and glide. Push and glide.

We'd been skating for about forty minutes when I saw a sharp left-hand bend up ahead. And then, as we rounded it, a spectacular sight came into view: a vast sheet of ice that stretched as far as the eye could see. Above it, the sky seemed to be clearing, the grey now punctuated with wispy white clouds. I felt almost tearful with relief.

'We did it!' Flora cried. 'We made it to the Danube!'

At the front of our little pack, Nathan did a running man victory dance – no mean feat on skates.

Even Saskia seemed emotional. 'I think that might just be the most beautiful thing I've ever seen,' she said, pressing her fingertips to her lips and blowing a kiss to the river.

Eager to try out the biggest rink any of us had ever seen, we kept on going. We dog-legged right, so that tributary and river were now running in parallel, with only a thin slice of land between them. As the two frozen waterways merged into one, I felt as if someone had lifted a great stone off my body. We had done the hard part. From here on in, it would be smooth sailing.

As we fanned out across the full width of the river, we quickly picked up speed. The icy breeze whipped against my face, stinging my cheeks and fuelling me with adrenaline. I felt almost weightless. The ice was so smooth, there was practically no resistance. For a few brief moments, I forgot the unbearable chain of tragedies that had brought us here and lost myself in the sheer beauty of the moment.

The others seemed to be enjoying themselves too. Flora and Saskia looked more relaxed than I'd seen them in days as they skated side by side. Suddenly, Saskia broke out of formation and treated us to an elegant pirouette, a ballerina on a frozen stage. Not to be outdone, Flora launched herself into a toe-loop.

'Bravo!' I called out as she landed. Our eyes connected briefly and something meaningful passed between us.

For the first couple of kilometres, we kept pace with one another, but, as our confidence grew, the temptation to go faster proved irresistible.

'See ya!' Nathan said, grinning cheekily as he broke away from the group, his strides long and powerful. Instantly, I took off after him, my body low to the ice like a speed skater.

Sensing me behind him, he slowed to let me catch up. We skated two abreast in perfect synchronicity, legs pumping, arms swaying back and forth. The world around us became a blur of motion, the frosted trees lining the riverbank whizzing by in a dizzying kaleidoscope of white and green. As we drove ourselves even harder, I experienced a powerful rush of endorphins – a reminder that I was never happier than when I was on the ice.

After ten minutes or so, I turned my head to check on Flora and Saskia. Surprised to see how far they'd fallen behind, I performed an abrupt hockey stop, shifting my weight to one foot, while turning the other foot perpendicular to the direction of motion and digging the edge of my skate into the ice.

'Hey,' I shouted to Nathan as he streaked ahead. 'We need to wait for the others.'

His feet stopped moving as he looked over his shoulder, but his momentum continued to carry him forward.

'What did you say?' he called back to me.

I started to repeat myself, but then something up ahead caught my eye: a large bird with a huge wing span, flying very low over the river. As its legs descended from its body, I realised it was coming in to land.

And Nathan was heading straight for it.

As I yelled a warning, he snapped his head back round. The bird was now standing on the ice directly in front of him, its wings still extended. In a desperate attempt to avoid it, he turned sharply to the left, but immediately realised he'd overcorrected. He tried to regain control by bending his knees to lower his centre of gravity. But it was too little, too late.

As the frightened bird took flight, Nathan's body slammed into the ice. The impact was so powerful, I felt the shockwave. I looked down, terrified the ice beneath my feet was about to fracture, but thankfully it held firm.

Up ahead, Nathan was lying on his side. His face was turned away from me and he wasn't moving.

My heart was in my mouth as I skated towards him. As I knelt down beside him, he lifted his head up.

'Are you all right?' I asked him.

His hand reached towards his right leg. 'I think so.'

I helped him into a sitting position, by which time Flora and Saskia had arrived.

'That was quite a tumble you took,' said Saskia as she squatted down beside us. 'You didn't hit your head, did you?'

Nathan gripped his right thigh with both hands. 'No, but my knee's hurting. It's probably just bruised; give me a few minutes and I'll be fine.'

I noticed that he was shivering. 'You're going to get cold sitting on the ice. Do you think you can stand up?'

'Yeah,' he said, 'but you'll have to help me.'

I eased off his backpack and handed it to Flora. Then Saskia and I got into position, one on either side of him. He wrapped an arm around our necks and between us we carefully lifted him up, using our leg strength to support most of his weight. I saw how he cringed as the foot of his injured leg made contact with the ice. I had a horrible feeling he was more badly hurt than he was letting on.

'Follow me,' said Flora, as she began skating to the opposite bank with Nathan's backpack. 'There's a big rock over there he can sit on.'

By the time Saskia and I had escorted Nathan to the bank, he was as white as a sheet.

'Does anyone have any pain meds?' he asked, as we gently lowered him onto the rock.

'I have some ibuprofen,' said Flora, taking off her backpack.

As she hunted for the tablets, I took out my water bottle.

'I'm so sorry,' I said as I handed it to him. 'I shouldn't have distracted you like that.'

He pushed back his hair with his hands. 'No, it's on me. I should've reacted quicker.'

'I blame that damn bird,' said Flora. 'What's the stupid thing even doing here in the middle of winter? I thought herons were supposed to be migratory.'

Nathan took the blister pack she was offering and shoved two tablets in his mouth, swallowing them down with a mouthful of water. As he handed the tablets back to her, she took a sharp intake of breath.

'Shit, Nathan, have you seen the size of your knee?'

We all stared at his leg. In his slim-fitting trousers, the swelling was obvious.

'There's no way that's just bruised,' said Saskia. 'Whatever you've done to it, you'd be crazy to carry on skating.'

It was sensible advice. Every skater knew that if you sustained an injury, you rested up. There was no point being a hero; you'd only end up aggravating the injury and prolonging your recovery time.

Nathan tilted his head back and stared at the sky; took a deep breath. I was expecting him to raise an objection and when he didn't, I knew he must be badly injured.

'Yeah,' he said at length. 'Even if I wanted to carry on, I don't think I could.'

'So what's the plan?' asked Flora. 'Should one of us stay here with him?'

'No,' Nathan said forcefully. 'You three go on without me; I'll be fine here on my own. You can come back for me later.'

Tears welled up behind my eyes as I remembered what had happened to Gabrielle. *She* had fallen on the ice too, and now she was dead. And Melissa. Left on her own in the forest. Easy prey. Then there was the weather, of course. Now that Nathan wasn't moving, his core temperature would drop quickly.

My chest heaved; the thump of my heart felt too fast, my face too hot. I didn't want to leave Nathan. What if something happened to him while we were gone?

I reached into my backpack, hunting for my phone. 'Maybe we can get a phone signal here, then we can call the emergency services.'

The others started scrabbling for their phones.

'I've got nothing,' said Flora, holding out her phone to show us.

It was the same for all of us.

'Just go,' Nathan said, and I heard the pleading edge in his voice.

I frowned. 'Let's just think about this for a moment.'

'Please, you don't have much time.' He pointed up at the sky.

At first, I wasn't sure what he meant. But then I saw the fingers of sunlight that were forcing their way through the clouds.

At any other time, I would've been overjoyed to see the sun, but not now. It wouldn't be strong enough to melt the whole river, but it was certainly capable of creating patches of frozen slush. Patches that wouldn't be visible until we were right on top of them.

Nathan reached out and took my hand. 'Listen to me, Libby,' he said, looking deep into my eyes. 'You're the fastest, strongest skater out of all of us. I need you to get the other two to the town; I need to know that all of you are safe.'

I thought for a few seconds. No one could possibly have tracked us all this way and the town was probably only eight or nine kilometres away; we could be there within the hour. As soon as we got to the police station, we could send help back for Nathan. He wouldn't be alone for very long.

'All right then,' I said with a heavy heart.

Not caring that the other two were watching, I leaned forward and placed a kiss on Nathan's cold forehead.

'You stay safe too.'

27

When we got back onto the ice, the mood had changed. Our earlier lightheartedness had evaporated and we were fuelled by a new urgency. It wasn't just Fred who was relying on us now; it was Nathan too.

The three of us pushed ourselves hard, legs and arms pumping, breath forming delicate clouds of mist above our heads. And all the while, the sun continued to burn through the clouds. It glistened on the ice, transforming the river into a field of diamonds: pretty, but potentially lethal.

I tried to set a pace that was manageable for us all, but after five Ks or so I could see that Flora was growing tired. Her upper body had started to slouch, her foot-work was becoming less precise. She did her best to keep up, but little by little, her speed slowed, until finally she stopped skating altogether. Of course that meant Saskia and I had to stop skating too.

'I'm sorry,' she panted. 'I'm absolutely shattered; I don't think I can go on much further.'

'We're really close now,' I told her, not knowing if this was even true. 'You've got this, Flora; I know you have.'

She doubled over, gripping her knees with her hands. 'My heart wants to keep going; I just don't think my legs are in the mood to listen.'

I looked up at the sky. Large areas of cobalt blue were now visible in between the clouds. Time was running out.

'Why don't you go on ahead and I'll stay with Flora?' said Saskia, evidently reading my concerns. 'We'll rest for a little while on the bank and as soon as she's caught her breath, we'll be right behind you.'

I almost offered to stay with them, but then I thought of Nathan, alone in the cold. 'Are you sure?'

Saskia nodded. 'When we get to the town, we'll go straight to the police station.'

'Fine; I'll meet you there.'

Since there was nothing more to say, I gave them both a quick hug, put my head down against the wind and started to skate.

I didn't like leaving them behind, but there *were* advantages to skating solo. It meant I could travel at my own pace; lose myself in my thoughts; imagine how good it would feel when I got to speak to Mum and Gran on the phone at the police station and let them know I was OK.

I had been skating for around twenty minutes when I spotted something on the left-hand bank: a large wooden sign. It looked like an information board, the sort of thing that might contain a trail map, or details about the local wildlife. Immediately, my spirits soared; it suggested I was getting closer to civilisation.

As I hurtled past it, I was aware of a small vibration, just below my right shoulder blade. I was puzzled for a moment, but then I realised my mobile phone was ringing. Finally – I was in range of a working mast.

Immediately, I stopped skating and pulled my phone out of my backpack. To my surprise, the name on the screen was Flora's. She'd suggested we swap numbers on our second day at Schloss Eis and I'd given her my phone so she could punch in her details.

Accepting the call, I pressed the phone to my ear. 'Hey, Flora, you managed to get a signal!'

I heard a ragged sob. 'Saskia's had an accident,' she blurted out.

A clamp tightened around my chest. 'What sort of accident?'

Another stifled sob. 'We were standing on the bank and something came flying through the trees – some sort of projectile; I didn't see what it was. It hit Sas in the neck and she fell over. I think she must have hit her head on a rock because her forehead's bleeding.'

I felt a sting of guilt like a poisoned needle in my sternum. I should've stayed with them. 'Is she conscious?'

'Yes, but she's very confused and her breathing seems laboured.'

'You need to call the emergency services. Right now.'

'I already did,' she wailed. 'I had to wait for ages before they put me through to someone who could speak English, only to be told it would be hours before help arrived. The operator said they're much busier than usual because of the bad weather. I told them we were in imminent danger, that Saskia had been deliberately targeted, but I don't think they believed me.' She was speaking quickly, her words falling over themselves like dominoes in a line. 'I think someone's been following us all the way from the castle. I think they're probably watching me make this call.'

My scalp prickled. 'Are you on the bank?'

'Yes.'

A thought detached itself from my mind and floated in the air in front of me, like a hologram: a figure wearing camouflage, hiding behind a tree; lining up his next shot.

'Can you get back on the ice?' I said urgently. 'You'll be safer there.'

'Saskia's in no fit state to skate and there's no way I'm leaving her.'

Something began to shift and splinter inside of me. This was all my fault. We should never have left the castle. How had I managed to get it so badly wrong? This was immediately followed by another chilling realisation. If someone *had* been following us, then they knew that Nathan was alone. With no phone signal and no weapon. Utterly defenceless.

I felt torn in a million different directions. I could continue on to the town and hope the police there would have the necessary resources to reach the remote locations where the other three were stuck.

Or I could try to rescue them myself.

I started to skate, the phone still pressed to my ear.

'Hang in there, Flora. I'm coming back for you.'

Despite my exhaustion, I skated faster than I had ever skated before. My vision had shrunk to pinpoints, my breath came hard. The only thought in my mind was getting to Flora and Saskia before the killer struck again.

As I approached the place where I'd left them, I could see Flora waving at me from the bank. My first thought was *thank God she's alive.*

'Where's Saskia?' I called out as she lowered herself onto the ice and started skating.

She didn't answer; she just kept barrelling towards me. As soon as she was near enough, she practically threw herself into my arms.

'Where's Saskia?' I said again, speaking through a mouthful of her hair.

Flora tilted her head back to look me. Her eyes were oddly blank, like an animal's; she must be absolutely terrified.

Suddenly, there was a sharp feeling, just beneath my ribs. Instinctively, I stepped back, thrusting Flora away from me.

When I looked down at my body, I noticed a tear in my jacket. I could see pale wadding spilling out through it. Confused, I put my fingers to the hole. 'How did that happen?'

Flora didn't answer. Then I saw what was in her hand: a silver dagger, its narrow blade glinting in the sunlight. It was the paper knife; the one Saskia had discarded on the bank.

Everything went very quiet and still inside my head. 'What have you done?' I said slowly.

She smiled at me with a kind of triumph. 'Oh, Libby.

Haven't you worked it out yet?' Her tone was lacking in emotion, a void where feeling should be.

A streak of something close to pure terror forked downwards from my brain stem, branching out across my entire body. We hadn't left the killer behind at Schloss Eis; we'd brought her with us.

Before I had time to digest this horrifying epiphany, Flora lunged at me with the knife again, her hand reaching towards my throat. But I had already kissed death long and hard enough to feel a nauseating intimacy with it – and now, with the spectre of my own death looming, I realised I wasn't ready to embrace it again.

I pushed off with my back foot, just like I had a million times before. But this time was different. This time, I was skating for my life.

As I flew across the ice, my brain felt like it was overheating as it tried to compute what was happening, but too many parts of the equation were missing.

Flora must've been lying when she said she was tired because she was right behind me. I could hear her laboured breathing and the rasp of her blades as they cut into the ice.

My muscles were screaming and my heart was hammering so hard it felt as if it was about to fly out of my body. I knew it was only a matter of time before Flora caught up with me. My eyes cast around the riverbanks. I was desperately hoping to see someone: a hiker, a dog walker; anyone who could help me.

But there was no one around.

The only person who could save me now was myself.

In the distance, I saw a tree lying across the ice. I'd passed it earlier on. It had fallen from the right-hand bank; a huge thing that spanned two-thirds of the river's width. I'd had to skate close to the left-hand bank in order to get around it.

A plan began to form in my mind.

I changed course, so that now I was hugging the right-hand bank, heading straight for the tree. As it got nearer, doubt bloomed inside me like a fungus. Could I really do this?

Lukas's words rang in my ears: *trust your instincts*. And my instincts told me that this was a risk worth taking.

I glanced over my shoulder. Flora had followed me over to the right-hand bank, just as I had hoped, and was now only a couple of bus lengths away.

I waited until the tree was almost within touching distance and then, with every last bit of strength in my body, I turned, jumped and rotated in quick succession, using my arms to draw a U-shape in front of me. The momentum propelled me upwards and then I was flying through the air, face down to the ice, all four limbs spreadeagled. The Butterfly Kick; it was just as well I'd had a chance to practise it earlier in the week.

My timing was perfect and I sailed over the trunk, landing on the other side with barely ten centimetres to spare. Flora, meanwhile, had skidded to a halt on the other side of the tree. For a brief moment, we stared at each other and the look on her face was one of pure hatred. The trunk was far too big to climb over and Flora's only option was to skate over to the opposite bank and make her way around the crown.

Knowing I'd bought myself vital minutes, I took off as if I were jet propelled. But I'd barely taken a dozen steps when I heard a scream. It ricocheted off the ice, reverberating in my eardrums.

I told myself to ignore it. It was a bluff. A twisted mind game.

But the screaming continued. It sounded anguished; almost primal. I slowed my pace and looked behind me. Flora was nowhere to be seen. I stopped skating altogether, my eyes scanning the right-hand bank in case she'd climbed up onto it, but there was no sign of her there either.

Then I spotted something, close to the crown of the tree: an arm reaching upwards, out of the water.

A dark tide of horror rose inside me. Flora had fallen through the ice. If she couldn't haul herself out, her chances of survival were non-existent. For a brief moment, I hesitated; remembered what she'd done to the others and what she had tried to do to me. Then I started skating towards her.

I found her bobbing in the middle of a small hole; her head and shoulders above the surface, her arms spread wide on the ice, holding her body in place.

'H-h-help me,' she stuttered. She was hyperventilating badly, her chest heaving, her facial muscles spasming.

Ignoring her momentarily, I checked the ice around

the hole for any fissures or patches of slush. Satisfied that it would hold my weight, I sat down behind her, my legs spread wide on either side of the hole.

'H-h-urry,' Flora urged, her teeth chattering madly. 'The c-c-current's p-p-pulling me.'

Plunging my hands into the icy water, I tried to reach under her armpits, but she was still wearing her backpack and the shoulder straps were in the way. I took a different approach, grabbing the straps instead and leaning backwards, pulling as hard as I could. The technique seemed to be working and Flora's upper body rose up out of the water. But then she started panicking, thrashing her arms, her hands scrabbling for purchase.

The next second, I was sliding backwards across the ice on my backside, the backpack still in my hands. Tossing it aside, I scrambled towards the hole on all fours, but it was too late. Flora was nowhere to be seen.

Suddenly, I saw a ghostly silhouette, underneath the ice. Flora's face, pale and stricken. She stared at me, her eyes wide and pleading for salvation, her hands pushing against the ice like she was trying to break through it. And then she was gone, carried away by the current.

I tried to get back on my feet. If I could outrun the current, maybe I could break a hole in the ice with the blade of my skate and grab Flora as she passed underneath it. But my legs didn't seem to be working properly. A build-up of lactic acid, probably; I had pushed myself to breaking point and now that I had stopped skating, it was all catching up with me. As I took a deep breath and prepared to try again, I noticed that the ice beneath my body was stained a pinkish-red.

Confused, I pulled off my right glove and reached a hand up under my jacket. When I took my hand away, I saw that my fingertips were bloody.

All at once, I was conscious of a deep and penetrating coldness spreading out from within me. My throat started to close, my vision grew fuzzy at the edges. I felt pain for the first time: a desperate, fiery ache that started under my ribcage and ended somewhere in my groin.

The last thing I was aware of, before the darkness descended, was a voice, calling to me from very far away.

28

I turned my head towards the window. The view from my hospital bed was a pleasant one. Snow still blanketed the ground, but, if the forecasters were right, warm air coming in off the Atlantic was about to usher in a period of much milder weather.

It was thirty-six hours since I'd been rescued from the river. An engineer carrying out emergency repairs to nearby power lines had heard Flora scream when she fell through the ice. As he'd rushed towards the river, he'd witnessed my frantic attempts to pull her out of the water. By the time he'd arrived on the bank, Flora was gone and I was busy passing out. When I failed to respond to his shouts, he'd courageously made his way onto the ice and stayed with me until rescuers arrived. It turned out Flora was lying when she'd said the emergency services were overstretched. She had never even made the call. Why would she, when she was the one who'd caused Saskia's injury, using the same knife she'd used to attack me?

I was rushed to hospital in a 4×4 response vehicle, where a full-scale trauma team was waiting to receive me. Everything seemed to happen at once. My clothing was removed; IVs were placed; heart monitoring pads were stuck to my chest. As I was wheeled off for a CT scan, I couldn't help fearing the worst.

Fortunately, my jacket had protected me, preventing the blade from piercing any vital organs. All I needed was suturing, antibiotics and pain management.

Mum and Gran were probably in worse shape than I was. They were beside themselves when they found out I was in hospital and all set to jump on a plane. With Munich airport still closed, I persuaded them to stay put, promising them that as soon as the doctors declared me fit to travel, I would be on the next available flight home.

Saskia was rather less fortunate than me. The first thing I did when I came round as they were stretchering me off the ice was beg my rescuers to find her. I showed them where to search on the map and gave them her phone number, hoping they'd be able to use GPS to pinpoint her precise location. An hour later, she was recovered, unconscious, from the riverbank, not far from where I'd last seen her. There was a single, deep stab wound to her neck.

While Saskia's condition remained critical, at least she was conscious now. Her parents were en route from Scotland; I heard they'd chartered a private plane. I could only imagine how they must be feeling. Bad enough that their daughter had been stabbed in the neck and left for dead, but to learn her attacker was a family member . . . that was something they must be struggling to come to terms with.

As for Flora, she was missing, presumed dead. Chances were her body wouldn't be found until the thaw set in.

I leaned towards the bedside cabinet, wincing as the stitches in my abdomen pulled tight. Easing the drawer open, I removed a small mirror, a comb and some tinted lip balm that one of the nurses had given me. I'd kill for some mascara, but all my make-up was back at the castle, together with the rest of my belongings. The police said I'd get my things back eventually, but not right now. Not while Schloss Eis was still an active crime scene.

Holding the mirror up in front of my face, I ran the comb through my hair, before applying the lip balm. I looked rather pale, so I added a dot of balm to each cheek and rubbed it in. I wasn't usually so image conscious, but Nathan was due any minute. He'd come to see me yesterday as well, but we didn't talk for long because two detectives were waiting to take a statement from me. Aside from a torn ligament in his knee, he was in good shape. The police had asked him to stay in the country temporarily, to help with their enquiries, and they'd put him up at a hotel, a short distance from the hospital.

As I returned the items to the drawer, I heard a light knock on the door. I called out a greeting and it opened to reveal Nathan, leaning heavily on his crutches.

'Hey, you,' he said with a warm, wide smile. 'How's it going?'

'Not bad, thanks. It looks like I'm going to be discharged in the next day or two.'

'That's great news.' He lumbered across the room and lowered himself into the chair next to my bed.

'How's the leg?'

He rested a hand on his knee brace. 'It hurts pretty

bad, but I'll live. My coach is organising some rehab for me when I get back to the States.'

'What about Saskia? Have you seen her yet?'

'Yeah, I've just come from the ICU. She seems to be aware of what's going on around her, but she can't talk because of her injury. Her parents were there; they flew in this morning. I spoke to them briefly; they seemed like nice people.'

'They must be absolutely distraught.'

'They are, but they know that if you hadn't gotten help for her, it could've been a whole lot worse.'

'And Fred? Have you managed to make contact with him?'

'Yeah, the mast's been fixed now; we FaceTimed a couple of hours ago. He's been moved to a guesthouse, not far from the castle; Annett's there too. The cops don't want them going anywhere until they have all the information they need. Fred says hi, by the way. He's very grateful for what you did; he said if it wasn't for you, we'd probably all be dead.'

I smiled awkwardly. 'I don't know about that.'

He reached out; gave my hand a little squeeze. Something inside me lit up, like a match struck in the darkness.

'Take the compliment, Libby; you deserve it.' He let go of my hand. 'Oh, and they've found Melissa. Fred took the police to her.'

There was a swirl in my gut. 'That's good; at least her family will be able to say a proper goodbye now. And Alexander?'

'Yeah, they've recovered him as well, but the bodies won't be released until the autopsies have been done. Same goes for Lukas and Gabrielle.'

As the light caught Nathan's face, I noticed the violet shadows beneath his eyes. I wondered if he was struggling to sleep. If he wished, like me, that he could excise the past few days like a tumour; forget any of it ever happened.

I stared down at my grubby fingernails against the starched white sheet, waiting for some sort of sense to flower from the dark, swollen bud my Bavarian experience.

'I see the story's broken in the media,' I said. 'I read a report on the Reuters website earlier. It looks like the police haven't released any of our names, or confirmed the number of deaths yet.'

'No, I think they want to keep the details under wraps for now. There's going to be a feeding frenzy when the full story comes out.'

'People are going to be heartbroken when they find out Lukas is dead,' I said sadly. 'I'm still trying to take it in myself.'

'I know. He didn't deserve what happened to him; none of them did.'

My head throbbed with a deep, sickening beat. 'Do you think Flora was responsible for all of it?'

'That seems to be the theory the German police are working on.' He drew his thumbnail back and forth across his chin. 'She really fooled us, huh?'

'Yes; she did.' The pain of Flora's betrayal felt as sharp as the stab wound she'd inflicted on me and, frustratingly, I still had no idea what had made her do it. 'Do you think we'll ever find out why?'

Nathan gave a long sigh that seemed to come from somewhere deep inside him. 'I don't know. I hope so; I don't think I can go through the rest of my life without knowing.' He looked at me and I saw the torment in his eyes. 'I keep replaying everything that happened at Schloss Eis; asking myself why I was so blind to the warning signs. It never even crossed my mind it could be Flora, I was too busy focusing on Lukas and Annett – two people who turned out to be completely innocent.' He broke off, as if the thought was too heavy to hold.

'There weren't any warning signs,' I told him. 'None of us could have done a thing to stop her and you mustn't feel guilty about it.' I knew I was speaking the truth; it was just a pity I couldn't take my own advice. I could only hope that, in time, both of us would be able to come to terms with what had happened.

He forced a smile. 'I hate thinking about what you went through on the river. I still can't believe you tried to save Flora; I don't think I would have been that selfless.'

The door opened and a nurse walked in. I silently cursed her for her appalling timing. There was so much more I wanted to say to Nathan.

'I need to change your dressing now,' she said in stilted English.

Nathan reached for his crutches. 'I'll go and grab a coffee. I can come back in half an hour – that's if you want me to.'

I tried to blot out the nurse hovering at my bedside with a stainless-steel tray in her hand; to pretend that Nathan and I were the only ones in the room.

'Of course I want you to.'

29

'How do I look?'

Gran smiled at me. 'Absolutely beautiful.'

'You don't think this lipstick's too much?' I said, frowning at my reflection.

'Not at all. That shade really suits you; it brings out the colour of your eyes.'

I turned away from the mirror. With any luck, the photographer would be quick. I hated having my photo taken, but, given the amount they were paying me, I could hardly refuse. Not that I would be receiving the cash myself. I had asked for it to be paid directly to Fred's family. It wouldn't cover the full cost of his brother's treatment in Switzerland, but it would certainly go a long way towards it.

The newspaper was also picking up the tab for two nights in this gorgeous boutique hotel. A car had picked Gran and me up yesterday afternoon and brought us down to London; Mum couldn't get the time off work, unfortunately. Gran and I had spent the morning relaxing in the hotel's spa, before returning to our room so I could get ready for my interview.

The trial had ended three weeks ago. In German murder trials, guilt is determined not by a jury, but by a panel of judges. I was one of the key witnesses. As the presiding judge announced a guilty verdict, he described my evidence as 'powerful'.

Up until a couple of months ago, I'd enjoyed virtual anonymity, but once the horrific details were laid bare at the trial, every media outlet wanted a piece of me – or at least that's the way it seemed. Eva, my coach, had put me in touch with a friend of hers who worked in PR. He said that if I didn't give at least one interview, the bombardment would continue indefinitely. He also explained that by granting exclusivity to a single publication, I'd be able to command a sizeable fee for my story. What's more, for a small percentage, he would do all the negotiating on my behalf. Reluctant as I'd been to go public, it was a no-brainer.

I went with a well-regarded British newspaper in the end. The female journalist I spoke to on the phone had assured me my story would be treated sensitively and stressed that she had no desire to re-traumatise me in its telling. I was probably more robust than she realised, my childhood experiences having left me more resistant to trauma than a lot of other people my age.

'Are you sure you don't want me to come with you?' said Gran, as I fiddled with my hair clip.

'No, I'll be fine. You stay here and make the most of room service.'

It would've been nice to have the moral support, but I knew Gran's presence would inhibit me; tempt me to downplay certain aspects of my story, for fear of upsetting her. I couldn't afford to hold anything back; the newspaper was paying me handsomely and would be expecting its pound of flesh. My PR had spent several hours running through practice questions with me and, while still a little apprehensive, I felt reasonably well prepared.

Satisfied with my appearance – or at least as satisfied as I was ever going to be – I set off for the first-floor suite where my interviewer was waiting.

The journalist was as nice in person as she'd seemed when we spoke on the phone. After turning on her voice recorder, she eased me in gently by asking how I'd got into skating in the first place. Having covered that, she enquired about my family. The PR had anticipated this and my pre-prepared answer referenced Dad's death, as well as paying tribute to Gran and her incredible support. It didn't involve any mention of Mum's alcoholism, or my difficult childhood; those subjects were definitely not for public consumption. Once the background stuff was out of the way, it was time to get down to the meat of the interview.

Journalist: How did you feel when the German police investigation confirmed what you had already suspected – that Flora Kavanagh was a cold-blooded serial killer?

Libby: It's hard to put it into words. Horrified. Dumbfounded. Sick to the bottom of my stomach. Even now, nearly a year later, I'm still trying to process it.

Journalist: As you know, Flora's body was never found; it's almost certain the river carried her out to sea. Does it make you angry that she effectively escaped justice?

Libby: I don't know about *angry*. I regret that she wasn't forced to face her victims' families in court. I also regret that she's not around to explain her actions. Despite all the stuff that came out during the trial, there's still so much we don't know. But I'm also relieved she's dead, because it means she can never hurt anyone again.

Journalist: Is there a part of you that feels sorry for Flora Kavanagh because, in some senses, she was a victim herself?

Libby: It's true that she was the product of her upbringing – but aren't we all? Lots of people face potentially destructive influences in their formative years. They don't all turn into murderers. Flora was an intelligent woman. When she committed those evil acts, she did so of her own free will. So no, I don't feel sorry for her. Not even a tiny bit.

Journalist: You said in court that when Flora attacked you, there was no doubt in your mind that she was trying to kill you. In that case, why did you try to save her when she fell through the ice? Was it a reflexive action?

Libby: If I'm being honest – no, it wasn't. I knew she'd already killed at least four people; I actually thought she'd killed Saskia too. It did cross my mind that

I could just leave her there to drown; in some ways, it was what she deserved. But, ultimately, I didn't want her death on my conscience. It's as simple as that.

Journalist: You say you knew she'd killed the others, but up until that moment, had you had any suspicions about her at all?

Libby: None whatsoever; Flora was the last person I thought would be capable of murder. I've seen some of the stuff that's been going round online – people saying we were stupid, that it must've been obvious it was Flora, and to a certain extent I get where they're coming from. But she was so clever, so believable. I think that unless you were there, you really can't appreciate that.

Journalist: So who *did* you all think was responsible?

Libby: We tossed around different theories; we were just clutching at straws really. I don't want to say any more than that because, ultimately, there was no truth in any of them.

Journalist: Kavanagh was the one who actually carried out the murders, but another person was found guilty of 'joint perpetration', as it's known in German law. What was your reaction when you discovered who the German police suspected of orchestrating the horrific events at Schloss Eis?

Libby: I was flabbergasted; I actually thought they'd got it wrong at first. It was only when they told me they had irrefutable proof of Helen Kavanagh's involvement and that they were pushing ahead with a prosecution that I realised it might actually be true.

Journalist: You must be very pleased she's currently serving multiple life sentences in a German prison right now.

Libby: For sure – and while no punishment can ever make up for what she did, I hope that the trial, and her conviction, has given the victims' families some answers, as well as a semblance of closure.

Journalist: Were you aware when you went to Germany that Flora Kavanagh and Saskia Blair were related?

Libby: Yes, I followed Saskia on Instagram; I still do. I'd seen a photo she'd posted of her and Flora together; the caption alluded to the fact they were second cousins.

Journalist: Were you also aware that Saskia was the daughter of Joanne Blair – or Joanne Murray, if I can use her maiden name?

Libby: I was. Joanne used to be a big name in British skating. She was someone I'd always admired.

Journalist: And Helen Kavanagh, née Murray. Was that a name you were familiar with?

Libby: No. I didn't realise Flora's mother had also been a talented skater in her youth. I can appreciate how upset she was when her career was cut short, but to find out it had made her so bitter and twisted that she spent the next thirty years waiting for an opportunity to get her own back on the skating community just blows my mind.

Journalist: And when you say 'skating community', it seems that included her own cousin too.

Libby: Absolutely. Even though they were related, Helen clearly couldn't bear the fact that Joanne had gone on to become one of the UK's most successful female skaters ever. It seems she kept her feelings pretty well hidden, though. Certainly, Saskia had no idea there was any bad blood.

Journalist: She told you that, did she?

Libby: Yes, Saskia and I are in touch regularly. We've spent a lot of time talking about what happened in Bavaria. I think we both find it therapeutic to share our feelings with someone else who lived through it.

Journalist: How Saskia's doing? I know she almost died in the attack.

Libby: Very well; she's skating again now. It'll be a while before she's able to compete, but her coach is confident she'll get there eventually.

Journalist: That's really good to hear. You said just now that Saskia was unaware of any problems between the two families. Do you know if she saw much of Helen Kavanagh when she was growing up?

Libby: She told me she could count on one hand the number of times she'd actually met her aunt. I think Joanne and Helen were pretty close as teenagers, but once Helen met her future husband and moved to Galway, they drifted apart. It was only when Saskia and Flora started meeting at competitions, four or five years ago, that the two branches of the family reconnected.

Journalist: Did Flora say much about her mother while you were staying at Schloss Eis? It's clear the two had a very dysfunctional relationship; I'm just wondering what Flora's upbringing was like.

Libby: She didn't mention her mother once. She related an interesting story to Saskia though.

Journalist: Oh? Can you share that with me?

Libby: She told Saskia she had a very high pain threshold and that it was all down to her mum's conditioning. When she was nine or ten, she'd sprained her wrist falling off her bike. Even though Flora's arm was in a sling, Helen insisted she keep up her skating. A few days later, Flora fell over during a practice session. The pain in her wrist was so bad she burst into tears. Apparently, Helen just stared at her emotionlessly from the side of the rink, not saying a word. Realising her mother wasn't going to offer any comfort, Flora picked herself up and carried on skating.

Journalist: Gosh, that really is tough love. No wonder Flora developed such a warped view of the world. Joanne and Helen grew up together in Dundee, didn't they? I believe they even trained at the same rink.

Libby: Yeah, ice skating is obviously in the genes. They're only a year apart in age, so they'd come up through the ranks together. I believe both of them were tipped as Olympic contenders at one time.

Journalist: Under cross-examination, Helen Kavanagh admitted that a fall on the ice during a skating competition, three decades earlier, had set into motion a chain of events that culminated in the murders of four people and the attempted murder of two others, including yourself. An expert fielded by the defence claimed she'd suffered previously undiagnosed brain damage during that fall. Her lawyer even argued – unsuccessfully, as it turned out – that this should be considered a mitigating factor. I think it's fair to say that ice skating is riskier than some other competitive sports. Speaking as a skater yourself, how unlucky was Kavanagh to suffer a career-ending injury at the age of just seventeen?

Libby: Skaters fall all the time, but usually the worst that happens is a few bruises. The difference in this case was that Helen crashed headfirst into the metal handrail that surrounded the rink. These days, most rinks have flexible barrier systems that can absorb and deflect the energy of a collision, but things were different back then. At first, she didn't appear to be badly injured, but later, in the dressing room, she collapsed. Although she seemingly went on to make a good recovery, the part of the brain that controls balance had been damaged, and as a consequence she never returned to competitive skating. So yeah, she was very unlucky.

Journalist: At the trial, Helen tried to justify her actions by saying that after her accident she'd felt unsupported by the skating fraternity. She claimed that her coach and her fellow skaters had basically turned their backs on her. Although she didn't specifically reference her cousin Joanne, the implication was that she also felt abandoned by her too.

Libby: That's the impression I got. I certainly don't think Flora would've attacked Saskia without her mother's encouragement. To be honest, I think everyone at Schloss Eis, even those who emerged physically unscathed, were on the Kavanaghs' kill list. Flora was determined to avenge her mother at any cost, and when she received Lukas's invitation, the pair of them saw the perfect opportunity. Finding out that Saskia had been invited too was just the cherry on the cake.

Journalist: Helen's lawyer said Flora had been acting independently in Bavaria, and that while his client had long-standing grievances against the skating world, she certainly hadn't masterminded the murders, as the prosecution claimed. Can I just ask, are you one hundred per cent convinced – as the judges clearly were – that mother and daughter were acting in concert?

Libby: Oh yes, I think the texts make that quite clear.

Journalist: Ah yes, the infamous texts, recovered from the phone that was found in Flora's backpack. I think the German police chief described them as the next best thing to a confession. Am I right in thinking Flora was wearing that backpack when she fell into the river – but it came off during your attempt to rescue her?

Libby: That's right; it was the backpack she used for skiing. If it hadn't been made of water-resistant material, the phone would've been completely wrecked and the police would never have been able to recover the data.

Journalist: From what I understand, most of the texts were written while Flora's phone had no connectivity and were only delivered to her mother the day of her death.

Libby: Yes. It's quite sickening, really . . . the thought that she was cataloguing everything she'd done, for her mother's benefit. I'm glad she did though, otherwise the German police might never have discovered Helen Kavanagh's role in all of this.

Journalist: Were you shocked at the forensic level of detail contained within those texts?

Libby: I was *beyond* shocked. They really do demonstrate a horrific level of premeditation. And what's even more scary is the way that Flora was able to think so quickly on her feet; to turn what was quite a fast-moving situation to her advantage. It's not like she or her mother could have done any prep work *before* she came to Schloss Eis.

Journalist: I don't suppose she knew the weather would deteriorate the way it did either.

Libby: She couldn't have done; even the meteorologists were taken by surprise.

Journalist: I have a printout of the texts here. I'd like to run through some of the content; get your thoughts on Flora's modus operandi; try to fill in a few of the missing pieces for our readers, if that isn't going to be too upsetting for you . . .

Libby: No, that's fine.

Journalist: OK, let's start with Gabrielle. On her third day in Bavaria, Flora tells her mother, almost gleefully, that she's considering sabotaging the castle's synthetic ice rink, in the hope that one of you would be, if not killed, then at least badly injured. Helen Kavanagh's reply makes it clear she's fully supportive of this plan. She even attaches a PDF, illustrating how the sections of a synthetic ice rink, very similar to the one in Lukas Wolff's home, fit together. And then, disappointed that Gabrielle had only sustained a broken ankle, Flora tells her mother in a subsequent text that she'd retrieved the packaging from a pre-prepared sushi meal, bought during her journey to Bavaria, from the wastepaper basket in her room. Crucially, that packaging contained a small plastic bottle of soy sauce. Were you aware that Gabrielle was severely allergic to soy?

Libby: Yes, we all were. Gabrielle had mentioned it at dinner on the first day. Later that same evening, someone – I think it was Fred – asked how bad her allergy was. Gabrielle made it quite clear that if she consumed anything containing soy, even a very small amount, it could be life-threatening. She actually got an EpiPen out of her handbag to show us. Looking back on it, that was probably the moment Gabrielle signed her own death warrant.

Journalist: Ugh, I've literally got shivers up my spine hearing you say that. In the next message to her mother, Flora says: '*I poured soy sauce into the water glass on Gabrielle's bedside table. I know she drank it because when I went into her room later the glass was empty.*' Flora also reveals that she stole the EpiPen from Gabrielle's handbag. It meant that, even if Alexander had been awake when Gabrielle started to go into anaphylactic shock, he wouldn't have been able to save her.

Libby: Yeah, Flora really did have all the bases covered. It breaks my heart to think that Alexander died believing he was partly to blame for what happened to Gabrielle.

Journalist: Can you help our readers understand how Flora managed to spike Gabrielle's water without anybody noticing? I gather there were quite a few of you in the room at the time.

Libby: I think the fact there were so many of us actually made it easier for Flora. She took advantage of the general confusion to act in plain sight. I was so focused on Gabrielle, I wasn't paying attention to what anyone else was doing and I'm sure it was the same for the other people present.

Journalist: I suppose she also took advantage of the trust you all had in each other?

Libby: Absolutely. When Gabrielle broke her ankle, we all knew it had the potential to derail her skating career. I'm sure I speak for the others when I say that in that moment I would've done anything I possibly could to help her. It never even occurred to me that one of us would be doing the precise opposite. Flora was very good at covering her tracks; she was always one step ahead. It was like the way she went back to the rink to fix up the ice panels after she caused Gabrielle's accident.

Journalist: I didn't realise she'd done that.

Libby: Yes, I think it was to muddy the waters; to cast doubt on Alexander's account of what had happened.

Journalist: Alexander, of course, was fated to be Flora's second victim. His was a horribly brutal death – and yet, in the text to her mother, Flora said: '*Killing him was child's play. He never even knew what hit him.*' It's followed by two laughing face emojis. How did you feel when that particular text was read out in court?

Libby: For me, it was one of the most upsetting moments of the entire trial. The way Flora relived what she'd done for her mother's vicarious enjoyment . . . it's almost inhuman.

Journalist: Her texts don't go into detail about the events leading up to the attack on Alexander. How do *you* think it might have unfolded?

Libby: The attack was very opportunistic; it wasn't something Flora could have planned out in advance.

She must've seen Alexander outside and followed him; she might even have offered to help him bury the food. But then, once his back was turned, she picked up the spade and . . . well, we know what happened then.

Journalist: Did you notice any change in her behaviour immediately afterwards?

Libby: Only that she appeared to be as shocked by his death as the rest of us. She pretended to be scared too, at the thought there might be someone stalking the castle grounds. That's one of the most disturbing aspects of this whole case – that she could kill someone and then behave as if she was as much in the dark as the rest of us.

Journalist: She was clearly a very good actress.

Libby: I think *psychopath* is the word you're looking for.

Journalist: Yes, it would've been interesting to see what a court-appointed psychiatrist made of her, had she survived. Of all the deaths, Melissa's appears to have required the most elaborate planning. In the texts, Flora reveals how she used a length of nylon wire, taken from Lukas Wolff's own fishing rod, to create a human trap. She told her mother she'd skied to the forest to set up the trap the day before it was actually deployed. I'm guessing it would've taken her some considerable time to do that. Did none of you notice her absence?

Libby: No, we weren't in each other's pockets 24/7. It wasn't unusual for people to spend time on their

329

own. I'm pretty sure Flora told us she was napping in her room that afternoon.

Journalist: And then the next day, with her trap in place, she suggested the others take the shortcut through the forest.

Libby: From what Saskia told me, they didn't take much persuasion. They all wanted to get to the village by the quickest route possible.

Journalist: Again, the texts don't reveal the precise sequence of events and it wasn't really explored at trial. Do you have any thoughts about how Flora managed to lure Melissa down the booby-trapped trail without drawing attention to herself?

Libby: Saskia said that when they got to the forest, Flora took off like a bat out of hell. Saskia, who's super competitive, was determined to keep up with her. I'm sure Flora had foreseen this. What she would also have known was that the two less experienced skiers in the group would fall behind.

Journalist: You're referring to Melissa and Fred.

Libby: Right. As soon as Flora had put sufficient distance between her and the others, she told Saskia the map had fallen out of her pocket and that she was going to go back to look for it. Saskia and I both think that was just a ruse, and what Flora actually did was ski back to find Fred and Melissa.

Journalist: But, hang on, wasn't Fred skiing down the trail at the same time to look for Flora and Saskia? Surely their paths would've crossed.

Libby: No, because this time they weren't on the same trail.

Journalist: Sorry, you've lost me.

Libby: In order for her plan to work, Flora needed to get to the other trail, the one where she'd strung the wire, without the other two seeing her. Saskia and I think she'd worked out an alternative route, one that circumvented the main trail?

Journalist: You think she recced the area the day before, when she was laying the trap?

Libby: I'm certain she did. I think that originally, she planned to wait a short way down the booby-trapped trail and then, when she saw Melissa and Fred approaching on the main trail, she was going to call out to them. I'm sure they would've followed her without a second thought; after all, she had the map. The three of them would've skied off down that slope at some considerable speed. All Flora had to do as they approached the wire was duck at the last second.

Journalist: You think she intended to kill both of them at once?

Libby: It sounds horrific, but I really do. But unbeknownst to her, Fred had already skied past the trail; Flora might even have glimpsed him through the trees, as she travelled in the opposite direction. When she spotted Melissa, sitting on a fallen tree all on her own, she decided to stick to her plan, except now there was only one victim instead of two. Her mission completed, she skied back the same way she'd come, arriving just seconds before Fred.

Journalist: It all sounds frighteningly plausible, especially as we know Flora was an accomplished skier. But one thing's troubling me, and I think our readers might pick up on this too. After Melissa was found dead, didn't Saskia mention that Flora had gone back to look for the map? If she had, it might've rung alarm bells for some of you.

Libby: Unfortunately not, but even if she had, I don't think it would've made a difference. Flora was an expert manipulator of people; she even managed to convince Fred that it had been *his* idea to take the shortcut through the forest. If Saskia *had* said something about Flora going back for the map, I'm sure Flora would've managed to talk her way out of it.

Journalist: The more I hear, the more I have this image in my mind of Flora as a spider who's patiently spun its web and all it has to do is wait for the unwitting flies to get caught.

Libby: Mmm, I know what you mean. But in some ways, Flora was more like a jellyfish. Light and translucent, with the ability to burn on contact. Only trouble was, her poison wasn't visible to the naked eye.

Journalist: That's a very interesting analogy; I'll use that quote in my piece. And her final victim: your host, Lukas Wolff. Flora's text to Helen simply revealed she'd locked him in his own freezer, alongside her first victim, Gabrielle. I suppose it isn't too difficult to imagine how she might have convinced him to go in there, moments before she slammed the door.

Libby: Yeah, there are all kinds of things she could have said to him. A couple of days earlier, Flora and I had spent half an hour emptying the freezer of food, so she had ample time to notice there was no emergency release. I must admit that *I* didn't notice, but then again I wasn't looking for ways to kill people.

Journalist: There has, of course, been a tremendous outpouring of grief in Germany in the wake of Lukas Wolff's death. What are your own feelings about the loss of such a legendary figure in the world of figure skating?

Libby: Lukas was one of my heroes. He acted with the best of intentions when he invited us all to his home, and it's an absolute tragedy that he was cut down at a time in his life when he still had so much to give the sport. He saw something in me that no one else ever has and, because of Flora, I'll never get the chance to say thank you.

Journalist: I know you only spent ten days or so with him, but were there any indications during that time that he was seriously unwell?

Libby: Why do you say that?

Journalist: You haven't heard?

Libby: Heard what?

Journalist: Oh, I'm sorry, I didn't realise. One of the

German newspapers managed to get hold of Lukas's postmortem through a Freedom of Information request; they published a story the day before yesterday.

Libby: But Lukas died of hypothermia; they said that at the trial.

Journalist: Yes, but the other postmortem findings weren't revealed in court. I guess they weren't deemed relevant.

Libby: What other findings?

Journalist: Lukas was suffering from stage four liver cancer; the pathologist estimated he had less than six months to live.

Libby: Are you serious?

Journalist: I can email you a translation of the article if you like.

Libby: Yes, please, I'd like to see it. Did Lukas *know* it was terminal?

Journalist: Apparently so. His brother, Stefan, was quoted as saying that Lukas had been battling cancer for several years and that it was the reason he'd quit coaching.

Libby: Wow. I had no idea Lukas was ill; he didn't say anything to us. Did Annett know?

Journalist: *Annett?*

Libby: Lukas's assistant.

Journalist: Oh yes, she was with you in the castle, wasn't she? I don't think anybody outside the family knew. Lukas was determined to keep his illness hidden from the world. Stefan also revealed something else; I should warn you, though, I think you might find it quite upsetting.

Libby: Go on.

Journalist: It seems Lukas had been planning to take his own life, if and when it all got too much. According to Stefan, he'd bought some strong painkillers on the black market, in readiness; quite a large quantity, it seems. Stefan believes he was the only one who knew what Lukas was planning. He wasn't very happy about the situation, but he felt it was up to Lukas to choose the manner of his own death. Are you OK, Libby?

Libby: Er, yeah, it's just quite a lot to take in, that's all.

Journalist: With the benefit of hindsight, do you think Lukas's illness was the reason he set up the training programme?

Libby: I'm sorry, I don't see the connection.

Journalist: I wondered – and I must stress this is pure speculation on my part – if, knowing how gravely ill he was, Lukas had made up his mind to pass on his trade secret before it was too late?

Libby: By trade secret, I assume you mean the Grim Reaper.

Journalist: Exactly.

Libby: Um, yes, I suppose it's a possibility. Sorry, is it all right if we stop the interview for a second?

Journalist: Of course. Apologies again, I didn't mean to blindside you. Let's break for twenty minutes, shall we? And when we come back, we'll talk about something much more cheerful. I'm dying to hear all about you and Nathan Carter. I understand the two of you are skating as a pair now; a little bird tells me you're about to sign a big sponsorship deal. Anyway, we'll save all that for later. I'm turning off my recorder now . . .

Thirty Years Earlier

30

Joanne Murray pulled a small cotton towel from her bag and began to wipe the moisture from her ice skates. Sitting on the bench seat opposite, her cousin Helen was busy doing the same.

'Training always makes me so hungry,' said Joanne. 'Fancy getting something to eat on the way home?'

Helen set down the skate she'd been working on and picked up its twin. 'Sorry, not tonight, Jo. I need an early night – and so do you.' She looked up and grinned. 'Big day tomorrow.'

Joanne began loosening the laces on her skate. 'Are you nervous about the competition?'

'No, I'm feeling pretty good about it, actually. I think I have a good chance of making the podium. Why, are you?'

'A little; I keep mucking up the take-off on my Axel. I don't know why; I never used to have a problem with it. It seems like the more I practise, the worse it gets.'

'Do you know what *your* trouble is?'

Joanne felt the different strands of her irritation tightening into one huge knot. It was the same whenever she knew her cousin was about to dispense some unasked-for advice. 'Go on.'

'You worry too much. Don't overthink it and it'll all come right tomorrow; you'll see.'

Easy for *her* to say, Joanne thought to herself.

On the face of it, the cousins had a lot in common. Both were ambitious, highly talented skaters, with a clutch of junior titles to their name. And yet, in certain critical areas, they were poles apart.

Helen was always brimming with confidence. She rarely suffered from self-doubt and when it came to competitions, she exuded an almost preternatural calm. Joanne was different. She knew she had the ability, but she struggled to get her anxiety under control, especially when she was competing. As she waited to step onto the ice, she could feel the nerves coiled tightly around her lungs, threatening to suffocate her and ruin her performance.

Their blood bond dictated that Joanne should be pleased for her cousin if she placed in the top three tomorrow. But if Joanne didn't make the podium too, she knew she would struggle to hide her true feelings.

In the beginning, it had been fun having a relative who was just as crazy about skating as she was, but slowly, drip drip slowly, things changed. Now, the more time Joanne spent with Helen, the more annoying she found her. Her cousin was always so upbeat, so relentlessly cheerful, so goddamn good at every new thing she tried.

Joanne was sick to the back teeth of hearing people at the rink tell Helen she was special, that she'd go far, that she was a Scottish national champion in the making. Her talent burned so bright, it was like staring at the sun; Joanne almost had to shield herself from its glare.

Last night she'd dreamed she'd killed Helen; with an ice skate, of all things. She'd woken up, skin clammy with revulsion. Then came the wave of relief that it was only a dream, followed by a backwash of guilt for having imagined it in the first place. But then, as she lay there in bed, she'd asked herself: weren't dreams supposed to be the unconscious expression of a real desire?

'I'd better nip to the loo before we head off,' said Helen, standing up.

As Joanne watched her cousin disappear, she knew what she had to do. Reaching into her skate bag, she pulled out the small screwdriver she always carried with her. A series of screws secured the blades of her skates to the soles of her boots. Every month or so, she would check to see that none of them had worked loose. It was good practice for every skater and had been drilled into Joanne from a young age. It had been drilled into Helen too, but Joanne knew her cousin was less diligent in her checks.

Reaching towards the opposite bench, she picked up Helen's right skate. She would only loosen the screws a small amount; nothing that would be obvious from a cursory glance.

Each counterclockwise turn felt like a victory, a step closer towards ensuring her own success. Joanne knew the potential outcome, but in that moment the desire to eliminate her biggest rival outweighed every other thought in her mind.

She'd barely had time to tuck her screwdriver away when Helen reappeared.

'Everything OK?' her cousin asked as she packed her skates away.

Joanne smiled. 'Couldn't be better.'

Everyone in the skating community thought the Murray cousins were such great friends, but, even if Helen didn't know it, they'd been growing apart for a while. Now that the thin thread holding them together had snapped, now that Joanne had finally plummeted to the dark waters below, the ones she'd been so scared of, she realised she wasn't drowning. Her head was above the water and she was swimming for the shore.

Acknowledgements

Thank you to the enormously talented team at Headline, especially my superlative editors, Lucy Dauman, Isabel Martin and Sophie Wilson, as well as the phenomenal Foreign Rights duo of Grace McCrum and Ruth Case-Green. I am also indebted to Sherise Hobbs, Joe Thomas, Patrick Insole, Bethany Wickington and Ana Carter.

To protect their secrets, she must expose theirs . . .

Amy Mackenzie's business may be thriving, but while she
rubs shoulders with the rich and famous, she is always
on the outside looking in.

But when her most glamorous clients, James and Eleanor Elliott,
hire her to provide the flowers for a lavish party, Amy gets a
taste of what it means to be part of their world. Until a guest
at the event suffers a violent and shocking death.

And Amy finds the finger of blame pointing at her.

As the florist fights to clear her name, it isn't long before
she uncovers some ugly truths about the Elliotts. But they aren't
the only ones with secrets. Amy has a dark past of her own,
and by the time she realises it's caught up with her,
it might just be too late.

Available to order

HEADLINE

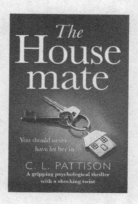

YOU LET A STRANGER INTO YOUR HOME

Best friends Megan and Chloe have finally found the perfect
house. And when they meet Samantha, she seems like
the perfect housemate.

YOU DON'T KNOW WHAT SHE'S HIDING

But Megan thinks there might be more to Samantha than
meets the eye. Why is she so secretive? Where are her friends
and family? And why is she desperate to get close to Chloe?

YOU'RE ABOUT TO FIND OUT

When strange things start happening in the house, Megan
and Chloe grow more and more alarmed. They soon realise
that letting a stranger into their home – and their lives –
might be the worst idea they've ever had . . .

Available to order

HEADLINE